UNCOMPLICATE IT

Uncomplicate It

by

Kel McCord

2025

UNCOMPLICATE IT

ISBN 13: 978-1-63679-864-6

This Trade Paperback Original Is Published By
Bold Strokes Books, Inc.
P.O. Box 249
Valley Falls, NY 12185

First Edition: August 2025

Credits
Editors: Radclyffe and Cindy Cresap
Production Design: Susan Ramundo
Cover Design By Inkspiral Design

Acknowledgments

In the beginning of our marriage, my wife told me that we needed to be each other's biggest cheerleaders. She is much better at this than I am and has embodied that for the last ten years. With every new hobby I have taken on, she has never asked "Why in the world would you want to do that?" but instead has found ways to help. From marathon running, beer brewing, to the summer I thought I could grow kiwis, to now writing, she has not only been my biggest fan, but has helped in amazing ways. I can't thank her enough and couldn't do any of this without her love and support.

I have the greatest best friend a person could ask for. While it may seem silly to be forty years old and still refer to someone as a BFF, I won't stop. Kara has earned that spot and no one will take it away. Without her pushing me to get started, I never would have written anything. She challenges me in the right places while providing the compliments I need, both in writing and in life. She has read terrible drafts that no one should ever have to read, making her a true BFF.

Many parents tell their children they can grow up to be whatever they want to be. Some parents allow their children to grow into who they want to be. I was fortunate enough to have the latter.

Every author at BSB thanks the amazing team and that's because they are world class. I can't say enough good things about them. Thank you to Rad, Sandy, and Cindy for not only your encouragement but your patience with me throughout the entire process.

Thank you to you, the reader. Without you finding and taking a chance on the works of new authors, I don't get the opportunity to keep pursuing this dream.

Dedication

To my BFF
I didn't think we'd make it this far

Chapter One

Drip. Drop. Drip. The splatter of rain against the office window held Hollis in a trance. One raindrop hit the glass, then ran down, creating pools and streaks on the fifth-floor window. Hollis clicked the top of her pen three times, paused, then clicked it another three times. The motion soothed her as she scoured the report on her screen. A slight pang hit her shoulder. Ignoring it, she kept staring at the screen. Something bounced off her again. As she brushed her hand across her shoulder, she found a wadded white piece of paper.

"What the?" She brushed it off. As she turned around, several more wadded pieces of paper fell to the seat of her black office chair.

Three more pieces fell out when she ran her hands through her hair. Flicking away a long strand, she swiveled all the way around to face her office mate and friend, Harrison, who had a hand over his mouth to conceal his giggling.

"Seriously?" She finger combed her hair to find any more stray pieces of paper.

"You are way too serious over there," Harrison said, still laughing, his dark brown five-o'clock shadow making its usual end-of-week appearance.

Hollis picked up one piece of paper and dropped it at the first sign of dampness. "Are these actual spit balls?"

"I had to get your attention somehow." His brown eyes twinkled, leaving Hollis to decide the origin of the paper wads.

Hollis rubbed her temples. "You do realize that this is due in an hour, and if I'm late, you're late. This is *our* department."

Harrison waved his hand dismissively. "Everyone knows you do all the work anyway."

The large office remained relatively undecorated, even though Harrison and Hollis had just hit their one-year anniversary at Fitwear. Sure, Hollis had brought her diploma and a few other generic trinkets. The one framed photo she kept was of her college softball team, right after they won the first playoff game in school history. Her captain's C had torn off her uniform as she slid into home, headfirst, for the go-ahead run. She actually preferred the office to look unoccupied. She always joked that if she got fired, she wanted all of her possessions to fit in one box. She would not be making a second trip to collect her belongings.

Hopefully, she wouldn't need to pack that box with a new boss starting. Fitwear, the Raleigh based athletic company, wanted a West Coast presence and had opened HQ II, just outside of Portland, Oregon. Hollis, like many other transplants, had jumped ship from one of the competitors in the area to a promotion with the up-and-coming company. It had taken her three tries to find the right office in the brand-new building on her first day. When she had, she'd been surprised to see it already occupied by the middle-aged, balding white man sitting across from her now. She'd backed out and checked the door. Two brown nameplates had been freshly installed—Hollis Reed and Harrison Scott.

"That's right," the man she now knew as Harrison had said. "Looks like we are in this together."

"Okay?" Hollis was hesitant.

"I only have one rule." Harrison leaned back in his chair and clasped his hands behind his head.

"What's that?" Hollis questioned her decision to take a new job.

"If you can't say anything nice, pull up a chair and sit next to me." He pointed to the office chair at the desk directly across from him.

"I think we're going to get along just fine." At that, she'd sat down at her new desk and adjusted the office chair.

Harrison rolled over in his chair and stuck out his hand. "Harrison Scott."

"My dad told me to never trust a man with two first names," she said, taking his hand.

"Lucky for you, I have two last names."

He grinned, a charming smile on a handsome face.

"Hollis Reed."

"Hollis." Harrison looked to the ceiling. "That won't do. Can I call you Holly?"

"No, you may not."

"It's just that I used to date a guy named Hollis. It didn't end well." His eyes looked unusually serious.

"And here I thought I was the diversity hire," Hollis said.

"I just opened up about my heartbreak and you don't even offer your condolences?" Harrison put a hand over his heart. "Besides, calling you Holly will help thaw this whole ice queen persona you have going on."

"First of all, you can't call me Holly, no matter the reason." She crossed her arms. "And second of all, I couldn't care less if you think I have an ice queen persona."

She stared at him, daring him to blink first. She'd worn her hair in a short, tight ponytail, and added a black blouse to complete her gray suit. She hadn't meant to dress so seriously, but she could see where he was coming from.

Harrison stared back. He put one finger up to his lip and made a thinking face. "I like you."

He'd blinked first.

"What a relief."

Now, she and Harrison oversaw the entire West Coast supply chain team. Under their leadership, the West Coast team quickly outperformed the rest of the country. The logistics of buying fabric from manufacturers and shipping it across the world was a problem Hollis enjoyed solving.

Despite Harrison being twelve years Hollis's senior, they'd also developed a deep friendship. When Hollis finally ended a relationship after recognizing her bad judgment in dating someone a little close to home, Harrison had decided that sunshine and sand were the only cure. He was right, but the HR department had plenty of questions when they returned from their Hawaiian vacation the month before. Once Hollis explained that while sometimes she and Harrison argued like an old married couple, they would never date each other, HR backed off, but still sent a friendly reminder that interoffice relationships were never a good idea. Like she needed any reminding.

Hollis wished she was sipping mai tais with Harrison on the beach now instead of stressing over this report. "We're getting a new boss on Monday, and we need to make a good impression."

"We're the dream team." Harrison leaned back in his chair. "Anyone worth their weight in salt will look at our numbers and just leave us alone."

"I still don't like to be late."

Harrison crinkled another wad of paper in his hand and threw it at her.

She swatted it out of the air. "Knock it off."

"What are you doing this weekend?"

Hollis rubbed her hands over her face. "Speaking of, are you coming to Sunday dinner? My mom doesn't understand why you don't come to every family gathering."

"That's right, that's this weekend. What's your mom making?"

"You know I can't ask her that. She gets offended." She raised her voice to impersonate her mother. "Does it matter what I'm making? Can't you just come for the company?" She sighed. "Seriously, I've tried to explain to her that you have your own life and can't come every time, but she'd kill me if I didn't ask."

"Of course I'll be there. Come to spin class with me tomorrow."

"Hell no." Hollis shook her head.

"Come on," he whined. "I want you to meet Greggory."

"Who's Greggory?"

"Just the man of my dreams." Harrison stared out the window with a dreamy expression. "He's the gorgeous spin instructor."

"I wouldn't be caught dead in a spin class. It's way too bubbly for me." She turned back to her laptop.

"I heard that corporate is starting to keep track of how often employees are using their gym membership."

Hollis turned back around. "That's absurd. Who did you hear that from?"

"You see that new admin in HR?"

"The brown-haired kid right out of college?" Hollis snorted.

"That's the one," Harrison said. "Turns out, it doesn't take much to get HR secrets out of him."

Hollis shook her head. "Please don't put those images in my brain."

"You don't want the new boss to find out you aren't using the gym like they want, do you?"

"Can they even do that? Is it legal?"

"Well, we are an athletic wear company, and they do strongly encourage an active lifestyle. If they're going to give a gym membership as a perk, then it is within their right to see who's taking advantage."

"That sounds like HR talk."

Harrison shrugged. "Not my best pillow talk, but also not my worst."

"Jesus. Is there anyone here you haven't slept with?"

Harrison managed an innocent face.

"I'm not against working out," Hollis said. "But I have a long run planned this weekend and just can't stand the idea of riding a bike going nowhere while some muscular guy shouts words of inspiration at me."

"We'll go to brunch after." Harrison rolled his chair closer. "If you hate it, I'll buy."

Hollis considered the invitation.

"Worst case, you get a free meal and an afternoon with me."

"I want to go to that place with bottomless mimosas."

Harrison stuck out his hand. "Deal."

CHAPTER TWO

I still cannot believe you talked me into this," Hollis said as Harrison joined her outside the fitness center. HQ II had built a state-of-the-art gym located across the street from the main office with three floors of brand-new workout equipment, multiple studios for classes, a basketball court, and an indoor track. Membership to this kind of facility would have cost hundreds of dollars a month under normal circumstances.

"I'm just trying to promote an active lifestyle among my coworkers," Harrison said.

"That sounds like more HR talk. Did you see the new guy again?" Hollis followed Harrison inside toward the spin studio in the back.

"A gentleman would never kiss and tell." He motioned zipping his lips shut. Then he quickly unzipped his lips. "But I am not, and I so did."

Hollis shook her head. "Isn't he like twelve?"

"I'll have you know, he just turned twenty-one." Harrison feigned outrage.

Hollis slapped his arm. "He's half your age."

"But legal and far from inexperienced." Harrison pulled open the door to the spin studio. "This is where the magic happens."

Goose bumps formed on her arms as she entered the over-air-conditioned room. Her knee-length yoga pants and black tank top did little to keep her warm. "I hope we won't have long to wait."

Harrison noticed her arms. "Don't worry. It warms up fast."

The bright lights reflected off the light wooden floor, and the floor-to-ceiling mirrors made the room appear larger than it seemed. Two rows of stationary bikes faced a single bike in the room's front.

Harrison pointed to two bikes right in front of the instructor's bike. "Here, this will give us the best view."

Hollis rolled her eyes. Participating was one thing. Embarrassing herself was another. She focused on the bottomless mimosas she knew she'd be getting in just over an hour as the room filled with other people milling about, waiting for the class to begin.

Soon enough, a short auburn-haired woman in black yoga pants similar to Hollis's and a matching blue tank top entered the room. She pulled a pair of shoes out of her saddlebag and bent down to put them on. Hollis couldn't help but stare. In her haste to hate spin class, she forgot about the part where it would be a room predominately filled with fit women. This particular woman had her wavy hair tamed in a ponytail and her olive skin reflected the lights of the room as she prepared herself for class. She seemed slightly older than Hollis, but not by much. She had the kind of sculpted arms that only came from sweat-ridden hours in the gym. Hollis had always been a sucker for a woman with toned arms.

Maybe this won't be so bad.

"Why is she changing shoes?" she asked Harrison, noticing that he too had changed his shoes.

He motioned to the black cycling shoes now adorning his feet. "They clip into the pedals so you can grip better, but don't worry, you don't need them until you get serious."

"This is a onetime deal." Hollis relaxed, watching the mystery woman fit a microphone headset to her face.

"No, no, no," Harrison muttered as he got on the bike.

"What's wrong?"

"That isn't Greggory." He motioned with his head to the woman up front.

"Obviously," Hollis said.

The woman clapped her hands together. "Alright, folks. Can you hear me okay?"

A few people in the back said yes.

She motioned to herself. "As I'm sure you can see, I am not Greg."

"That's an understatement," Harrison said under his breath.

Hollis chuckled.

"I'm Ainsley." She clapped her hands together again. "Greg asked me to fill in this morning. Not to worry, we'll have a great class. Ready?"

There were a few more yeses.

"Not even a little bit." Harrison sounded disgruntled.

"Before we start, are there any newcomers here today?"

Harrison waved his hand over his head obnoxiously. "Right here."

"What are you doing?" Hollis glared at him. She was going to get through this class and try not to embarrass herself. The last thing she needed was extra attention.

"What? If I can't stare at Greggory, at least you can stare at Ainsley."

Warmth flushed to her cheeks.

Ainsley stuck out her hand. "Hi. I'm Ainsley."

Hollis reluctantly took her hand. "Hollis."

"Welcome to the world of spin class." Ainsley made a sweeping motion with her hands, instantly reminding Hollis why she didn't want to do this in the first place. While this woman was great to look at, she was entirely too bubbly for this time of day. Nothing about riding a stationary bike could be this exciting.

"Have you ever ridden one of these bikes before?" Ainsley asked.

Hollis shook her head. "It's my first time."

"Great. I love introducing people to spin." Ainsley winked, and Hollis's stomach did an actual flip. Was the spin instructor seriously flirting with her? No. That would be too good to be true. That only happened in cheesy movies, not the real world.

Ainsley carefully grabbed Hollis by the shoulders and steered her body next to the bike. Her warm hands spread heat to Hollis's entire body.

"You want the seat to be right at your hip," Ainsley explained, and Hollis tried not to stare at her perfect cheekbones.

She touched Hollis above the hip and pushed her close to the bike. Hollis held her breath. She knew that close contact was normal in situations like this. Fitness trainers were always invading personal space, but that didn't change the fact that she enjoyed Ainsley's hand on her hip. Ainsley sized her up as she looked at the bike and then at her. "That looks good," Ainsley said.

Hollis hid her disappointment when she realized Ainsley meant the bike.

Ainsley patted the seat. "Hop up on here and we'll get your feet squared away."

Hollis climbed on the bike and struggled to get her feet in the straps of the pedals.

Harrison let out a laugh.

Ainsley scowled at him. "Hey now. That's not how we treat new people."

"Oh, it's fine. She's not new people to me."

"This is a space for encouragement. Try to find some." Ainsley turned back to Hollis and crouched to tighten the strap on the pedal, holding Hollis's foot in place as she worked. "Is this okay?"

A faint "yes," was all Hollis could get out. She stared at Ainsley's slender and commanding hands. Hollis focused her thoughts on spin class to try to get her mind off of ogling her. It hadn't been that long since she'd been with a woman. Was she seriously fantasizing about spin instructors? But Ainsley had to be much more than just a spin instructor, right? The way she commanded the attention of the room, and put Harrison in his place—skills like that would be lost on just this spin studio.

Ainsley bent down to tighten the other strap, she looked up. "Too tight?"

Hollis stared into her brown eyes. Good God, they were gorgeous. She shook her head and then remembered to speak. "No."

Her voice cracked.

Ainsley stood up and clapped her hands together. "Great. Anyone else need help getting set up?"

When no one needed help, she returned to the bike at the front.

Hollis let out a long breath. Harrison cleared his throat, and she looked over at him.

"She is totally into you," he whisper-yelled.

"What?" She furrowed her brow. "No. No way."

"I think you might like spin class after all."

Ainsley's voice came over the speakers. "Alright, folks, let's start with a slow warm-up."

Forty-five minutes later, Hollis's legs turned to mush. She wasn't new to physical activity, she just mostly ran or played sports that involved running. Marathon training took up any extra time she had. She never imagined that riding a stationary bike could be so taxing. She used her tank top to wipe the beaded sweat off her forehead. It turned a darker shade after mopping up her brow. She slowly put her shirt back down and noticed Ainsley only a few feet away. And was that her staring at her stomach?

"How was it?" Ainsley asked, quickly making eye contact.

"Very different than I was expecting," Hollis answered honestly.

"Don't be surprised if you're sore later today, or even tomorrow." Ainsley rocked on the balls of her feet.

"I'm sure I will be."

"So, I'm not usually this forward, but I'm trying something new." Ainsley paused. "Would you want to grab coffee?"

Hollis blinked. Why would she want coffee so soon after a workout? "I actually have brunch plans with him." She motioned with her thumb to Harrison.

"It doesn't have to be now. It could be another time. You know, like a date?"

Oh God! Hollis didn't know if she'd ever been asked on a date. She flipped through her memory quickly. Nope. Never. She'd always been the one to ask girls out. It was weird being on the receiving end. Not bad weird, just different.

Ainsley raised her eyebrows in question, and Hollis remembered to speak.

"I just got out of something kind of messy." Even though it had been over a month, Hollis didn't know if she was ready to get back into dating. She was definitely over Miranda, but dating led to feelings, and before she knew it, they would fight about how Hollis was so busy at work that she never made it home for dinner.

"I'm not trying to be pushy or anything, but I think you're cute, I get the sense that you might be into me too, and I'm only asking for something light. Just coffee."

"Yeah. I'd like that. This weekend is a little full for me, but maybe next week?" Something light she could do. It was time.

"I'm starting a new job on Monday, so my nights will be long and I have a work event on Friday."

"Me too. What is it with companies thinking I want to be social on Fridays?"

"I have no idea. So Saturday?"

"Saturday it is. Here." Hollis fished her phone out of the cup holder on the bike. "Why don't you plug your number in, and we can figure out a time and place later."

"Sounds great." Ainsley's skillful fingers worked quickly.

Hollis took her phone and shot a smiley emoji to her newest contact.

Ainsley lingered a second longer before leaving. She turned around and said over her shoulder, barely above a whisper, "Don't forget, my first timers are always sore."

Butterflies swirled in her stomach as she turned toward the exit. The air-conditioned air welcomed her as she left the spin studio. She had sweat in places she didn't even know possible.

Harrison clapped a clammy palm on her shoulder. "Well, I think it's safe to say you enjoyed that."

Hollis looked at the new number in her phone. Ainsley's name with a bike emoji next to it. As if she could forget where she met her. "I enjoyed certain aspects of that, yes."

"Let's go find the bottom of those mimosas, and since I won the bet, you're buying."

CHAPTER THREE

Gravel crunched beneath the tires as Harrison slowly drove up the road to Hollis's childhood home. "Would it kill you to at least drive five miles per hour?" Hollis asked, irritated that the drive was taking so long.

"If you wanted to get there faster, then you should have driven. You know I hate cleaning mud out of my floorboards." Harrison waggled his eyebrows in the annoying way he tended to do.

"Ew. I don't even know what that exactly means, but I know it's not good."

"Oh, it's good."

"Can we please talk about anything but sex before we go see my parents?"

"You're no fun." Harrison pretended to pout.

Finally, the car crawled to a stop as Harrison parked in the long driveway. Hollis's house was a sprawling ranch-style home with dark brown siding and a red metal roof. Daffodil buds poked through the ground and would spring to life on the first sunny day of the season. Harrison and Hollis entered together through the large wooden front door.

"Hello!" Hollis yelled. The aroma of handmade tomato sauce greeting them. The house could have been featured in a country living magazine. Knotty pine trim and custom wooden furniture adorned every room.

"In here, sweetheart," her mother called from the kitchen.

She led Harrison down the short entryway and turned into the kitchen. Although they lived in the home forty years, Hollis's parents continually invested in upgrades. The modern country kitchen housed state-of-the-art stainless-steel appliances.

Her mom stood at the farm sink, rinsing off dirty dishes. She wiped her hands on her red apron.

"Hi, Mom," Hollis said.

Her mother turned off the water and turned around. "Oh, hi." Hollis had little to no resemblance to her mother as she towered over her with a hug. Her mother released her daughter from the embrace and looked past her. "Harrison, thank goodness you're here."

"Gee. Thanks, Mom. Happy to see you too."

Her mother playfully swatted Hollis with the dish towel. "Last I checked, you don't know how to make roses for a charcuterie board."

"That is correct," Hollis answered. "And I probably never will."

Harrison took a step between Hollis and her mother, pushing her to the side. "Did you get the prosciutto like I mentioned?"

"I did. But I can't quite get the folds right."

"Step back and watch the master." Harrison wrapped his arm around Hollis's mom and led her to the counter. Hollis stared at them both, grateful and confused that her family had taken such a quick liking to one of her closest friends.

"Ooooff." Hollis nearly collapsed as something, or someone, took her out at the knees.

"Auntie Hollis!" Her nephew, Lyle, slammed into her and clung tightly to her legs. She ruffled the six-year-old's already mussed, dark brown hair as she slowly peeled him off her body. "Hi there, Lyle. What a greeting."

"Want to play a game?"

Hollis looked around for any kind of out. Normally, her nieces and nephews could busy themselves outside on the swing set her dad had built, but with the weather still on the cooler side, they were all stuck inside. "Uh…" She kept looking for anything that could distract her and cursed herself for never learning to cook. What a great excuse that would have been.

"Lyle, honey, you know Aunt Hollis doesn't do things for fun," Madison, her younger sister, said from behind.

"Excuse me?" Hollis raised her voice slightly as she turned to face her sister. "I do plenty of things for fun."

"Name one."

Hollis started to speak but was quickly shut down.

"And don't say running." Her sister smirked.

"Well, the things I do for fun shouldn't be mentioned in front of little ears."

Madison ushered Lyle toward a Lego set the other kids were building. Hollis watched them play and wondered if kids were something she actually wanted. Miranda constantly harped on her to settle down and start a family. But did she want a family? She was supposed to want a family, right? Hollis held in a heavy sigh as she played through all the emotions swirling in her head. She knew breakups were a bit of a mind fuck, but when would it end? How much time had to pass until she wouldn't think about Miranda in every situation? They weren't even that serious of a couple, at least Hollis hadn't thought so.

"Alright, everyone!" Her mother's voice boomed through the whole house. When it was time to eat, it didn't matter what was going on, everyone came to the table. Hollis's father ushered in the remaining grandkids and sat at the head of the table. "Oh. Harrison is here! What a delight."

"I'm here too, Dad." Hollis made her annoyance clear. If someone had taken a picture of her dad when he was younger and put it into one of those computer programs that showed what you would like as the other gender, the image would be an exact replica of Hollis.

"Yes, but did you teach your mother how to fold fancy ham into roses? I swear, she's talked about nothing but meat flowers for the past week."

"Okay, that's enough." Her mom talked over her dad, cheeks flushed slightly from embarrassment.

"So, Harrison, what's new?" Her dad asked as he took a bite of steaming lasagna.

"Well." Harrison paused, waiting for all eyes on him. "Hollis here has a new love interest."

"Oh really?" Her dad tilted his head.

"Honey, that's great!" Her mother beamed.

Her sisters both sat up, wanting to hear details.

"I'm sorry, what?" Hollis choked on her own bite of dinner.

"She's a spin instructor. Totally not her normal type, but I told her to go for it anyway." Harrison looked pleased with himself.

"You should bring her for our next Sunday dinner," her mother suggested.

Hollis lifted her hands, palms out. "Okay, I think we need to all slow down here."

"Yes, of course," her mother said. "It's way too soon to bring her. I know, I know. I just get excited. Well, when the time is right, she is welcome."

"Ainsley. Her name is Ainsley," Harrison chimed in.

"We can't wait to meet Ainsley," her dad said.

Hollis let out a deep, calming breath as she stared daggers at Harrison. "I'm afraid that Harrison has misled you all. I am not seeing anyone at the moment, let alone a spin instructor."

"Sure," Madison said with an exaggerated wink. "Of course not." She winked again.

"But other than that," Harrison gained everyone's attention again, "there's nothing new and exciting with me. Same old, same old."

Hollis wanted to scream. First, her family was inviting Ainsley to family dinner and now they didn't believe that she wasn't dating her? They had barely exchanged numbers and hadn't even finalized a place for Saturday. This. This was why she didn't do relationships. No woman, no matter how good she looked in yoga pants, was worth this level of drama.

Chapter Four

"It's a new boss, not a first date," Hollis told herself Monday morning after fussing with her outfit three times. The company-wide memo stating that a new executive was coming to run the entire HQ II division was the only information Hollis had about her new boss. Corporate remained cryptic about the entire situation. Hollis and Harrison had tried to internet-stalk their new manager, but the memo didn't even give a name. Harrison tried to pull strings in HR, but corporate kept this news secret. Hollis settled on a teal silk blouse and her favorite black slacks. She straightened her hair and put on just enough makeup to look more awake than this Monday morning brought. She was at least going to feel good about herself today to help her project confidence.

The early spring sun poked its head above the trees as she made the quick seven-minute walk to work. It wasn't necessarily a walkable commute, but there were sidewalks through the neighborhoods from her apartment to HQ II. The new building became a business draw for the suburban town, and now a strip mall and other establishments popped up left and right. The cool air smelled like spring and she thanked her lucky stars the rain held off. She hated the days she took the time to do her hair, only to have it messed up by the typical Pacific Northwest drizzle. At 7:50 a.m. Harrison already sat in his chair. He wore his favorite black suit with a powder blue tie. Hollis figured he was going with the same strategy today. "You're in early." She didn't think Harrison had beaten her into the office since her first day.

"Here." Harrison stuck out a coffee and handed it to Hollis.

"Thank you." She took the warm cup, grateful for the extra boost of caffeine. "What's the occasion?"

"You want to feel good or do you want honesty?" Harrison looked her in the eyes.

Her heart rate quickened. What did he know that she didn't? "Let's go with feel good." Whatever bad news he had, she would find out eventually.

Harrison grinned. "You're my friend and I like doing nice things for you."

Hollis spit out a sip of hot coffee. "Now, if that's not a load of bullshit."

She reached in her drawer for a napkin. Luckily, she missed her shirt and started wiping up her chair.

"Honest reason is there is a cute new barista down front."

"What happened to the new guy in HR?"

"Oh, Hollis." He shook his head. "A man like me cannot be tamed. I need more than one man to keep me interested."

"Listen to yourself."

"I'm trying to envision a situation with HR guy and cute barista." Harrison stared out the window.

"Does this mean I'm going to be getting coffee from you more often?"

"At least for this week." He checked his watch. "We should go. We don't want to be late for the all-team."

Hollis followed Harrison into the large conference room and took a seat next to Harrison. The room had two rows of chairs set up in an auditorium-like setting. All team meetings happened once a month and the CEO video-conferenced in to make the small HQ II team feel like part of the larger company.

Hollis saw three chairs at the front of the room. "Did you know he was going to be here?"

Harrison leaned over and whispered, "HR guy did tell me that a big guest was coming today, but I didn't think this big."

Sitting in a perfectly fitted navy blue suit, looking over papers in his hands, was Andrew Williams, the Fitwear CEO. Hollis had never actually seen him in person, and he looked just as charismatic in the real world with his brown hair gelled into place and cut to accentuate his strong jaw line. The lights flickered signaling the start of the meeting.

Andrew approached the podium at the front. "Good morning," his deep voice filled the room. "As you all know, today is a special day at Fitwear. We just hit our one-year anniversary for HQ II." He stepped back and applauded the room. "My goal for HQ II has always been for it to be a continuation of the good work we do in Raleigh, not to be its own entity. You all have done an amazing job bringing our brand to the West Coast. So amazing, that we're ahead of schedule in every major market."

Harrison and Hollis looked at each other and nodded. It was their work that brought the company ahead of schedule and they knew it.

"And because of that, we are bringing an additional level of leadership to this division. To help you all continue the great work you're doing and to keep moving this company forward."

Hollis leaned to Harrison's ear. "If we are doing such a good job, why do we need a new babysitter?"

"And with that, I want to introduce you to the new president of HQ II, Ainsley Jones!" Andrew stepped back, motioned to the woman standing at the doorway to the side of the podium, and invited her inside.

"Holy shit." Hollis's favorite spin instructor looked like a completely different person from the woman Hollis saw in yoga pants on Saturday. Her auburn hair was down, and she wore a black pencil skirt, cream blouse, and matching black jacket. Hollis noticed loose curls in her hair and wondered if they were natural or if Ainsley woke up early to do her hair this morning. She confidently approached the microphone, shook Andrew's hand, and then placed both hands on the podium.

"Thank you all for your warm welcome," she started. Her voice still held that bubbly spin-instructor tone, but came out more subdued. "As Andrew mentioned, this team has done amazing work over the last year. I am proud to be joining you and for this opportunity to help Fitwear continue to exceed expectations. I'll be getting to know all of you over the next several days. I promise I'm not going to make any big changes." She let out a slight laugh. "I just want to get to know you all."

She looked right at Hollis as she said that. Had she noticed Hollis specifically? She probably didn't even see her in the dark room.

"Thank you all again and I look forward to learning more about this team." She stepped away and Andrew continued the meeting. Hollis couldn't focus on a single thing during the presentation.

The lights came back on and Hollis couldn't move. She could have sworn Ainsley still looked at her as the meeting ended.

Harrison stood up. "Are you coming?"

"Holy shit," she said, just above her breath.

"I know right?" He leaned down. "Now you can have the hot spin instructor and the hot boss fantasy."

Hollis slapped his shoulder. "Jesus. Not everyone is trying to sleep with everyone at work. After Miranda, I'm never sleeping with another coworker again."

He raised his palms up. "It works for me."

Hollis sat in her desk chair and put her hands over her head. She hadn't stopped thinking about Ainsley since Saturday morning. It didn't help that Harison mentioned her being Hollis's new love interest. She couldn't stop thinking about the moment when she tightened the straps around her foot and asked, "Is this okay?" Hollis let out a long sigh and rubbed her hands over her face.

"You need to get it together," Harrison said from behind her.

"I'm fine. I'm just surprised." She turned around to face him and pressed her fingers to her temples. "Of all the people I could have imagined as our new boss."

There was a knock at the door. She looked up and the dream woman looked back at her.

"Hey, you two." Ainsley's voice was friendly.

Hollis started to stand.

"No, no." Ainsley stopped her. "Don't get up."

Good. Her knees couldn't stand if she wanted to.

Ainsley looked back and forth from Harrison to Hollis. Her eyebrows shot to her hairline. She snapped her fingers. "You two were in spin class."

Harrison raised a hand. "Guilty."

Ainsley held Hollis's gaze and smiled. "I don't normally meet employees like that."

"I don't normally get suckered into spin class." Hollis glanced at Harrison.

Ainsley laughed. "It wasn't that bad, was it?"

Hollis loved the sound of Ainsley's laugh. She wanted to record it and listen to it on repeat. She wanted to say whatever it took to get her to laugh again.

"No," she said. "It was much better than I was expecting."

"I have to be honest." Ainsley stepped into the office and lowered her voice. "I was really nervous. I haven't taught in years. Greg called me in a bind and if you know Greg, he's impossible to say no to."

"I'd sure like to," Harrison mumbled.

"What was that?" Ainsley asked.

"The class was great. We'll make sure to tell Greg you were an excellent stand-in." Harrison flashed his perfect smile. It always helped him get away with everything.

Ainsley clapped her hands together. "Well, I should be going. I'm just making quick rounds right now. Be looking for calendar invites for later today."

On her way out, she turned around, her arm leaning against the doorframe and looked directly at Hollis. "I'm really looking forward to getting to know the team."

Hollis held her gaze. Ainsley held her eye contact a few beats longer than was professional, but Hollis didn't care. Her stomach swirled, staring into her brown eyes. She would have stayed there all day if she could.

Ainsley continued down the hall.

Hollis let out a long breath. "Holy shit."

Harrison let out a laugh. "This is bad."

Hollis looked at him. "What's bad?"

"You've got the hots for our new boss, and you know it."

"I do not," Hollis said.

"Mm-hmm. A hot woman asks you out for the first time in God knows how long, and you're going to pretend you *aren't* interested?"

"I don't have to pretend." Hollis bristled. "I'm not interested anymore."

"Riiiight. And I'm going to start dating women."

Chapter Five

Hollis worked through lunch, not that she could bear to eat, anyway. The stress of a new boss had her stomach tied in knots. She'd been in the corporate world long enough to know that new bosses meant changes. It wouldn't be fast, but she knew they were coming. There would be new reports to fill out, new meetings to attend, and what she feared most, restructuring. Was a new president coming on board to combine her role with corporate? She wasn't naive enough to think that a new person in charge would keep everything the same. She and Harrison had a great thing going, and she shuddered to think that Ainsley Jones would take that away.

Then there was the realization that Ainsley Jones was her boss now. Just saying her name brought heat to her body in places not suitable for work. Beautiful Ainsley Jones was her new boss. She was going to have to work hard to get over this crush if she had any hope of keeping her career.

"Here you go, Holly."

Hollis was brought back from her daydream as a protein bar hit her keyboard. "What have I said about calling me that?"

"You didn't mean it."

Hollis opened the protein bar. "I most certainly did." She took a bite. "Thank you, by the way."

"I figured you needed something inside you."

Hollis choked on her bite.

Harrison snorted. “Something besides coffee. You know what I meant. Get your mind out of the gutter.”

Hollis regained her breathing as a ding sounded from her laptop. “Are you freaking kidding me? Did you get one of these?”

“Meet and greet at four p.m.,” he said.

“Mine’s at four thirty. She’s meeting with us separately?”

“Damn. Power move.”

Technically, the working hours went to five p.m., but there was an unwritten rule in the Pacific Northwest that when spring came and the sun finally arrived, the workday ended early. Hollis had hoped to sneak out closer to four and end the day at a happy hour outside somewhere. The reality hit her that this unwritten rule might change with her new boss.

“Of course, she’s meeting with us separately,” Harrison said.

“Why is that so obvious?”

“You know these corporate types.” He sat up in his chair. “She’s going to follow the typical formula of no changes for thirty days. She’ll say she’s just getting to know the team or drinking from the firehose or whatever buzzword she wants.”

Hollis laughed. She liked Fitwear, but she and Harrison both shared a distaste for corporate bullshit. Yet another reason she needed to stay far away from dating Ainsley Jones.

At 4:29 p.m., Hollis shifted uncomfortably in the armless black leather chair outside the large corner office. While the office was on the same floor as Hollis, she had actually never been to this section of the floor. It made sense that the new president would have the large, vacant office. She couldn’t decide what was worse, the fact that her new boss had asked her out, or the fact that Hollis would have to turn her down. What if Ainsley held that against her? For all of her thought that dating could ruin her focus on her career, maybe saying no to dates was just as bad. She let out a breath. She couldn’t go into this meeting with her mind dialed up.

A new assistant sat behind the desk directly outside what was now Ainsley Jones's office. He seemed young. Hollis thought twenty-two, maybe twenty-three. He wore a tight-fitting gray suit with a skinny black tie. In his right ear, Hollis noticed a small black, Bluetooth earpiece. She thought it looked extremely dorky, but it was probably necessary for the position he held.

The door opened, and the room filled with Ainsley Jones's magnificent laugh. Her still wrecked stomach did a somersault.

"Yes, we'll do that sometime," she said as Harrison left her office.

"I'm holding you to that." Harrison pointed directly at her and flashed a grin.

Ainsley laughed again. "Parker, Ms. Reed, here is my last appointment of the day. You can go ahead and head home now if you like."

Parker nodded. "Thank you, Ms. Jones."

Hollis noticed Harrison catch Parker's eye. Harrison held out his hand. "Parker, is it? I'm Harrison Scott."

"Shall we?" Ainsley motioned for Hollis to enter her office.

Hollis had never known there was this kind of view from this side of the building. The Willamette River reflected the sun outside the floor-to-ceiling windows and Hollis wished she was somewhere with a drink in her hand watching the water flow instead of in this meet and greet. Ainsley headed behind her desk, removed her black suit jacket, and hung it on the back of her office chair. "Sorry, I was getting warm."

"It's fine," Hollis said.

Ainsley motioned to the conference room table next to Hollis. "We'll have a seat over there."

Hollis side stepped over to the table and noticed as Ainsley bent forward to grab papers off of her desk. Her cream blouse flowed beautifully off the curves that Hollis had seen in that tank top on Saturday. She saw Ainsley's collar bone exposed and realized she had undone a few more buttons on her blouse since this morning's meeting. She tried to shake the images that had been living in her brain all weekend, but being this close made it difficult. How would it feel to run her fingers along that exposed collarbone? Was Ainsley's skin as soft and smooth as it looked?

Ainsley tapped a pile of papers together and made eye contact with Hollis. "Were you sore after your first time?"

Hollis's mouth became dry. "I'm sorry, what?"

"Your first time at spin class?" Ainsley clarified. "Most people are sore after the first one."

Hollis let out a small breath. "Ah yes. Of course. Actually, I was a little sore."

Ainsley sat down across from her.

"I normally just stick to running, but that class definitely worked muscles I haven't used in a while."

Ainsley let out a small laugh and Hollis relaxed, the built-up tension from the day releasing in Ainsley's presence. "You runners are all the same."

"How's that?" Hollis asked.

"You think that running is the only suitable exercise and forget that cross-training is the only way you're going to actually get any faster."

Hollis furrowed her brow. *How do you know that?*

"Let me guess, you're a marathon runner?" Ainsley asked.

Still confused, Hollis responded, "How'd you know?"

"It's my superpower," Ainsley said. "Maybe it's because I've been in this industry so long, but I can guess anybody's exercise of choice."

"That's a heck of a superpower."

"Cross-training. Trust me." She picked up the stack of papers and tapped them on the table.

Hollis narrowed her eyes. "Thanks for the advice."

Were they really not going to talk about the elephant in the room? Maybe it wasn't as big a deal as she was making it out to be. Ainsley probably asked out dozens of women. She took in a breath and for the first time inhaled Ainsley's perfume. It was floral and intoxicating. Hollis wondered how her scent could still be this strong at the end of the day. Had she freshened up for this meeting? No. That wasn't possible.

Ainsley returned the papers to the table. "Anyway. That Harrison is quite a character."

"He is. And a great partner."

"So how is it that we have two people doing the work for one department?" Ainsley's tone changed and Hollis wondered why her department was under the microscope.

"I don't know that I'd put it like that."

"How would you put it?" Ainsley made direct eye contact with Hollis.

Hollis thought this was a meet and greet, a typical, "so tell me how you got here" or "why you like working here" situation. She didn't expect that her actual position would be in question on day one. But if Ainsley was thinking about sweeping changes, of course she'd be scrutinizing everyone's position. "Well, for starters, our department is over one hundred people."

Ainsley gave a small nod.

"Most of them are out in the field, but we have a dozen process owners who sit here," she paused, searching carefully for the right words. "I don't need to tell you that our supply chain is complicated."

Ainsley nodded in agreement.

"So, with all the moving parts, it takes both of us coordinating our efforts. I'm sure you can see that our results speak for themselves."

Ainsley sat back slightly. "They do. And honestly, I was very impressed with the summary you submitted."

Hollis sighed in relief. She worked hard on that summary, knowing she would need to impress the new boss.

"I can tell that you take your work seriously," Ainsley said.

"I do."

"But some people could argue that the results of your department are because you have two people doing the work of one."

"But—"

Ainsley held up her hand. "I'm not saying I think that. I'm just saying, one could argue." She made a sweeping motion with her hand. "When you have two people in this kind of position, it would be expected that the results would be head and shoulders above everyone else."

Hollis's heart beat hard in her chest. Was she the last meeting of the day because she was getting fired? If she'd gone on that date already, would this be a very different meeting? She hesitated before responding. "I guess I never thought of it that way."

"I'm still getting to know the team." She gave a forced laugh. "I'm still drinking from the firehose."

Hollis wanted to burst into laughter, but she composed herself. A bird chirped and she looked to the window; of course there were birds out on this beautiful day. No. No birds. The sound chirped again. This time Ainsley took notice.

"Oh my God." Hollis patted her thigh as she realized the chirping was coming from her. "I am so sorry. I thought I put this on silent."

"Go ahead," Ainsley said.

Hollis fumbled with her phone as she pulled it out of her pocket. As she went to change the settings, her eye couldn't help but focus on the texts scrolling across the screen. *The Ex.* She had changed Miranda's name in her phone after the breakup. She was tired of looking at it. She figured if she saw texts or calls from *The Ex*, it'd be easier to ignore them. She should have deleted the number altogether, she should have blocked her, but she hadn't. She knew she should look away and focus her attention on her new boss, but the text was long:

So I found a few of your things as I was cleaning my place. It's too much for me to bring to work and have you carry home since you refuse to drive and all. I'm tired of looking at your things, so tell me when I can bring your stuff by your place.

Hollis just shook her head.

A picture of a tri-colored Australian shepherd filled the screen, followed by:

Jasper misses you : (

"I'm not sharing custody of a dog," Hollis said under her breath.

"Is everything okay?" Ainsley motioned to her phone.

"I am so sorry about that." Hollis tried to regain her bearings and remember she was still at work. "Just some annoying personal things."

"Is that your messy situation?" Ainsley gave a hint of a smile.

"It's nothing important." She double-checked her phone was set to do not disturb and put it face down on the table.

Ainsley eyed the phone, and then Hollis. "So, what would you change?"

"I've been working on owning the part that's mine."

Ainsley arched one of her perfect eyebrows.

"I didn't communicate well enough. I thought that I was clear that I wasn't ready for a big commitment. My career has always been my focus, and I didn't want anything or anyone to take away from that. Looking back, I may have led her on by entertaining conversations I shouldn't have. It doesn't matter now. I ended it because I need to refocus on work right now."

Ainsley nodded in agreement. She seemed to be listening intently, and Hollis appreciated having her full attention.

"She always harped on me for working too much. The thing is? I love my job, so it never feels like I'm working too much. It just feels right. She told me she wanted to start a family, but I wasn't around enough for that kind of commitment."

"And you didn't want a family?"

"Not necessarily. My timeline now is professional for the next five years. And…" Hollis hesitated.

Ainsley said quietly, "And something else?"

"She had a picture of the perfect family and the perfect house and I realized I had made a mistake. We were not at the same place in life, and I should have seen that sooner. I should have seen a lot of things sooner." She sighed. "The dog was a compromise. And another mistake."

Ainsley snorted.

"Then she told me I wasn't even around enough to properly care for a dog." Hollis put both her palms up. "Whatever that means. So, then she told me I had to choose between work or her."

"And you chose work?"

"Oh my God." Hollis's cheeks flushed. "I just realized you weren't asking about my ex." Why on earth would Ainsley care about any of this? The question was about work. She wanted to slap herself on the forehead but refrained.

"Well, originally I had meant what would you change about Fitwear, but getting to know my employees is part of the job."

"I can't believe I just word vomited all over you."

Ainsley let out a laugh. "It's really okay."

"Are we going to talk about Saturday?" Hollis couldn't keep her work life and personal life sorted in her brain.

"You said you didn't mind spin class," Ainsley joked.

"I meant that part right after class."

"Right." Ainsley stiffened.

"I think I'm going to have to change my answer given that we now work together. I don't like to mix business and pleasure and I think—"

Ainsley broke in. "Regardless of why, it doesn't matter now. It would be extremely unprofessional, so how about we just try to move past that? Okay?"

"I'm going to take a deep breath and try this again." Hollis looked down at the conference table and fought the urge to hide under it. Maybe being open and honest with her boss wouldn't be the worst thing in the world? Nope. Sharing the intricacies of why she and her ex-girlfriend broke up and then rejecting her boss for a date was absolutely the worst thing in the world. She exhaled to the count of three. "Brick-and-mortar stores."

"Brick and mortar stores are dead." Ainsley shook her head.

"That's what they want you to think. It's all in the marketing. If we had stores where customers knew they could try on products or exchange and return them for free, it would take us to the next level."

Ainsley stayed silent.

"People are hesitant to buy clothes online if they can't try them on. Think about it. Are you going to commit to running twenty miles in a pair of leggings if you don't know how they fit?"

"I'm not committing to running twenty miles period," Ainsley scoffed.

"You know what I mean." Hollis dismissed her comment. "Once someone gets a product they like and knows it fits, they are hooked. We see it in the repeat customer data."

"Where is this going?"

"It's the return process." Hollis saw Ainsley start to interject and cut her off. "I know, I know. We offer free returns and shipping labels and all that. But it still requires work on the part of the customer. They have to repackage the item, get the label on it, and then take it to the post office or whatever. If you are a stay-at-home mother of three, do you want to drag your kids to the post office of all places?"

"I guess not." A look of thought consumed Ainsley's face.

"We have the supply chain network in place. We have proven we can get product anywhere in the country at any time. Now all we need is the real estate. If we had brick-and-mortar stores in a few strategic locations, I guarantee you they would be profitable in the first year."

"Really?"

That was it. Profitability finally got the new bosses' attention. She should have led with that. Profitable departments rarely faced restructuring. "Absolutely. And the framework is already there. We just need the right marketing team and real estate strategy to make it a reality."

Ainsley sat back and Hollis could tell she was thinking about her words. Hollis wondered if she had said too much. She was passionate on the subject. She knew she got excited when she was passionate, but the reality was it was a good idea, and she would have shared it, eventually.

"That could work."

"Like I said, it's all in the marketing and real estate strategy. Definitely not my area of expertise, but the pieces are all there. Someone just has to put them together." She interlaced her fingers on both her hands.

Ainsley looked at her watch. "It's getting late, and I'm sure you have a home life to get to."

Hollis thought of the empty studio apartment waiting for her.

"I'll be getting to know the team more over the next sixty to ninety days. I think you'll find I'm a manager who likes to get in the weeds and work with her team."

Hollis fought the urge to roll her eyes.

"And I want to talk more about this brick-and-mortar idea."

"Of course." Hollis wondered if Ainsley was already planning the kind of changes Hollis wouldn't like.

CHAPTER SIX

Harrison waited in his desk chair when Hollis arrived the next day. He pushed a coffee into Hollis's hand.

Hollis took the drink. "Is this a thing now?"

"At least until my cute barista friend gets a real job." Harrison straightened a stack of papers off his desk. He dressed to impress in a black suit with a dark red tie.

"You ask him out yet?" Hollis pulled out her laptop.

"Well, I was a little busy with Parker last night."

Hollis shook her head. "I knew he didn't stand a chance."

"Hey," Harrison said, "I figured getting some intel on the new boss would be a good thing. Speaking of, how was your meet and greet?"

"It was fine." Hollis was still processing last night's meeting and the complete fool of herself she'd made in front of the boss.

"That's it?" Harrison sounded disappointed. "That's all I get? It was fine."

"It was a normal meeting," she said hesitantly.

"Spill it."

Hollis replayed the entire meeting for him. She started with the accusation of them having two people to do the work of one. Then the embarrassing details of the text from *The Ex* and then ended with sharing the idea Harrison had already heard a million times.

Once she had finished, Harrison sat back in his chair. "Damn."

"What?"

"So now what?" he asked.

"What do you mean?"

"She's clearly into you."

"Are you forgetting the part where I brought up Saturday and she said we should try and move past?"

"She had to say that. You know, being the boss and all."

"What the actual hell are you talking about?"

"No woman is going to care to listen to you drone on and on about an ex unless they are into you."

"She just felt bad for me." Hollis thought about it. Was she into her? Plus, even if she wanted to ask her out, Ainsley had shut that down.

"She could have stopped and redirected the conversation several times. She was interested in hearing where it went. I would say that means she's into you."

"She's the boss," Hollis said. "You can't ask the boss out."

"Maybe you can't," Harrison mumbled. "This is perfect. Don't you see it?"

"How is this perfect?" Hollis tried to push images of Ainsley's sculpted arms out of her mind. How could she ever focus knowing what those arms looked like under her suit jacket?

"She can't get mad at you for working too much. The more you work, in theory, the better you perform, and that makes her look good. Perfect!" Harrison clapped his hands together.

"This will never work." Not to mention the fact that she was done with relationships.

"She probably works more than you do. You can have romantic dinners by computer monitor light." Harrison droned on, but Hollis couldn't listen to him anymore. She needed a plan and fast.

"Alright," she finally cut him off. "Can we get back to work now, please? We can discuss my dating life, or lack thereof, another time."

Harrison picked the stack of papers off the desk and threw it in Hollis's lap. "We need to crack some skulls."

"What's this?"

"New inbound SOP that went out today. There are eight typos. I highlighted them for you." He pointed to the red marks on the page.

"Eight typos in a standard operating procedure?" Hollis shook her head as she read through the stack. "This is bad. How big was the rollout?"

"Whole West Coast division," Harrison answered. "Oh, and get this, one of the typos was Fitwear."

"Shit." Hollis hated for her department to look sloppy. She especially hated Ainsley to see any kind of mistake coming from her department, after she thought they were overstaffed, anyway. Hollis was going to make sure that everything out of the supply chain department was perfect for the foreseeable future. "How do you want to play it?"

Harrison stroked his chin. "I'm thinking bad cop, worse cop, with all the process owners."

"Okay. When?"

"Weekly meeting that's scheduled for today?"

"I'll get my speech ready."

"I have a question." Harrison leaned forward, elbows on his knees, staring at Hollis intently.

Hollis nodded his direction.

"If you and Ainsley are both type A ice queens, which one would be on top?" He burst out laughing.

Hollis flushed red with embarrassment. "Shut up." She turned around and tried to shake the image of Ainsley on top out of her mind.

Harrison and Hollis stood in silence waiting for the elevator. Hollis knew the mood Harrison was in and she couldn't handle any more jabs about their new boss heading into this meeting. The elevator doors opened, and Hollis swallowed hard as she looked at Ainsley Jones, who stood engrossed by her phone. She wore a navy suit with a stark white blouse, and a gold necklace.

Ainsley looked up from her phone as she exited. "Hey, you two."

"Hi." Hollis gave an awkward wave.

Ainsley's eyes grazed across her body from head to toe. Or at least she thought she did. Hollis hadn't put as much effort into her look today, but still looked professional, wearing light gray pants and a sky-blue blouse. She held Ainsley's gaze as she definitely caught her looking. Her cheeks flushed just slightly. Ainsley's auburn curls bounced back and forth as she passed. The curls were definitely natural.

The second the elevator doors closed, Harrison turned and faced Hollis. "You still think she's not into you?"

"Shit." Hollis looked down. "I didn't even say good morning or anything."

Harrison laughed.

"I should have at least said something. Instead, I barely managed a word." She put one hand over her face. "What a numbskull."

"For what it's worth, she thinks you're a good-looking numbskull." Harrison laughed again.

"Oh God." Hollis closed her eyes and replayed the exchange in her mind. Could she have a single interaction with Ainsley, without making a fool of herself?

The elevator dinged, and the doors opened. "Get your game face on." Harrison motioned for Hollis to exit first.

❖

Hollis laughed as she sat in her chair. Harrison replayed the meeting the whole way back.

"And then," he laughed. "David's face when you said, Fitwear is literally on your shirt," he mocked Hollis's voice and burst into laughter again.

"I think they got the message." Hollis truly treasured her job. Even when her team messed up, like they had today, they owned their mistakes and fixed them. Most days she still couldn't believe she found a company that she loved and a job that she actually enjoyed.

She and Harrison had their roles dialed in and only scratched the surface of what they would accomplish.

"Do you have a minute?"

Hollis turned around at the familiar voice. She remembered to speak this time. "Hey."

Ainsley looked directly at Hollis. "Did you get my email?"

Hollis looked over her shoulder and saw an unopened email at the top of her inbox.

"We just got back from a meeting," she said. She prided herself on being on top of her inbox and clearing it to zero every day. "I see it right here. I'll get on it right away."

"Great." Ainsley tapped the door frame with her hand. "Come by my office once you're up to speed."

"Of course."

What was so urgent? She glanced at her watch. 11:01a.m. The email showed a timestamp of 11:00 a.m. Ainsley would have had to hit send and then come over here immediately.

"Oh God, she's one of those," she said to her laptop and put her head in her hands.

"One of what?" Harrison asked.

"One of those people who hit send on an email and then come over to ask if you got it." She spoke into her hands.

In all of her worrying over a new boss, she had never considered that she would work for a micromanager. She had been fortunate in the last year having a boss not only in a different state, but a different time zone. Since she and Harrison hit all of their metrics and outperformed most of the country, they had been left alone, which was exactly the way she wanted it. A sinking feeling came over her as she thought about how those days were over. She glanced over the email. It made little sense and seemed rather cryptic. She stood to head toward Ainsley's office.

"Say hi to your girlfriend for me."

"Knock it off," she snapped over her shoulder.

Parker typed on his laptop outside of Ainsley's office. He had a smile across his face that wasn't there the day before. Harrison had that effect on men. She cleared her throat. "Ainsley asked me to come by."

Parker nodded but didn't look up. He pushed a button on his earpiece. "Yes, Ms. Jones. Ms. Reed is here to see you." He pushed the button on his earpiece. "Go ahead and go in."

"Thanks." Hollis took a deep breath and opened the door. Ainsley sat behind her large mahogany desk with a dark wooden credenza desk behind her. She added a few pictures Hollis noticed weren't there the day before. Ainsley wore black-framed reading glasses that Hollis hadn't seen. Her stomach did the flip that was becoming more and more familiar in Ainsley's presence. She thought she had composed herself, but the glasses gave a new layer to Ainsley's look that she wasn't prepared for.

Ainsley looked up and motioned for Hollis to have a seat at the conference table they had sat at yesterday.

Get it together. She needed to get her mind right and focus on work. She took a seat and waited.

Ainsley walked across the room—more like floated. She pulled out her chair and sat. "I'm sorry about earlier."

Hollis wrinkled her brow, not expecting an apology. "I don't think you have anything to be sorry for."

"The whole did you get my email thing. That's not me." She sounded apologetic.

Hollis let out a long breath. "Oh, thank God."

Ainsley raised an eyebrow.

"You're the boss. And you can manage whatever way you like, but I'm not used to that level of micromanagement."

"I see."

"I'm actually not used to a whole lot of interaction with my boss. Our last meeting was actually more than I'd ever shared with a boss." Good God, why did she have to bring up one of her most embarrassing interactions?

"Really?"

"I tend to keep work and my personal life separate. Sharing too much tends to blur those lines." Hollis could tell that Ainsley was looking right at her.

"Well, I hope that we can have a close working relationship. I'm certainly not a micromanager, but I do like to be hands-on."

Hollis's mouth went dry.

"Anyway, I'm sorry about before. I just needed you." Ainsley shook her head, flustered. "That came out wrong. I needed to see you."

Hollis squinted at Ainsley. Was it possible that she made Ainsley just as nervous as she made her? Was there even a remote possibility that Ainsley's body was as revved up as Hollis's at that moment? She wasn't crazy, was she? There was something here. Something much more than a new boss wanting to have a professional relationship.

"I'm normally much more together than this," Ainsley said.

Hollis decided to throw her a bone. "Time change?"

"Yes. I'm having a much harder time adjusting than I anticipated. Anyway, I need your help."

"How can I be of service?" Hollis asked, then regretted her word choice. It sounded silly. She sounded silly. Overeager.

"I've been thinking about the brick-and-mortar idea you were telling me about last night." Ainsley leaned forward.

"I'm sorry if I overstepped on that. I know it's not my department, and it's a half-baked idea."

"No." Ainsley shook her head. "It's a great idea. I've been thinking about it all morning."

Hollis sat up a little taller.

"Do you have any numbers to support the data?"

Hollis shook her head. "Nothing definitive. I have a few reports, but I haven't done a full budget or anything."

Ainsley narrowed her gaze. "Is that something you think you could pull together?"

Hollis thought about it. "I need to pull data from a few different places, but I don't see why not."

"I want to pitch this idea to Andrew."

"Really?" Hollis met Ainsley's gaze. Her eyes, she realized, were not just brown—but brown with specks of gold. She caught her mind wandering and refocused.

"Yes. And we have a big meeting next week to talk about all the projects for the next fiscal year. If your idea is as good on paper as I think it is, it's a home run."

Hollis knew it was a brilliant idea, and she appreciated validation.

"I know it's a quick turnaround, but is there any way you can get me numbers by Monday? They can be rough. Directionally correct is fine. That will give me a few days to put something together before the meeting with Andrew."

Hollis would have agreed to anything after looking into those eyes. "I can make that happen."

"Great." Ainsley clapped her hands together. "Let me know if you need anything."

You have no idea.

Chapter Seven

Hollister Elizabeth Reed, it is Friday night and time to quit working," Harrison admonished her from across the office.

"You know that's not my name." This joke was beyond old. For whatever reason, Harrison enjoyed making up middle names for Hollis, and it annoyed her to no end. Harrison stood, laptop bag over one shoulder and ready to go.

"I really need to get this finished tonight." She had meant to finish the report for Ainsley much earlier in the week, but fires kept popping up.

"Even your phone thinks it's time to quit working. That thing has been lighting up all afternoon." Harrison motioned to Hollis's phone on the desk.

"Oh, that's just Bobby."

"Bobby? Is that short for Roberta?" He waggled his eyebrows.

"What? No."

"You haven't really been with butches before, but I guess I can picture it." Harrison stroked his chin.

"Oh my God, no." Hollis squeezed her eyes shut. She didn't have time for Harrison right now if she had any hope of finishing work tonight. "My old boss, Bobby."

"Oh. So you have a thing for bosses."

"I don't have a thing for anyone," Hollis snapped.

Thankfully, Harrison noticed the shift in her and backed off. "If the new boss sees you working late on a Friday, she's going to expect it."

"I know. But if she sees me working on a Saturday, she'll expect that too. This is the lesser of two evils."

"Okay, but we have that mixer tonight. You know the one for the new president?" Harrison said suggestively.

"I know, I know. But we both know I was going to show up late, stay for my two company provided drinks, and leave early."

"Gosh, you are no fun," Harrison said dramatically.

"If you leave now and let me finish this, I will stay for three drinks."

"Let's not get too crazy. I'll save you a seat."

"Get out of here so I can actually get some work done."

Hollis rubbed her hands over her face and stared at her screen. She was trying to pick back up where she left off, but it was Friday night, and her eyes burned from staring at screens all week. Someone moved at the door.

"For fuck's sake, Harrison, I'll be there as soon as I'm done."

"Is that how you talk to all of your coworkers?"

Her stomach dropped as she recognized Ainsley's voice. Maybe Harrison had gotten really good at impressions in the last five minutes. She closed her eyes as she turned around, wishing she had just cussed out anyone but her new boss. She slowly opened her eyes to see Ainsley standing at her office door. "Harrison's more of a brother than a coworker."

Ainsley quirked her eyebrow.

"You know, we're a big happy family here at Fitwear." Hollis awkwardly tried to make a joke.

"You're working awfully late."

Hollis was thankful for the topic change. She'd been trying to avoid her new boss since the awkward interaction on Monday, but no matter how hard she tried, she couldn't act like a normal person in front of Ainsley. Hollis figured if she put enough space between them, she could get over her initial attraction. She needed to focus on the fact that Ainsley was a bit of a micromanager and not what her ass looked like in yoga pants. Hollis leaned back in her chair. "Well, I got a new boss this week and on top of my already busy schedule, she gave me a special project with a tight deadline." Hollis could have sworn she saw a smile come across Ainsley's face. "And I don't want to work this weekend, so here I am."

"I see." Ainsley nodded. "Any big plans for this weekend of yours?"

"Only if you count running twenty miles on Sunday as big plans."

Ainsley let out a laugh and flicked her wrist. "Runners."

"Most people don't get it," Hollis said.

Ainsley crossed her arms. "Oh, I get it. Are you training for anything?"

"A marathon at the end of May," Hollis replied.

"Huh," Ainsley said as if thinking. "Isn't it a little soon for twenty?"

Maybe Ainsley really did get it. "It's a new strategy I'm trying."

"Does this new strategy involve cross-training?" Ainsley prodded.

Hollis chuckled and met the brown eyes gazing at her.

Ainsley leaned into the doorframe, arms still crossed. "So, if I could convince your boss to move the deadline to let's say, Tuesday, would that mean you could leave now for the company get-together?"

"You can try," Hollis joked. "But she's a real hard-ass."

Ainsley let out a laugh. "I can be very persuasive." She narrowed her focus on Hollis.

"If I could have until Tuesday, then that would mean that I could start my weekend now and head straight to the welcome party for the new president." Hollis rocked back and forth slightly in her chair.

"How about I talk to your boss and, as a way of saying thank you, you head over with me? I'm still getting to know the area and I don't want to get lost." There was a slight hesitation to Ainsley's question.

"Okay." Hollis nodded. It was hard to deny the feelings forming inside her. She knew better than to spend more alone time with someone she could potentially fall for, let alone her boss, but when it came to Ainsley, she couldn't stay logical. She struggled to stick to her plan.

❖

The gray sky looked like it could rain at any minute as they left the Fitwear entrance. The weather had been unseasonably warm all week, and everyone had gotten spoiled seeing the sun four days in a row. Now that the weekend was here, the sun decided to go back into hiding. Hollis didn't mind as she was happy it was getting warmer and lighter out every day.

"I would have been happy to drive," Ainsley said.

"And be stuck in a car for ten minutes only to stress about finding a parking spot? I think not." Hollis would take walking to driving any day.

"So, do you not drive?" Ainsley asked.

Hollis laughed. "I drive." She paused. "I just don't like to."

"You just walk everywhere?" The concept sounded foreign coming out of Ainsley's mouth.

"Everywhere I can," Hollis said. "My last job was a forty-five-minute commute one way. With no traffic, it should have been twenty. So now, I walk as much as I possibly can. Plus, it helps me get my steps in." She held up the fitness tracker on her right hand.

Hollis opened the door to the bar for Ainsley and followed her in. Legends was her go-to and also happened to be a great gathering place for work events. It was only slightly unfortunate that now all of her work colleagues could run into her on any given night, but it was close to her apartment, had a great beer selection, and the food was always good. It was an upscale bar with high-top tables and exposed wood beams for décor. Hollis led her to a large group of tables in the back where her coworkers were already several rounds in.

Ainsley picked up one of the printed drink menus and studied it in her hand. "I have missed IPAs." She kept reading over the list.

"They try in North Carolina. The brewery scene is up-and-coming, but they still haven't figured out how to make a good IPA. No, the best IPAs come from home."

Hollis looked at her. "So you're not from Raleigh?"

"God no. I'm from here."

"Really? I guess I just assumed."

"Well, technically I'm from Vancouver." She turned the paper menu over and kept reading.

"Oh, so you're one of those." Hollis playfully drug out her words.

Ainsley looked at Hollis over the menu. "What does that mean?"

"Oh, just one of those Washingtonians who think that Vancouver is great and Portland is trash."

"No." She shook her head. "I'm not one of those. I have no animosity toward Oregon."

"Hey, boss!" Harrison appeared, an empty martini glass in his hand. "This is perfect. I was just headed to the bar to get a drink, and you have an empty hand. What are you drinking?"

Ainsley pointed to a triple IPA on the menu. "It's really okay. I can get my own drink."

"Nonsense." Harrison put an arm around Hollis. "The boss should stay and mingle and Holly and I will take care of the drinks."

Ainsley snickered as Hollis whipped her head toward Harrison. "Seriously? Can you just call me my name?"

Harrison steered her to the bar.

"Hey, Trevor," she called to the tall, gangly bartender. His black "Legends" T-shirt showed off his tattooed arm sleeves.

"What are we having tonight, Hol?" he asked.

"The regular for me, and that triple hopped whatever." She pointed to the tap.

"For your date?" He smirked as he poured the glass.

"Right?" Harrison interjected. "Wouldn't they look so cute together?"

Hollis ran her hands over her face. "You have to stop. I didn't even want to come to this in the first place. Now let me have my two company-paid-for drinks in peace and then go home."

"Buzz kill." Harrison motioned with his thumb toward Hollis.

Hollis and Harrison returned, drinks in hand, and Hollis swore she saw a flash of relief in Ainsley's eyes. It must have been hard to be the newcomer to such a close-knit team.

"Thanks." Ainsley brushed Hollis's hand slightly as she took the beer from her.

"So, boss, what do you think of HQ II so far?" Harrison asked.

"The team seems great." Ainsley gave a non-answer. "But that's enough about work. This is supposed to be about us all getting to know each other better."

Hollis tried to mask her eye roll as coworkers seemed to come out of the woodwork for a few minutes with Ainsley. If she wanted to climb the corporate ladder, she should learn to schmooze better, but today wasn't the day for learning new skills. As the conversation slowed, Ainsley's eyes widen in excitement. "Is that shuffleboard?"

Hollis turned around. She had never noticed that there were shuffleboard tables in the back, despite the fact that she was here once a week.

"We have to play!"

"I've never actually played," Hollis admitted.

"It's so fun." Ainsley's excitement picked up. "I'll teach you. It's easy. We just need two more people."

Hollis hesitated. The last thing she wanted to do was embarrass herself, but Ainsley's enthusiasm was infectious. She could talk her into doing anything. "Harrison!"

Harrison appeared with Parker in tow. "You rang?"

"You're on my shuffleboard team."

"You really know how to make a guy feel special."

Hollis looked to the young receptionist behind him. "This is perfect. Parker, you're with Ainsley."

"Sure thing." Parker and Harrison took the other end of the table.

Ainsley took the pucks, or whatever she had called them, and laid them out on the table. "The goal is to get as close to that number three on the other side of the table as possible."

Hollis looked at the long wooden table. It was a light wood, and had a one, two, and three clearly marked off on both sides. The bottom was dark leather with an overhang to catch the pucks that sailed off the ends. She stared at Ainsley's hands as she laid the metal pieces on the board. Four had red tops and the other four had blue tops. Her slender fingers skillfully lined the pucks on the board.

"Red or blue?" Ainsley asked.

Hollis was too distracted thinking about those hands to listen. "What's that?" She needed to focus.

"Do you want to be red or blue?" She held a red puck in one hand and a blue in the other.

"Um, red." Hollis didn't care.

"Good. Because I'm always blue." Ainsley bent slightly over the long wooden table. She squinted, aiming at the lines on the other end of the table. Hollis couldn't believe she'd never noticed this gigantic table before. Ainsley slowly glided the puck back and forth in her hands and released it. It floated down the table, sailed past the one mark, past the two, and landed squarely in the three section. Ainsley clapped her hands together and stood up.

"Whoa! Nice work, boss!" Harrison yelled from the other end of the table. "I didn't realize we were about to get hustled." Parker laughed way too hard at that joke.

"I'm in trouble," Hollis said.

"I'm sure you're a fast learner." Ainsley gave her a wink.

Hollis stood where Ainsley was and slid the puck back and forth in her hands. It was heavier than she expected. She took a deep breath, slid the puck back, and released. It zoomed to the other end of the table and hit the back with a loud thud.

"That was a little hard," Ainsley said.

"That's what he said!" Harrison couldn't help himself.

"You think?" Hollis stepped aside to let Ainsley take her next turn. She noticed that the jeans she had changed into hugged her just right and extenuated her slight curves. Ainsley's next shot glided across the table and landed within inches of the first one. "You are, like, really good at this."

"Too many college nights with Greg in bars instead of studying."

"I think you turned out alright." Hollis approached the end of the table. Ainsley leaned in right behind her. Their legs almost touching, and heat radiated from behind her.

"Let me help," Ainsley said.

Hollis sucked in a breath. Ainsley bent over and put her hand on top of hers. Ainsley's electric touch sparked energy through her entire body. She tried to control her heart rate; she didn't want Ainsley to feel her racing pulse. She looked up, unsure of what Harrison would make of this situation. Fortunately, he was so busy flirting with Parker, he didn't notice anyone else at the bar.

"The trick is in the release," Ainsley said just above a whisper into Hollis's ear.

It would be so easy to turn and kiss her. She shook her head again. Ainsley moved their hands slowly back and forth and then released the puck. It went slowly, but made it across the table and landed close to the two.

"Much better." Ainsley took a step back.

Hollis turned around to face her. "Having a good teacher helps."

They took turns playing back and forth. Ainsley and Parker—well, mostly Ainsley—killed in all three games. Normally, Hollis would hate losing, but for some reason, with Ainsley she didn't care.

"Well, I don't think we'll be joining shuffleboard leagues anytime soon." Harrison met up with Ainsley and Hollis at the middle of the table.

"This game has leagues?" Hollis barely knew shuffleboard existed before tonight.

"How do you think I got so good?"

"Ah! So you did hustle us. I knew I liked you," Harrison replied. "I think I'm going to head out."

Hollis noticed the bar had cleared of Fitwear employees and was more or less the usual Friday night crowd.

"Will I see you at spin class tomorrow?" Harrison looked between Hollis and Ainsley.

"Maybe," Ainsley said. "Greg does owe me lunch for covering for him last week."

"Not a chance in hell," Hollis said. "See you Monday."

Harrison left, and Parker followed without saying a word.

"Is that a fire pit outside?" Ainsley looked to the back patio behind them.

"Yes."

"I am not ready to go home yet, and another drink by the fire sounds amazing. What do you say?"

How could Hollis say no to an offer like that? Another drink outside with a beautiful woman? With your boss, she corrected herself. You are not with a beautiful woman, you are with your boss. Your boss who might very well intend to cut your position.

"I'll go grab us refills, you go grab us seats," Hollis said.

CHAPTER EIGHT

Thanks." Ainsley took the beer from Hollis and took a small sip. She wiped foam off her upper lip, and Hollis tried not to stare. "This is really good."

"I'm glad you like it. I've been coming here for years, and it's finally starting to take off." Hollis took a sip of her beer. She leaned back into the tan Adirondack chair surrounding the propane fireplace. Ainsley had snagged the last two spots, and the fire warmed Hollis's legs as a chill infiltrated the air. She set her drink on the large chair arm. Something brushed past Hollis's feet. A tri-colored Australian shepherd jumped up and placed two paws on Ainsley's chair.

"Well, hi there," Ainsley said and scratched his head. The dog's tail whipped back and forth.

"Jasper?" The dog panted excitedly. "Shit."

"It's okay." Ainsley leaned down closer to scratch the dog. "I love dogs."

"It's not the dog." Hollis looked around frantically. "It's the owner."

"I am so sorry." Hollis recoiled from the speaker like she had just heard nails on a chalkboard. "He just gets away from me sometimes."

"Oh, it's okay," Ainsley replied. "He is just so cute." Ainsley made a baby voice.

"Oh my gosh. You're Ainsley, the new president. This is even more embarrassing."

"Nonsense." Ainsley continued scratching Jasper behind his ears.

"I'm Miranda Smith. I work in accounts payable."

Ainsley stood to shake her hand. "Great to meet you."

Hollis held her breath hoping that if she stayed still Miranda wouldn't see her and would leave. That trick allegedly worked on T. Rexes, maybe it worked on ex-girlfriends too?

"Hollis?"

Dammit. It didn't work. "Hi, Miranda."

"Already talking work with the new boss I see."

Hollis stayed in her chair. "You know me. Always working too much." Something looked different about Miranda, but she couldn't quite put her finger on it. She'd been avoiding Miranda since the breakup, making sure not to linger in common spaces too long. "You changed your hair." Hollis finally put the pieces together noting the new bangs she sported. Hollis didn't like it. Not that it mattered since it wasn't her place to care about Miranda's looks anymore.

Miranda gave a shrug. "Yeah, I needed a change. A fresh start, you know?"

Hollis nodded. "I do."

"Some of us need sunshine and sand, some of us get by with a new haircut."

Miranda's point was not missed. She was referring to the breakup trip Hollis had taken with Harrison. Hollis took a deep breath. She needed to compose herself and not let Miranda get under her skin.

"You know what's great about accounts payable? No long after-hours meetings, no angry customers, just bills to be paid."

Hollis steadied her breath. She broke it off with Miranda in part because she couldn't keep having this fight. Relationships were supposed to be fun.

Ainsley broke the tension. "It sounds like we're lucky to have someone so on top of our finances." Ainsley was ever the diplomat.

Miranda snapped her fingers and Jasper healed at her side. "Hey, since I've got you, when can I bring that stuff by your place?"

Not this again. Was there really anything she needed? "Can't you just donate it?"

"Believe me, I thought about it. But it's a pair of running shoes, some fancy running jacket and a couple of books."

So that's where that jacket went. Hollis ended up at Miranda's place mid run when she had been inspired to take part in a different form of cardio. By the time she left, it had been too warm to need her favorite running jacket. "I don't care. Tomorrow?" She wouldn't allow Miranda to see how much she wanted that jacket back.

Miranda made a thinking face. "Tomorrow won't work. It's JayDee's birthday, remember?"

Hollis sighed. "Okay, next Saturday?"

Miranda pulled out her phone to look at her calendar. "I think I can make that work. What time?"

"Anytime." Hollis was over this.

"I need a time, Hollis. I'm not going to bring it by and leave it outside your door," her tone was condescending.

"How about ten?"

"Are you sure you won't be out running?" her disgust was clear.

"I'll make sure I'm done in time," Hollis said.

"Great. Ten it is." She waved at Ainsley. "It was so nice to meet you." She pulled at Jasper's leash as she left.

Hollis let out a long breath and sank back into her chair. She resisted the urge to chug the rest of her beer.

"Wait." Ainsley shot Hollis a look.

"What?"

"Don't slouch," Ainsley said just above a whisper.

Hollis sat up straight. "Okay?"

Ainsley smiled tightly and still got the words out. "Don't let her see you slouch."

"Got it." Hollis wasn't sure what was happening, but decided to play along.

Ainsley motioned to Hollis's beer. "Take a long sip of your drink. Do it slowly." She spoke like a ventriloquist through her smile.

Hollis grabbed the drink, relishing the cool glass in her hand. Her face was flushed. She wasn't sure if it was from anger, or the fact that Ainsley giving stage directions was kind of sexy. She took a long drink and tension started to leave her body.

"You so totally won that exchange. The ex, I presume?"

"Yes. And I did?" Hollis wasn't aware that it was a competition until Ainsley said something. But that was the first time she had interacted with Miranda since she'd called things off. It surprised her how uncomfortable it made her feel just seeing her.

"Oh God yeah. The whole haircut and sad dog thing." She was motioning with that beautiful hand. "That is a girl who is clearly not over you."

"That is the last thing I need right now."

"So Miranda's a coworker?"

"I told you it was messy."

"I thought you didn't like to mix business and pleasure?"

"Anymore."

"Oh. So I'm too late?"

Hollis swallowed hard.

"Kidding of course."

"Right. Trust me. Mixing work and relationships doesn't work. It was the perfect arrangement until it wasn't. At first it was fun seeing Miranda at work. We could go out on lunch dates and sneak the occasional kiss by the printer. But then the nights I would work late, she'd come by the office door, sighing, asking when we could leave."

"I didn't know you and Harrison worked so many late nights."

"Usually just me, to be honest."

"Oh, so does Harrison leave you to do work alone a lot?"

Dammit. This was exactly why getting involved with Ainsley couldn't happen. They could never just be two women just having a drink on a Friday night. Work would always come between them. She would have to answer delicately so as not to throw Harrison under the bus for a department Ainsley already thought was overstaffed. "Harrison is great at his job, but at this phase in his life, he's not looking for more." That answer seemed safe.

"And you are?"

"Absolutely. Now is the perfect time for me to focus on my career. No romantic attachments, no large financial commitments, no pets."

"I see." Did Hollis notice a hint of disappointment?

"And Miranda's right, accounts payable doesn't work long hours. So when I did, she didn't get it. She didn't get a lot of things."

"It seems that way."

The air shifted between them. It was no longer the lighthearted easy banter but had turned to something more serious. Ainsley seemed worlds away. That was for the best. They could never be anything but boss and employee. Trevor broke the tension when he arrived with a tray of food.

"I took the liberty of ordering us something," Hollis said, only just realizing that might have been presumptuous on her part.

"Great!"

"These are the best sweet potato fries you've ever had." She picked one up from the basket and popped it in her mouth.

Ainsley leaned back in her chair and took a slow bite of a sweet potato fry. "You're right. These are delicious."

Hollis took pride knowing she hadn't oversold her favorite bar snack.

"Okay. No more work talk." Ainsley took a sip of her beer.

"Okay?"

"It's just that at these functions or when coworkers meet up, it always turns to work talk. Everyone tonight tried to resist, but I've been basically talking about work with everyone since we got here. Even when we talk about your ex, it's about work." Ainsley's lighthearted nature was back.

"Low blow, but fair."

"I just want a few minutes of feeling like a normal girl at a bar having a drink."

"That sounds good to me. So…" She pondered what kind of question to ask, and decided to start out with a safe one. "When did you become a spin instructor?"

Ainsley laughed. God, Hollis loved that laugh. So light and breezy, like there wasn't a single care in the world. "My best friend Greg got me into that." She paused to grab another fry. "These are really good."

"I told you. But I have a feeling you becoming a spin instructor has more to it than simply Greg asking you to."

"Well, it's a long story that involves *my* ex."

"You know more than you should about my last relationship. I think it's only fair you tell me about yours." Hollis couldn't help herself. Even if dating the boss was off-limits, she needed to know more about her. "Kayla and I dated for seven years," Ainsley started. "We met right after college. She actually moved with me when I got the job in Raleigh."

"How long were you at HQ in Raleigh?" Hollis asked.

"Oh gosh." Ainsley paused. "I just hit ten years, so about that long."

"You've certainly made your mark in ten years."

"The plan was always for me to open HQ II. We just had other projects getting in the way."

Other projects like cutting other departments? Hollis wondered what the job would have been like if Ainsley had been there from day one. Would she still like it as much? One of the biggest perks was the autonomy she had, and she wondered if she and Harrison would have accomplished as much with someone looking over their shoulder at every turn.

"Suffice it to say, she didn't take the move well. Even though it was her idea," Ainsley punctuated that last part. "She never really embraced Raleigh. We tried to make it work. We tried for four years. But how do I put it? She felt like she wasn't getting enough attention from me, so she found it somewhere else. Someone else, I should say."

"Damn."

"She said I was emotionally unavailable."

"Were you?" Hollis cocked her head to one side.

The corner of Ainsley's mouth turned up to a smirk. "That's not the point."

"Oh really? Then what is the point?" Hollis tried to keep her tone playful.

"That she should have talked to me first instead of falling into bed with the first girl who called her pretty." Ainsley rolled her eyes.

Hollis had never been cheated on but could only imagine what it would be like to be three thousand miles from home and have the one person who was supposed to support you, betray you.

"I'm not saying that I didn't push her away. But it would have been nice if she'd completely ended things before moving on with someone else."

Orange flames flickered across the lava rocks of the firepit. At least Miranda hadn't cheated. "I'm sorry. That must make the breakup even harder."

"Lesson learned."

"Really," Hollis said. "What was that?"

"That I'm not the serious relationship kind of person. I *do* prefer work to almost everything else."

Hollis ignored the sudden surge of disappointment and forced a laugh. "We have that in common."

Ainsley studied her for a moment. "I guess we do."

"So, back to the original question of how you became a spin instructor?" Hollis changed the subject before the conversation headed somewhere it shouldn't. Like what other things they might have in common outside work.

"After Kayla moved out, Greg told me I needed a hobby. Apparently, my short rebound fling didn't count." Hollis kept herself from digging into that. What would a short fling with Ainsley Jones be like? "He's always been big into spin class. I started going and then the two of us decided to become instructors together. We were on opposite sides of the country, but it really helped us stay connected. He does it much more regularly than I do."

"Harrison loves his class."

"That doesn't surprise me. He's really great at it."

"Well, I've only been to one class, but I think you were pretty great at it, too." Hollis took a long drink of her beer.

"It's definitely not me, but it's fun."

"What do you mean?"

"The whole bubbly over-the-top thing. It's not who I normally am, but it's fun to fill the role. It's like taking on a new persona. People expect that out of a fitness instructor and it's fun to play pretend."

Hollis could have listened to Ainsley speak all night. It's all she wanted to do. She wanted to hear everything she had to say about anything. She needed to learn everything about her.

Ainsley continued. "I actually went on and became a certified fitness trainer."

"Really? How did you find the time?"

"The company paid for all the classes." She shrugged. "They want an active lifestyle, you know."

Hollis rolled her eyes. "I've heard that a time or two."

"I actually coached a team in training for the Raleigh marathon five years ago. There were twenty of us and I got every single one of them across the finish line."

The more Hollis learned, the more she liked this girl. Well, not girl, per se, Ainsley was an actual adult. Hollis thought about it. She had never dated or even been with someone older than her. She had always been the older, responsible one. She was the one with the successful career and younger girlfriends. The idea of being with someone as put together as Ainsley Jones excited Hollis more than she expected. Ainsley was the kind of woman who actually changed her sheets once a week, not just when they felt dirty, and she could probably fold a fitted sheet without just rolling it into a ball.

"That's pretty amazing," Hollis said.

"I did one full marathon, but now with my knee, a 10K is as far as I can get."

Hollis shook her head sympathetically. "That sucks. Did you do something in particular?"

"A sprained MCL that just never quite healed." Ainsley brushed the question off. "But it's okay. I really enjoy biking and have gotten into other things." She paused and took a sip of her beer. "This race you have coming up in May. How many marathons will that be for you?"

Hollis looked at the dark sky and counted in her head. She should know this. Each one had been a painstaking achievement, yet she could never recall on command how many she had done. "Seven?" She squinted as she said it.

Ainsley let out that beautiful laugh. "You don't even know?"

"I'm pretty sure this will be seven. It blurs with all the halfs and fulls."

"So, you're one of those crazy runners then?" Ainsley titled her head to the side.

"Yeah. I guess I am."

"I like a little bit of crazy." Ainsley looked into Hollis's eyes.

The moment stretched between them, and despite the way her heart raced, Hollis couldn't contain a yawn. "Oh God, sorry."

"Should I ask if it's me?" Ainsley asked, sounding half-serious.

"Absolutely not! I mean—no. It's not you at all. No." Hollis clamped her jaw shut before she said anything more.

Ainsley looked at her smartwatch. "I guess it *is* getting late."

Hollis looked at her own watch. Ten p.m. "Workdays and all."

"I should probably get going. I better close out." There was that hesitation again in Ainsley's voice.

"I'll head out, too." Hollis didn't want the night to end, but didn't want to push it. At the end of the day, Ainsley was still her boss and that's all she could ever be.

Chapter Nine

The air was cold as they left the bar. Hollis hadn't brought a jacket, being fooled yet again by fake spring in Oregon. She noticed Ainsley hadn't brought a coat either.

"I'll go with you back to your car," Hollis said.

"Thanks."

Hollis could see the smile forming on Ainsley's face even on the dimly lit path. The silence wasn't uncomfortable but almost relaxing. As she thought about it, she realized that she hadn't even known Ainsley a week, and yet her familiarity was growing closer with her than with anyone else in a long time. Dreamily, she looked up at the clouds. "Oh no," she said aloud.

Quicker than either of them was prepared for, rain started pouring from the sky. The wind picked up and blankets of rain blew sideways. "Come on." She reached her hand out and it pleasantly surprised her when Ainsley took it without any further questions. She started running and Ainsley kept up with her hand in hers. "Just up here." Ainsley wiped rain from her eyes and nodded, her mascara just beginning to run.

Hollis slowed her pace as soon as she was under the cover to her apartment complex. She wiped the rain from her forehead and looked to Ainsley. It looked like she had just stepped out of the shower fully clothed. "This is me. Come on up." She nodded toward the door and again, to her surprise, Ainsley didn't protest.

After the short elevator ride, she opened the door to her small apartment and motioned Ainsley inside. It was technically a one-bedroom, but barely bigger than a studio. It was a fairly new complex that had been built in the last few years. The small white kitchen sat behind the matching island which doubled as a table. The dark wood floors and high ceilings helped give the appearance of the space being larger than it was. A gray couch sat in the corner of what Hollis called the living room, facing a TV and a corner desk set up next to it. She had a single wingback chair for when she didn't feel like sitting on the couch. It wasn't much, but it was only her and she liked the small space.

"I'll grab some towels." Hollis headed for the bathroom. "That came out of nowhere." She tossed a grey towel across the room to Ainsley.

"Yeah, I wasn't expecting that." Ainsley dried her hair.

Hollis looked out the window over the couch. The rain reflected off the streetlights coming down in sheets. "It's not letting up anytime soon. Let me get you something to change into. You can wait it out here."

Ainsley titled her head. "Not to sound rude or anything, but I doubt you have anything my size." Ainsley motioned to the fact that she was at least six inches shorter and significantly smaller than Hollis.

"Don't you worry. I'll be right back." She took off her wet shoes and socks so as to not track any more water into the apartment. She returned minutes later and handed Ainsley a long sleeve T-shirt and black pair of yoga pants.

"Please tell me these aren't Miranda's."

"God no," Hollis said. "They are samples from the new line last spring. Sorry that the shirt is…" she paused thinking of the right words. "A little colorful." It was an electric blue shirt with lime green accents. Hollis motioned to the bathroom. "You can change in there. I'll throw your clothes in the dryer while we wait for the rain to stop."

Ainsley just nodded and headed to the bathroom. Hollis went to her bedroom to change. She breathed out a long breath. How was it possible that she had Ainsley Jones alone in her apartment? She took a moment to compose herself. They were just waiting out the rain. It didn't mean anything. It couldn't mean anything. She quickly changed out of her wet clothes and into the nicest pair of sweats she could find.

Hollis stood in the kitchen when Ainsley came out of the bathroom. It was just yoga pants and a long-sleeve shirt, but Hollis couldn't help but think Ainsley would look great in anything. "I know they decided not to go with that shirt pattern, but after seeing it on you, I think they made a mistake."

Ainsley let out a laugh. She looked down. "It's a little loud."

"You're making it work." Hollis motioned to the soaking wet clothes in her hands and took them from her. "I'll throw these in the dryer, and we can have a drink on the couch while we wait?"

"Sounds great." Ainsley headed for the couch.

Hollis grabbed two beers out of the fridge and took a seat at the opposite end from Ainsley, leaving a full cushion length between them. "It's not as hoppy as you might prefer, but it's still pretty good."

Ainsley examined the can in her hand, reading the label. "I'm really not that picky."

Hollis popped the top to the can and took a long drink. Ainsley's auburn hair looked great even after the rainstorm.

Ainsley broke the silence first. "So why running?"

"What do you mean?" Hollis didn't understand the question.

"Of all the ways you could spend your free time, why distance running?"

Hollis paused, still pondering. "No one has ever asked me that before." She saw Ainsley look at her intently. She had Ainsley's full attention and she loved it.

"Well, I'm asking."

"I played team sports my whole life." Hollis thought back to her first T-ball team. She was five when she swung a bat for the first time and had been in love ever since. "I actually went to college on a softball scholarship."

"Oh really?" Ainsley seemed impressed.

Hollis motioned to the Portland State emblem on her sweats. "Played all four years."

"Impressive."

"But there's something different about individual sports. I'm a team player, don't get me wrong, but with running, it's all me. There is no one else to depend on."

Ainsley remained quiet, focused on Hollis.

"With other sports, people are always trying to find new equipment, or tricks to make them better. With running it's not like that. I know there are fancy shoes and things like that, but for the most part, for a runner like me, it's just me and my feet and seeing where they can take me."

"I've never thought about it like that."

"It's a mental challenge more than anything, and that's what drives me." Hollis had never said any of this out loud before. No one had ever cared enough to ask. "What about you? What are your hobbies? Besides substitute spin instructing, that is."

"Oh, I don't have time for hobbies." Ainsley took a sip of her beer.

"What do you do in your free time then?"

"I don't have a lot of that either."

"Oh, come on. Everyone has free time. What do you do when you aren't working besides sleep?" Hollis wanted Ainsley to open up to her.

"Okay." Ainsley let out a small breath. "But it's kind of embarrassing."

"Now you have to tell me."

"I don't know." Ainsley looked down at the couch. "I don't want you thinking less of me."

"There's only one way to find out."

Ainsley looked up slowly. "I love watching reality TV."

"Wait. Really?" Hollis didn't know what she was expecting but it wasn't that.

"Really. The more obscure, the better."

"Like what?" Hollis couldn't picture Ainsley sitting down to watch any of the latest reality TV shows.

"All of it. I like the cooking shows, the game shows, the dating shows. I even like the ones where they swap family members. My favorite one is where they send everyone to an island and they either find a date or get voted off."

"I don't think less of you, but I am surprised."

"It's just..." Ainsley paused. "There are so many real problems in the world today, and yet someone signed off on spending millions of dollars to send a bunch of pretty twenty-somethings to get drunk and try to find love at first sight. I don't know how to explain it. It's mind-numbing and sometimes exactly what I need."

"That makes sense."

"Only Greg knows that about me."

Hollis loved knowing something about Ainsley that the rest of the world didn't. She wanted to know all of the things about Ainsley. "I'm not going to lie." Hollis changed the subject. "I'm really curious about that rebound fling you mentioned before."

"Well." She played with the tab on her beer can. "She was really young, and it didn't last long."

"How young?"

"Twenty-three." Ainsley wrinkled her forehead at the admission.

"How old are you?" Hollis couldn't stop the question. She knew better than to ask a woman her age, but the words were out before she could stop them.

"Thirty-five," Ainsley said definitively.

Hollis was only thirty; five years wasn't that big of a deal. She caught herself thinking that way and tried to stop. "That's a little bit of a difference," she settled on saying.

"Do you know who Rachel McCreedy is?"

"You mean Olympic marathon runner, Rachel McCreedy?" Of course, Hollis knew who she was. She was on countless covers of running magazines. She had recently broken the world record for the women's marathon time and was heavily favored to take gold at the next Olympics.

Ainsley nodded and raised her eyebrows.

It clicked into place. "You slept with Rachel McCreedy?"

"I did." Her voice had a hesitancy to it, like she was admitting to something she shouldn't.

Hollis rubbed a hand over her face. "Damn. Rachel McCreedy." How could Hollis compete with someone like that? Of course,

Ainsley Jones would have a fling with an Olympian. "She's an amazing runner. It's impressive what she's been able to do." She put one arm on the back of the couch, outstretched.

"I don't know..."

"What do you mean? She broke the world record marathon time!"

"If your job was to eat, breathe, and sleep something, don't you think you'd be good at it?"

Hollis just stared into her brown eyes. She didn't know where this was going.

"All I'm saying is she's good at her job. Lots of people are good at their job." As Ainsley moved her hand she brushed Hollis's arm on the back of the couch.

That touch sent a charge of energy, and Hollis caught her breath. Hollis set her can on the ledge of the window behind the couch and Ainsley followed suit.

"Last weekend." Hollis brought Ainsley's attention back to her eyes. "You said you were trying something different when you, um..."

"When I asked you on a date?"

"Yes. That." Hollis still didn't know how to process being asked out.

"Greg said I need to put myself out there more."

Hollis snorted. "I have a friend who does the same."

"But I don't get it," Ainsley continued. "He doesn't like my rebound flings, but then he says I'm not dating enough. I don't know how to make that man happy."

"I oddly know exactly what you mean." Hollis couldn't keep up with all the things Harrison thought she needed to try in her life.

Ainsley played with her fingers on the back of Hollis's hand. "I have to admit that I've been avoiding you this week."

I've been avoiding you too. She wanted to say it out loud, but then recognized that that was a silly thing to be in competition over. "Yeah?"

"It threw me when I saw you on Monday. I couldn't stop thinking about you the rest of the weekend. Do you have any idea how difficult it was to focus on teaching a class with you in the front row?"

Hollis didn't think she had ever held anyone's attention in that way. It surprised her to think that Ainsley could be distracted by her and not just the other way around.

"I was really looking forward to our date tomorrow." Ainsley let out a short sigh. "Then I saw you on Monday and things got," she trailed her fingers on the back of Hollis's hand again, "complicated."

"Right. Complicated." Hollis looked down at her lap.

Ainsley inched closer to Hollis. "I know, I shouldn't have asked you to stay later tonight, but I was having such a good time and didn't want it to end."

Hollis shifted closer. Ainsley was like a magnet to her soul and Hollis couldn't resist her pull if she tried. "But?"

"It got complicated." Ainsley looked directly into Hollis's eyes.

"Right." Hollis nodded. Hollis tucked one leg under the other and looked down at her thigh. When she looked back up, Ainsley was inches from her face. Hollis inhaled her scent. The mix of citrus and floral becoming more and more familiar. Ainsley moved in closer. Hollis closed her eyes and leaned until there was no space between them. Ainsley's lips were soft. Softer than she had imagined. The world stopped. Nothing else seemed complicated in that moment. It didn't matter if Ainsley was her boss or the Queen of England. All Hollis could focus on were the incredible lips doing incredible things to her. The kiss was hesitant at first, but Hollis leaned into her and kissed back. Ainsley's lips were gentle and knew exactly what to do.

It was wrong. So wrong. Kissing the boss was wrong. But why did it feel so right? Why did kissing Ainsley feel so natural? Ainsley let out a breath, and Hollis pushed her tongue into her mouth. Ainsley let out a small moan, and it was the encouragement that Hollis needed. She reached her hands down and grabbed her hips, swirling her tongue in her mouth, pushing things further. Hollis wanted to do more but also wanted to stay in this moment forever. This was the best kiss she had ever had. It was the right amount of soft and pressure. She could get lost in Ainsley's lips. She dug her hands in, resisting the urge to work her way up Ainsley's shirt, which she so badly wanted to do. She would take things slow.

Ainsley bit Hollis's bottom lip. Hollis let out a small sigh and Ainsley drove her tongue back into her mouth. She used the full force of her muscle and was completely in command. Then, just as quickly as it had started, it stopped. The kiss was over. Hollis opened her eyes, confused.

"God dammit," Ainsley said.

"What?" Had she done something wrong?

Ainsley rubbed her hands over her face. "Part of me was really hoping you'd be a bad kisser."

"Okay?"

"Because if you were a bad kisser, maybe I wouldn't want to kiss you anymore."

"I see. But?"

"But you're not a bad kisser." She brushed her fingers through her drying hair. "So that makes things—"

"Let me guess. Complicated?"

"I'm sorry." Ainsley shook her head. "I shouldn't have done that. I just couldn't not know any longer what kissing you felt like."

"It's okay." She needed Ainsley to know that even if things were complicated, it was okay. In fact, she didn't care how complicated or messy things got. All she cared about was Ainsley.

"I should be going."

Hollis looked out the window. The rain appeared to have stopped, at least for now. "Okay," Hollis said. She desperately wanted her to stay, but knew she couldn't push it. Hollis headed toward the dryer. She quickly folded the clothes and handed them to Ainsley, who was already putting her shoes on at the front door.

"Thank you for drinks," Ainsley said.

"You're welcome." Hollis wanted to talk more. She wanted to talk about that kiss. She wanted to do more than kiss, but Ainsley had drawn a line. She couldn't cross it—could she?

The door closed behind Ainsley and her question went unanswered.

Chapter Ten

Monday morning came, and Hollis entered an empty office. Things must be over between Harrison and the cute barista. The trees just below her office window finally filled out with green leaves. Winter was officially over, and not a moment too soon.

Harrison interrupted the quiet by dramatically slumping in his chair. He let out a long sigh. Hollis didn't budge. It was too early for Harrison's drama.

"Aren't you going to ask me what's wrong?"

"I'm assuming that since you didn't buy me coffee, things are over with the barista?" She didn't look up from her laptop.

"He got a real job."

"Oh?" Hollis still didn't move.

"He's going to be an investment banker, so I had to call it off."

At this, Hollis turned in her chair. "So the cute young guy who's into you starts a successful career, so you end it?"

"Exactly."

Hollis shot him a look.

"This only works when I'm the sugar daddy."

"Seriously?"

"It's a whole thing. You wouldn't get it."

"Clearly."

"So, I guess I'm back to the HR guy and Parker."

"Here's a thought." Hollis raised a finger at him. "You could date someone who doesn't work here. Or someone, you know, age appropriate."

Harrison shook his head. "Age appropriate is different for gays."

"That's an exaggeration—or maybe a rationalization."

"Greggory taught spin class again on Saturday." His voice sounded dreamy. "You know who else was there?"

"His boyfriend?"

"Ha. Ainsley." Harrison raised both eyebrows. "She asked where you were."

"She did not." Hollis shook her head.

"She did! Scout's honor." He held three fingers up in a salute.

"What did you say?" Who knew what embarrassing thing might have come out of his mouth.

"Just that you were probably running or something equally boring."

"Thanks for supporting my hobbies." She rolled her eyes.

"Seriously Hol, who runs for three hours alone? It's like so mind numbing."

"Maybe your mind just isn't interesting enough." She wanted to ask what Ainsley said back but this wasn't middle school.

"Oh, it's interesting."

Hollis just shook her head.

"Maybe Ainsley would give me Greggory's number."

"You can't ask our new boss for her best friend's phone number."

Harrison narrowed his eyes. "Who said he was her best friend?"

"Did I say best? I meant friend." She faced her chair toward her computer.

Harrison rolled across the office and spun her around. "What do you know?"

"I don't know what you're talking about."

"Hollister Marie, I know when you're lying." He stared into her eyes.

"That's not my name."

"Tell me."

"There's nothing to tell." She held her hands up.

Harrison rolled his chair back a few feet. "I'm going to let this go for now, but don't think we aren't coming back to it." He pointed a finger at her.

She let out a breath as quietly as she could. Harrison could pry anything out of her, she knew that. She knew eventually he would learn the details of Friday night, but for now she wanted to keep the memory to herself. As she turned back to her screen, a new calendar meeting popped up, "From Parker Grant on behalf of Ainsley Jones." Her stomach filled with butterflies just reading Ainsley's name. Her mind flashed back to Friday. Friday night was all she thought about all weekend. The firepit, the run through the rain, the glorious, earth-shattering kiss. She was sure she was remembering it as better than it was, but in the moment, it was the most amazing kiss ever. Soft lips, firm hands. Hollis could get lost in Ainsley Jones.

She picked up her phone off the desk and scrolled through her recent text conversations until she found the thread with Ainsley. It was just after she had finished her run on Sunday. She got back to her apartment and pulled her phone out to sync her Garmin running watch. Then she saw it. A message from Ainsley Jones. All it said was: *Hey*

Hollis pictured her voice saying it in a soft, welcoming, tone. She responded. *Hey*

Bubbles formed to signal Ainsley's response. She pictured Ainsley, sitting at home, curled on the couch holding the phone with both hands.

How was your 20 mile run?

Hollis didn't recall anyone ever asking her about a run. She was constantly defending this lifestyle. She had to explain to her mother that she wasn't ruining her knees. She reassured Harrison that spending that much time alone wasn't unhealthy. Then there was the constant explaining to Miranda. She needed to move on from that. She typed a response to Ainsley.

Honestly? Not great. My legs felt sluggish and my lungs were weak. I just didn't have it today.

She could have just responded with a simple, "good" or some other response, but she got the sense like Ainsley honestly wanted to know, even if was just in a personal trainer capacity. Her phone buzzed.

Damn. That sucks.

The phone buzzed again, instantly.

How far off race pace were you?

Hollis smiled. How was it that a woman as stunning as Ainsley Jones was speaking her language?

3 minutes.

Ainsley replied.

Ouch

Hollis gave a small laugh, then replied.

Ya. Well a bad run is better than no run.

A response came instantly.

You don't actually believe that crap. Do you?

Hollis actually laughed out loud. She didn't believe that crap for one second, but she was trying to keep things light. She wrote back.

LOL. No. I was just trying to stay optimistic.

Text bubbles appeared and disappeared for almost a full minute.

Enjoy the rest of your Sunday. I just wanted you to know I was thinking about you.

Hollis sat in her office rereading that last text. She never had responded. She didn't know how. What did it mean that she was thinking of her? How was she thinking of her? Hollis hadn't stopped thinking about her since Friday. Was she thinking of her in the same way?

On the one hand, she wanted to confront Ainsley. She wanted to know exactly what Friday meant and more importantly, when could it happen again?

But on the other hand, she needed to be practical. Ainsley Jones was her boss. Hollis had worked hard for her career, and she was proud of what she had accomplished. She couldn't throw away her years of work for a woman. Even if that woman was smart and sexy as hell. No, Hollis needed to push any thoughts of Ainsley Jones out of her mind. She was going to get over her, one way or another.

"Do you believe this crap?" Harrison said.

Hollis was shaken from her thoughts. "What?"

"This ten a.m. meeting." He pointed to his laptop. "It's recurring."

"Okay?"

"She's going to check in on us every Monday?" Harrison's voice was full of disgust.

Hollis wasn't following.

"This is how it starts. First, it's new meetings. Then it's new reports and whatever else corporate bullshit she wants. She'll probably demolish the whole team before sixty days is even up."

"What are you talking about?"

"I heard from some guys in Raleigh that her specialty is "efficiency." She comes in, cuts teams in half, and then moves on to the next project."

"Are these actual people or just some guys?"

"These are reliable sources."

He might be right, and Hollis knew it. She had hoped that Ainsley wouldn't make big changes right away. One weekly meeting wasn't a huge change, and maybe more communication would be a good thing. She thought about mentioning this to Harrison but he could not be reasoned with in this state.

"If she even tries to make me fill out a checklist, I'm out." Harrison pointed to the door.

"Easy, tiger." Hollis tried to calm him down.

He clapped his hands together. "I'll be out faster than the men's figure skating team."

Hollis just shook her head.

❖

Hollis and Harrison sat next to each other at the long conference table for the ten a.m. meeting. As she looked around the table at the other department managers, she realized that while they all led teams in this building, they had never had a meeting together.

The attention shifted to Ainsley as she entered the room. She wore a neatly tailored maroon pantsuit with a black camisole under it. It accented her auburn hair, bringing out the various shades in her curls. Any hopes that Hollis had had earlier in the day of just getting over her left as soon as that door opened.

Ainsley took the chair at the head of the table and started the meeting right away. "Good morning all."

There were nods and other greetings.

"This is going to be our first Monday meeting." Ainsley had a hint of her spin instructor persona as she spoke. Hollis stared at her red lips. She remembered the way they brushed against hers. She couldn't focus on anything but kissing those lips. She blinked and tried to get her head back into work mode.

"You all have done a fantastic job over the last year."

Harrison leaned over and whispered in Hollis's ear. "Here comes the but."

"But," Ainsley said.

Harrison jabbed Hollis in the arm. She brushed his hand aside. She didn't want Ainsley to think they weren't paying attention.

Ainsley continued. "You all are known as the Wild West back in Raleigh." She gave a laugh to lighten her tone. "My role here is to get us all on the same page. We have had amazing success across the country, but we need a unified approach." She paused and passed out a stack of papers along the table.

Harrison looked at one and rolled his eyes.

"This is the report that I'll be asking all departments to send out every week." Ainsley signaled to the paper. "Don't worry, it's not a checklist." She gave a small chuckle, but no one laughed along.

Hollis couldn't help but notice Ainsley's hands as she held the report in front of her. She had painted her nails a shade of maroon that matched her outfit. Hollis pictured Ainsley sitting on the edge of her bathtub painting her fingernails. She wondered if she had painted her toenails too. She pictured her carefully blowing on her fingers to make the polish dry faster.

Hollis remembered nothing else that was said in the meeting. She was thankful that she had Harrison and his steel trap memory. While his opinion would be jaded, he would at least remember any takeaways.

Hollis reminded herself repeatedly that she loved her job. She would not put her career in jeopardy over whatever this was. She needed to push Ainsley from her brain. She needed to not let her take up so much space in her mind. But as she watched her sit at the end of the table, she knew this would not be an easy task.

Chapter Eleven

"So, I've been thinking about your love life, or lack thereof." Harrison slumped down into his office chair.

"Do you really have nothing better to think about?"

"HR guy wasn't as interesting as I hoped." Harrison shrugged. "Anyway, do you remember what you told me the night after the luau in Oahu?"

"You mean the night of a thousand rum runners?" Hollis shuddered at the memory of falling over the steps back to the hotel room. Harrison had insisted she drink away her feelings, and apparently after the breakup, she still had a lot. "I don't remember a whole lot."

"Well, on the beach, you told me that you never actually loved Miranda. You just loved the idea of being in a relationship. Does that ring a bell?"

Hollis could remember getting back to the room and finding sand in places it shouldn't be, but she had no recollection of this heart-to-heart.

"You said you wanted to be settled down and married like your sisters and you jumped at the first girl who you could maybe make that happen with. Think about it, Hol, you jump into relationships too fast."

Hollis crossed her arms.

"Have you ever slept with someone you haven't been in a relationship with?"

Hollis realized she hadn't. Even when a relationship might not have been a good idea. Miranda came to mind.

"So stop saying this Ainsley thing is because you don't want to date a coworker and admit it's because you are terrible at relationships."

"Hey now." Hollis sat all the way up. "I'm not terrible at relationships."

"Oh really?"

"Okay, fine." Hollis was maybe not great at relationships, but didn't want to go down that path right now. "There is nothing wrong with only wanting to sleep with one person at a time and wanting a commitment from that person before I do!"

"I'm not saying there is. The problem is you jump in too fast. You bring your U-Haul to the first date!" Harrison burst out laughing at his own joke.

"Ha. Ha." She didn't have the patience to correct him on the fact that she had never actually lived with a girlfriend.

"I have just the solution."

"I can't wait to hear it." Hollis rolled her eyes.

"You need to get with someone you would never in a million years have a relationship with. You need to sleep with a girl, or a hundred girls, or whatever, and realize that you don't have to marry someone just because she laughs at your dumb jokes."

"This sounds like a horrible plan."

"Okay, maybe not sleep with. But at least go out on dates with more than one woman. Have you ever even dated around?"

Hollis couldn't imagine trying to keep track of partners like Harrison did on a regular basis. She had a hard enough time keeping track of herself.

"I know just the place. You're coming out with me Thursday night."

"What makes you think I'm free Thursday night?"

"You're free every night. The only thing you ever do is run."

The last thing Hollis wanted to do was sleep with a stranger, but maybe Harrison had a point about dating around a bit. She did tend to jump into relationships too fast and what had that gotten her? She hesitated before responding. "Fine."

"Great!" Harrison clapped his hands together. "I'll pick you up at six and make sure you bring a flannel."

"A flannel?"

"Oh don't act like you don't have sixteen hanging in your closet. Lesbians love flannels."

"You're such an ass." Hollis figured she had one—or possibly two.

❖

Harrison pulled into the parking lot at exactly six p.m. Hollis opened the passenger door and slipped inside.

"Good. You remembered." Harrison eyed the red-striped flannel in Hollis's hand. She had opted for jeans and a plain black T-shirt, not knowing entirely where Harrison would take her.

"What's with the getup?" Hollis took in Harrison's own outfit noting his blue flannel and matching blue handkerchief tied tightly around his neck.

"Gotta look the part!" Harrison gunned the gas pedal and Hollis's head flew back against the headrest. "Yeeee-haw!" Harrison yelled and took off on the main road.

After a short drive, Hollis relaxed as Harrison finally brought the car to a reasonable speed. A tall marquee with a cowboy boot in various stages of wear welcomed them to whatever establishment they were at. "The Rusty Spur?" Hollis looked at Harrison as she noted that the flashing lights on the sign were to make the boot look like it was moving. Maybe it would have worked if over half of them hadn't been out.

"Like I said, we need to set you up with a nice girl who you would never want to be in a relationship with." Harrison pulled a black cowboy hat out of the back seat and placed it on his head.

"How did you even get into those jeans?" Hollis could see parts of Harrison she never wanted to in his tight Wranglers.

"The more important question is, who's going to help me out of them?" Harrison opened the front door and motioned for Hollis to enter.

It took a moment for her eyes to adjust to the darkened bar. While she knew it was illegal to smoke inside, she couldn't escape the smell of cigarette smoke filling the room. Neon lights buzzed with various beer labels and NASCAR numbers that Hollis had no idea who they were. Harrison led her to a long bar in the middle of the room that looked onto a dance floor. A few old spinning lights that Hollis recognized from middle school dances illuminated the floor in all colors.

"Oh good. We aren't late." Harrison sat on a stool next to her.

"What exactly is this place?"

"It's a country-western bar."

"I gathered that much." Hollis looked around and realized now why Harrison had instructed her to bring a flannel. At least she would blend in a little more.

"They give line dancing lessons on Thursdays."

"I am not line dancing." Hollis stood to leave. She could catch a rideshare home. It was one thing for Harrison to bring her to this run-down hole in the wall. It was quite another to expect her to dance.

Harrison reached for her wrist and pulled her back down. "Easy now. You don't have to dance. You can just watch."

Hollis put her head in her hands. "I can't believe you talked me into this."

"It's far too early in the night for a pretty girl like you to be crying." A female voice next to her said. "Is this guy bothering you?"

Hollis pulled her head up slowly. "More than you know."

"Look here, mister, if you're going to be causing trouble, I will have you removed." The woman's voice held authority. Hollis turned to meet the face of the voice and noticed striking blond hair pulled into a low ponytail. Tassels and sequins adorned her purple shirt. It looked like something a rodeo princess might wear.

"He's not bothering me any more than normal." Hollis tried to defuse the tension.

"Are you sure?" The woman wasn't convinced.

"He's a friend of mine."

"Is that so?" The woman eyed Harrison suspiciously.

"Gross, not like that," Harrison interjected. "We're coworkers and my friend here needs a night out to relax. She's wound too tight for her own good."

"I see." The woman relaxed.

Was it jealousy Hollis saw when the woman thought she and Harrison were together?

"I'm Jo, by the way." She stuck out her hand.

Hollis shook it and the warm hand squeezed hers back. "Hollis. And that annoying friend is Harrison."

"Pleasure to meet you, Hollis. I take it you don't come here often?" Jo looked her up and down.

"Is it that obvious? All Harrison told me to bring was a flannel."

Jo burst out laughing. "It's going to take more than that flannel to make you into a line dancer."

"Oh, I don't think I'll be dancing tonight."

"That's too bad."

Harrison pushed his stool back from the bar. "They're starting the lessons now and I need to get this achy breaky heart moving."

"Is he always like that?" Jo asked.

"Worse normally."

Jo reached for her glass of beer and took a long sip.

Hollis took in her soft features and thought maybe Harrison wasn't wrong. Maybe a few drinks with someone like Jo would be a good thing. Certainly she wouldn't end up with a country dancer. Or maybe she could? Dammit. She needed to stop. She was here to have a few drinks and relax, not find her next girlfriend.

Jo set her glass on the bar. "So, why does that friend of yours say you need a night out?"

"I haven't gotten out much since my girlfriend and I broke up, and he thinks it would be good for me."

"I see." Jo paused and downed what was left in her drink.

Hollis didn't know if the pause was because she was uncomfortable with the word girlfriend. Hollis hadn't thought twice about being honest, but maybe in this bar she should be on guard.

"That kind of conversation warrants a drink. How about I buy you one?" Jo motioned to her own her empty glass.

Hollis relaxed. Jo wouldn't offer a drink if she wasn't at least interested in talking more. Surely she hadn't scared her off yet. "That sounds great."

Jo put both hands on the bar and pushed herself up. "What are you having?"

"Whatever you are." Hollis didn't want to ask for a beer menu or have her new friend think she was a beer snob wanting to know the ABVs in the drinks on tap.

Just as Jo left, Harrison sat back down. "Okay, I think I got it," he said, slightly out of breath.

"Why exactly are we line dancing again?"

"Oh, no reason." Harrison craned his neck to look at the front entrance. "Yes. Perfect timing."

"What is?" Hollis tried to see what or who he was looking at, but the bar filled with people ready to line dance.

"Oh shit. I didn't think about that." Harrison turned around.

"Didn't think about what?" Hollis glared at him.

"Hey, you two."

No. It couldn't be. How could she be in this dive bar, of all places?

"That." Harrison sighed and turned around. He plastered his signature grin back on. "Oh, hey."

Ainsley looked from Harrison to Hollis. "I didn't expect to see you two here tonight."

"Same." Hollis glared at Harrison again. How could he put her in this position? Tonight was supposed to be about finding girls who weren't Ainsley, not watching her strut around in her own pair of tight Wranglers.

"This is my friend Greg." Ainsley motioned to the man standing next to her. "Greg, I think you've met Harrison from spin class, and this is Hollis. She also works at Fitwear."

"Oh my God, are you kidding me?" Hollis tried to keep her voice at a whisper.

"Is everything okay?" Concern filled Ainsley's voice.

"I'm so sorry. Yes. Hi, Greg. I've heard so much about you." Hollis stuck her hand out to shake Greg's. Of all the schemes Harrison had to meet guys, this was by far the worst.

"Greg is quite the line dancer," Ainsley said with a slight chuckle.

"I don't know about that." Greg finally spoke up. "I seem to remember you dancing circles around me the last time we went out."

"Speaking of." Harrison turned to Greg and made eye contact. "There's one step I'm having a hard time with. Maybe you could help me out before the real fun starts?"

"Of course." Greg followed Harrison to the dance floor, leaving Ainsley and Hollis very much alone.

Hollis took a deep breath. "Is Greg a line dance instructor too?"

Ainsley laughed her glorious laugh. "He should be. He just can't help himself when someone needs help."

"I can see why Harrison is so enamored with him." Hollis said as Harrison attempted to grape vine and then spin in a circle.

"So…now that we aren't at work, we should probably talk about the other night."

Hollis swallowed hard. All she'd wanted to do was talk about the kiss. "I know. But not here." She couldn't get into it now and risk Harrison finding out.

Ainsley nodded in understanding, and Hollis locked gazes with her brown eyes. God, how she wanted nothing more than to kiss those lips again.

"Here you go, beautiful." Jo reached her long arm around Hollis and set the beer down.

Hollis turned away from Ainsley and forced a smile at Jo. "Thank you."

"I didn't interrupt anything did I?" Jo asked defensively.

"No," Ainsley answered quickly. "Hollis and I are just coworkers catching up."

Just coworkers. The words stung more than Hollis was prepared for. Just coworkers who would never be kissing again. No matter how much either of them wanted it.

"Is this like a work function or something?" Jo frowned.

Hollis shook her head slightly. "Just a weird coincidence."

"Will I see you out there?" Ainsley asked and locked eyes with Hollis once again.

"Oh, she's promised me the first dance." Jo stood up a little straighter.

"I'm just here to observe tonight. It'll take a lot more of these to get me out there." Hollis raised her beer glass and took a sip. She tried not to gag as the light beer hit her taste buds. She should have known it would be some kind of light beer, but she wasn't expecting it.

"Oh, I can make that happen." Jo's voice turned flirtatious.

"I'll see you later." Ainsley exited as quickly as possible. Hollis tried not to stare as she walked away, but she should really be a model for those jeans.

"So the last breakup was bad?" Jo broke the silence.

Hollis pulled her eyes from Ainsley and met Jo's. Jo had nice eyes. Sure, they were not Ainsley's, but Jo was perfectly nice. There was absolutely nothing wrong with Jo. She had introduced herself. She had threatened to kick Harrison out of the bar. She had bought her a beer. So why couldn't Hollis get her mind off of Ainsley?

"It's not that it was bad." Hollis realized she'd stayed silent for too long. "It's more I've realized we wanted very different things, and Harrison thinks I should date around a bit. You know, play the field?"

"I do." Jo nodded. "So, you're looking for something a little more casual?" Jo playfully ran her fingers on the back of Hollis's palm.

Hollis stared at the fingers. What was happening? "Uh."

"It's okay to not know what you're looking for." Jo picked up her beer glass. "Sometimes just having fun is the most fun." She took a slow sip of her beer.

Hollis hadn't intended to have one light beer, let alone more. Every time her glass was empty, Jo had a refill at the ready. It was a good thing too, because Hollis needed something to distract her from Ainsley's surprisingly smooth dance moves. Not that Hollis was surprised Ainsley was a good dancer, Ainsley was good at everything. What surprised Hollis was that Ainsley could make even line dancing seem sexy. She'd sway her hips just slightly, then thrust them before clapping the heel of her boot and performing some kind of spin.

Greg had abandoned her for Harrison almost immediately, but that didn't slow Ainsley one bit. She danced with everyone at the Rusty Spur within an arm's reach.

"Alright," Jo said as she slid another beer to Hollis. "You have to at least do one dance."

Even the slight buzz couldn't get her on the dance floor. "I told you, I didn't come here to dance."

"Scared you might like it?" Jo egged her on.

"Are you really resorting to grade school tactics?"

"Or are you scared you'll be bad at it?"

More like scared she'd embarrass herself in front of Ainsley.

"Oh! This song is the best!" Jo jumped out of her chair. She reached for Hollis. "Come on. You have to learn how to boot scoot!"

"How to what?" Hollis didn't budge.

"Just come on." With one last tug, Jo was able to get Hollis off her stool. Hollis didn't know why, but she decided to just go with it. What was one dance?

Jo took a place at the end of the line forming and motioned for Hollis to stand next to her. "Okay. Just follow me and you'll be fine. Start with a grape vine to the right."

Hollis found the beat of the music and grapevined behind Jo's lead.

"Now to the left."

Hollis followed the line in front of her as it was time to kick, stomp, and twist just a bit. It seemed silly, but with a whole bar of people dancing together, it was almost fun.

"Now you do a quarter turn and start again." Jo clapped her hands as she started the grape vine again.

I can do this. Hollis could totally do this. Casually date. Line dance. She was unstoppable. After all, Jo was nice. They had a pleasant conversation. They'd shared a few drinks. Maybe she should ask her out again. Nothing serious. Just dinner. "Oooof." The air left her lungs as she crashed into a body in front of her. "Sorry." She tried to catch her breath as two arms steadied her.

"You're supposed to turn the other direction." Ainsley helped Hollis regain her balance.

The music stopped in Hollis's mind and the only thing she could focus on was Ainsley. Ainsley with her strong grip keeping her in place. Ainsley's lips that she had kissed not that long ago. God, what would it feel like to be able to kiss them again? The fire raged inside her. She wanted nothing more than to reach for Ainsley. She pulled herself together. "Sorry, this is my first time," she said.

"Another first-timer?" Ainsley said with a knowing smile. "First times are becoming our thing."

The dancers around them continued and when Hollis had steadied herself, Ainsley motioned for them to jump back in. Hollis finished the dance, slightly less confident and more careful to follow the people around her this time.

"You did great!" Jo clapped a hand to her shoulder. "That wasn't so bad, was it?"

Hollis looked for Ainsley, but she had disappeared into the crowd. Probably for the best. "Do you want to get out of here?"

"My place isn't too far, if that's what you're thinking."

"Sounds perfect." Hollis needed to be anywhere but in the same room as Ainsley. "Let me just tell Harrison I'm leaving."

Hollis found Harrison engrossed in conversation with Greg. "I'm going to take off."

Harrison studied her. "What, you aren't having fun?"

"Jo and I are going to take off."

"Ah. Okay. Well, don't do anything I wouldn't do."

"That is a short list." Hollis shot Greg a warning glance and made her way to the front door.

After a quick drive, Hollis found herself sitting on the couch of Jo's living room. She could tell Jo tried to take care of her rundown house by adding decorations to cover the worn down wood floors and old walls. Jo returned from the kitchen behind Hollis and handed her a bottle of water.

"Thank you." Hollis opened it and took a long drink.

"I know it's not much, but it's home." Jo motioned to the living room.

"It's great."

Jo sat next to Hollis, their thighs touching. "You're great." She inched closer.

Hollis put the water on the end table. As she turned back, she was met by a pair of lips. Slight panic rose in her as she wasn't expecting Jo to be so forward. She calmed her heart rate and settled into the kiss. It was nice. That was it. There was no fire. No passion. It was nothing compared to the kiss with Ainsley. Nothing like the best first kiss she'd ever had not even a week ago. She moaned, thinking of Ainsley's lips crushing against hers.

Jo took the groan as an invitation and moved her hands toward the top of Hollis's jeans. She slowly started to unbutton them.

"Wait." Hollis pushed Jo away carefully.

"Everything okay?"

"I can't do this." Hollis buried her head in her hands. "I'm sorry. I thought I could, but I can't."

Jo scooted to the other end of the couch. "Is there someone else?"

"Kind of."

"The cute coworker?"

Hollis looked up from her hands. "Is it that obvious?"

"It's not not obvious," Jo joked. "Come on. I'll take you home."

"No. It's okay. I'll just call for a car or something. You already went to a lot of trouble tonight. I'm not going to make you drive across town."

Jo eyed her cautiously. "You sure?"

"Positive. Thank you for a fun evening. I really did enjoy myself."

Jo led her to the front door. "I'm at the Rusty Spur almost every Thursday. Come find me if things don't work out with her."

Hollis stood on the porch waiting for the car to arrive. Things couldn't work out with Ainsley. There was no scenario where getting together with a coworker, let alone her boss, would be a good idea. But the thought of going back inside to Jo just didn't feel right. Even though Jo had been perfectly nice and a welcome distraction for the night, she would never be Ainsley.

CHAPTER TWELVE

Hollis sat at home, already changed into her comfiest sweats before five p.m. on Friday. She was exhausted from the work week. Not so much from the work part, but from trying to get over Ainsley. Just when she thought she could push her from her mind, she would see her in the hall, or pass her by the elevator. Thinking of those soft lips filled her stomach with butterflies and she'd have to start the process of getting over her all over again. She did her best to avoid her, but with their offices on the same floor, seeing each other was unavoidable. Then there was the run-in last night. The Rusty Spur set her back big time, as now all she could think about was Ainsley grapevining in tight jeans.

But Hollis had a plan. She was going to take the weekend and hibernate. She was going to crawl into her apartment and emerge on Monday fully over Ainsley Jones. A certain sadness formed within her. She was grieving a relationship that never was. She was grieving the idea of being with Ainsley. She was going to take the weekend to eat junk food and watch until the end of Netflix. Then on Monday, that would be it. She would move on. She would even let Harrison take her out again. She hadn't been with anyone since Miranda. Even though she hadn't been able to go any further with Jo, maybe with a few more dates she could. But for now, she was going to hibernate.

Harrison's picture filled the screen on her phone. She took a breath and answered, "Hello."

"Hollister Joanne Reed."

"That's not my name." She made sure he could hear her eye roll.

"Are you coming out or not?"

"I'm already in my sweats. I'm in for the night."

"It's Friday night, it's sunny, and you're inside in sweats?"

Hollis sighed. "I don't have it in me tonight."

"What's going on with you?" Harrison held genuine concern in his voice.

"I just need a weekend to get my mind right." She wasn't ready to share her Ainsley drama yet.

"What the hell does that mean?" Harrison sounded annoyed.

"It means I'm eating fried food alone in my sweatpants tonight instead of acting as your wingman."

Harrison scoffed. "You are the worst wingman in the history of wingmen."

"Did you even get Greg's number last night?"

Harrison sighed dramatically. "I was so busy dancing I totally forgot. A good wingman would have reminded me."

"Then you won't miss me, will you?"

Harrison sighed again, even more dramatic this time. "I'm going to let this go. But…" He paused for dramatic effect. "You owe me one night at happy hour next week and you're going to tell me whatever the hell this is. Got it?"

There was a knock at Hollis's door. "My food is here. I have to go."

"You didn't answer me," Harrison said, annoyed.

"Got it. Happy hour next week. My treat."

"Damn right it's your treat."

"Have a good night, Harrison." She went to hang up.

"And, Hol?"

She held the phone back to her ear.

"I know you ordered two dinners. Try not to eat them both tonight."

"I'll try my best," she said through a laugh. He'd been her friend long enough to know. She riffled for her wallet in her laptop bag.

There was another knock at the door. "I'll be right there," she yelled as she grabbed her wallet. She pulled the door open, and said while looking for cash, "Is tip included or not? I can never remember."

She took a step back as she realized it wasn't her food.

"Tip is not included." Ainsley grinned.

Hollis stared. What was Ainsley doing here? She'd changed into jeans and tennis shoes. Had she walked here from work? This was definitely not part of the plan Hollis had for the weekend.

Ainsley held up a small plastic grocery bag. "I wanted to return these. I thought it might raise questions if I did it at work."

"Right," Hollis said, disappointment overcoming her. Ainsley was just returning that ugly shirt. Of course, she would have no need for it. Ainsley handed her the bag and then continued to stand there.

"I have a bottle of wine open," she said before she could change her mind—or before Ainsley disappeared. "It would make me feel better about drinking the whole bottle if you had a glass." She caught Ainsley looking at her black sweatpants. "Yeah, I'm drinking in my sweats on a Friday night."

"I'm not judging."

"So, you'll join me?" Hollis held the door open, waiting. "Unless you have plans, that is."

"No." Ainsley took a step into the apartment. "No plans. Plus, we need to talk."

Those dreaded words. Hollis shut the door, and when she turned around, Ainsley was right there. Inches from her. Hollis dropped the bag and wallet from her hands.

Ainsley grabbed Hollis's face with both hands and kissed her. Ainsley stretched on her tiptoes to reach Hollis. This kiss was more forceful than the first one. Ainsley was commanding, but not overbearing. She slowly moved Hollis until her back hit the front door. Hollis leaned into the door and slightly bent her knees, making it easier for Ainsley to reach her.

Hollis pulled Ainsley closer until their bodies touched. This was night and day from the kiss with Jo. This was what a kiss was supposed to feel like. Ainsley held her hands firmly on Hollis's face. Ainsley pulled back slowly and kissed Hollis on the cheek while rubbing her hands down her body, landing squarely on her hips, playing with the elastic of her sweats. Hollis let out a breath. Ainsley kissed up her cheek, then worked her way up to Hollis's ear and let out a long, slow breath. Hollis's knees went weak, and the heat grew in her body. She gripped Ainsley tighter and pulled her in closer. She needed there to be no space at all between them.

Ainsley breathed again into Hollis's ear and Hollis moaned. Ainsley kissed a path from her ear back to her lips. She bit down softly on Hollis's bottom lip. Hollis couldn't stand it much longer. She caressed the warm skin under Ainsley's shirt and slid both palms onto the small of her back.

Ainsley worked up under the front of Hollis's T-shirt. She kept one hand entwined in her sweats and the other slowly moved up her shirt until it was on top of her bra. Hollis panicked as she realized she was wearing an old sports bra, and certainly nothing she would ever want Ainsley to see.

They both jumped at the knock at the door.

"No, no not now," Hollis said under breath.

Ainsley took a step back and smoothed out her hair with her hands.

Hollis bent down and picked up her wallet. "That's the food I ordered." She looked at Ainsley. "Don't move."

"I can't," Ainsley said.

Hollis worried that she would leave in a hurry or something. She definitely needed her to stay. She wanted whatever had been happening to *not end*. Not yet. Maybe not ever.

She opened the door, paid the kid for the food, and left a large tip. She turned around and exhaled in relief. Ainsley had stayed glued to her spot. "I'm going to get us that glass of wine. Please stay."

"Alright." Ainsley's voice was soft.

Hollis motioned to the couch. "I'll be right back."

Please don't leave.

Hollis put the food on the island. She downed the remaining wine in her glass like a shot and poured them each one. She sat beside Ainsley on the sofa.

"I'm sorry," Ainsley said as she took a glass of wine.

"Why?" Hollis held Ainsley's gaze.

"All I've thought about since last Friday was kissing you again. I thought for sure I was romanticizing it. Remembering it better than it was."

"And?"

Ainsley sighed. "And you're a better kisser than I remember."

"So that makes things…?"

"Complicated."

"I haven't stopped thinking about you since Friday either."

"Yeah?" Ainsley's voice was shaky.

"I'm drinking alone in sweats on a Friday night as part of my plan to get over you." Hollis grimaced as the words came out. It sounded ridiculous out loud.

Ainsley laughed that wonderful laugh. "You're trying to get over me?"

Hollis nodded.

"Is it working?"

"It's complicated."

Ainsley inched closer. "I know this sounds silly, but I just…" She paused and bit her bottom lip. "I just can't stop thinking about you and more than just the kiss, I mean. You're someone I feel myself opening up to and I can't explain why."

"It's not silly." Hollis clasped Ainsley's arm lightly. "Because I feel the same."

"You do?" Ainsley's eyes looked hopeful.

"I've been trying not to," Hollis said. "I've been trying to tell myself it's all in my head, but…" She hesitated. If she said what she wanted to say that she'd wanted to know Ainsley from the first moment, had imagined kissing her for weeks, would she cross a line she'd never be able to retreat from?

Ainsley rubbed her hands over her face. "I swear I never do this."

"Do what?" Hollis asked.

"Kiss my employees." Ainsley shook her head. "Follow them to their apartment and then kiss them in their home."

A warmth grew in her chest. It was oddly reassuring knowing that she hadn't done this before. Hollis set her wine glass on the ledge behind the couch, took Ainsley's glass from her, and set it next to hers.

"I want to kiss you again," she said confidently. Lines could move, couldn't they?

Ainsley looked up at her, concern and confusion on her face.

Hollis reached for her hands and pulled her closer. "Uncomplicate it," she said, barely above a whisper.

Ainsley gave the faintest of smiles.

Hollis pulled Ainsley on top of her, so her knees rested on the couch, straddling her. She whispered again, "Uncomplicate it."

Ainsley kissed her. Hollis held her hips tight, wrapping her fingers in the belt loops of her jeans. She reached up to meet Ainsley's lips. Her stomach flipped again, and heat radiated to her center with the weight of Ainsley on top of her. She kissed Ainsley back deeply. She wanted to kiss her in a way where Ainsley would see there was nothing complicated about this at all.

Ainsley pulled back.

"What?" Had she pushed her too far, too fast?

Ainsley shook her head, flustered. "If we're going to do this, we need rules."

"Like sex rules?"

"What? No." Ainsley paused. "Well, maybe."

"Like a safe word or something?"

"I'm not talking about consent—but we can if you want to." Ainsley pointed a finger between the two of them. "Rules for this. Whatever this is."

"What kind of rules?" Hollis would have agreed to anything in that moment.

Ainsley leaned back slightly on Hollis's thighs. "No one at work can find out. At least not yet."

"Okay," Hollis agreed.

"Not even Harrison." Her eyes widened meaningfully.

"Got it."

"And we need to keep things professional," she went on. "We can't be flirting or making eyes or anything with other people watching."

"Making eyes?" Hollis laughed.

"You know what I mean." Ainsley's tone turned serious.

"I do," Hollis said. "And you're right, of course."

"And nothing in any work emails or anything. We need to be strictly professional."

"I totally agree."

Ainsley let out a long breath.

"We need to not talk about work outside of work," Hollis said.

"Sure." Ainsley nodded.

"You are the boss at work, but you aren't the boss once we leave." Hollis gripped her tighter.

Ainsley laughed. "Oh, I'm still the boss."

Holy shit. That was hotter than Hollis had prepared for.

Ainsley sighed. "Okay."

"Okay?"

"I think if I know I'm going to get to kiss those lips later, then I'll finally be able to focus at work." Ainsley sat back up on her knees.

Hollis looked up into her desire-filled eyes. She couldn't wait much longer. "It's important that you're able to focus."

Ainsley leaned down and kissed Hollis again. Hollis loved the kissing, but she needed more. She needed to feel Ainsley.

Ainsley kissed up her neck until her mouth was at her ear again. "Let's move to your bedroom."

Hollis swallowed hard. She carefully lifted Ainsley off of her and led her by the hand down the short hall to her room.

Ainsley pushed Hollis to a sitting position at the end of the bed. She crawled on top of her lap and resumed the position they were in on the couch. Ainsley playfully bit her bottom lip and then pulled back. She stayed just out of reach. Ainsley ran her hands up Hollis's side and removed her shirt in one motion.

Hollis's face flushed as she sat in her old sports bra. The straps were hanging together by threads. "I wasn't expecting anyone to see this tonight," she said sheepishly. Out of reflex, she sucked in her stomach.

"It's coming off anyway," Ainsley said into her ear and then removed the bra over her head. Hollis's small breasts fell free and Ainsley took one in each hand, slowly massaging them. It was rare for Hollis to not to take the lead in the bedroom. While she hadn't had many partners, she had always been the one to initiate sex in her previous relationships. She was always the more dominant, controlled one in her relationships, but with Ainsley, it was different. Ainsley was calling the shots, and Hollis was surprisingly okay with it.

Ainsley pulled back and slid her hands from Hollis's breasts to her shoulders. She looked her up and down exposing Hollis. "I have been picturing you topless all week."

Hollis looked away, embarrassed.

Ainsley grasped Hollis's head with both hands. She leaned in until her lips were just above her ear. "It's better than I imagined."

Hollis pulled her head back and looked up at her. "It's a little unfair that you're still fully dressed."

"I hate for things to be unfair." Ainsley sat up slightly and undid the first button on her white blouse. "Is this better?"

Her voice was sexy as she slowly undid the next button.

Hollis could barely contain herself. She held her hands tight on Ainsley's ass, keeping her in place. "It's getting better, but still not fair."

Ainsley undid another button, making her white lacy bra visible. "How about now?"

Hollis swallowed hard. "Getting warmer."

Ainsley didn't break eye contact as she slowly undid the rest of her blouse. With her shirt completely open, Hollis got a full view of her body. Hollis caressed Ainsley's ass and stroked all the way up her soft skin until she reached her shoulders. Then she slowly slipped the blouse down her arms and let it fall to the floor. "Getting warmer," she said.

Ainsley leaned back down to kiss Hollis. Hollis reached her right hand behind Ainsley's back and undid the clasp of her bra. Ainsley seemed slightly surprised as she pulled back. She gave

Hollis an approving nod and allowed the bra to fall to the floor as well.

"Now it's fair," Hollis said as she got her first look at Ainsley's magnificent breasts. She pulled Ainsley in closer with her hands on the small of her back and took one nipple into her mouth. A throaty moan escaped from Ainsley as her nipple grew under Hollis's touch. She sucked and flicked and took pleasure in the sounds coming from Ainsley. With one hand, she undid the button to Ainsley's jeans. The angle was wrong, and she couldn't get her hand under her waistband.

"I need to touch you," she said.

"Not yet," Ainsley replied. She pushed Hollis back until she was lying on the bed. She lay on top of her, their bare skin touching. Ainsley continued to kiss her and held both her breasts in her hands. She took a thumb and forefinger of one hand and made Hollis's nipple turn hard.

Hollis let out a small cry. Warmth flooded between her thighs, and she needed to feel Ainsley.

Ainsley pushed herself up with her arms and met Hollis at the end of the bed. She easily removed Hollis's sweatpants and underwear with one motion, and dropped them to the floor. She undid her jeans and slid them off as well. Was that black thong the kind of underwear Ainsley always wore to work, or was she hoping for Hollis to see it?

"Move up on the bed," Ainsley said as she removed her thong. Now she was naked and all Hollis could do was stare.

"Up," Ainsley repeated.

Hollis quickly pushed closer to the headboard, still sitting on top of the white down comforter.

"Good. You listen." Ainsley crawled up the bed to join her.

She ran her hands the full length of Hollis's body. Hollis's heart rate quickened under Ainsley's touch. Ainsley continued rubbing her hand up Hollis and then paused when she got to her inner thigh. She held her palm there for a moment, and then grazed her throbbing clit. "Is this okay?"

"Oh God," Hollis breathed out. "You have no idea how many times I've fantasized about you saying that."

"Oh really?" She slid her hand easily around the apex of Hollis's thighs, moving her wetness around.

Hollis let out a breath.

Ainsley increased the pressure with her palm. "You didn't answer me." She held her entire palm over Hollis's center. "Is this okay?"

"Yes," Hollis breathed out.

Ainsley stroked her palm back and forth and slowly entered Hollis with her middle finger. "Is this okay?"

"Yes," Hollis moaned. "God yes."

Ainsley's finger glided easily in and out. She picked up her pace, and Hollis arched her back. Ainsley rested one hand on Hollis's hip, holding her in place, and added a second finger. "Is this okay?" Her voice was low and husky.

Hollis squeezed her palms into her forehead. The pressure inside her building stronger by the second. She had fantasized about Ainsley touching her in this way and it was even better than she could have imagined. The feel of her hands, the sound of her voice, her smell. Hollis was right on the edge and Ainsley was pushing her closer with each thrust. She arched her back and pushed her hips upward, her chest heaving. Ainsley's hand holding her in place was driving her crazy. Sounds she didn't recognize escaped from her. She couldn't keep them in. This was the boost Ainsley needed, and she quickened her pace.

Her entire body contracted and her hips convulsed uncontrollably. She clamped her eyes shut and stars filled the darkness behind her eyelids. She relaxed her body and fell back onto the bed. She strained to catch her breath as Ainsley cuddled up next to her, laying her head on Hollis's shoulder, Ainsley's own skin slick with sweat.

Hollis put her arm around Ainsley. "Wow."

"Was that anything like you fantasized?"

"Better." Hollis still struggled to catch her breath.

Ainsley stroked her hand up and down Hollis's bare chest slowly. She rubbed her hand from navel to collar bone.

Hollis tried to comprehend what had just happened but her brain was fuzzy. "Give me just a minute before your turn," she said between breaths.

Ainsley let out a laugh. "This isn't shuffleboard."

"What do you mean?"

"There aren't turns," Ainsley said into her ear. "Roll over."

"What?" Hollis still wasn't following. Of course, there were turns. Sex had always had turns. Usually, she would initiate and then her partner would return the favor. Hollis had had plenty of good sex in her life, but she was realizing now that it was always transactional. There was always a give and take. Was that why all of her relationships had failed?

"Roll over," Ainsley said it again, slowly, punctuating her words.

Hollis gave in and slowly rolled onto her stomach.

"Good," Ainsley said. "I was afraid you couldn't follow directions."

Hollis gave a nervous laugh. Ainsley grabbed her hips and set her up slightly. Hollis shifted her body weight onto her elbows. The new position stirred up unfamiliar feelings during sex. She was feeling anxious, exposed. She had never done anything in this position before let alone give up this level of control. It surprised her that her stomach could still do flips this soon after her first orgasm and at how turned on she was by Ainsley being in charge.

Ainsley squeezed Hollis's ass and she let out a gasp. Ainsley continued running her hand over Hollis's ass and in between her thighs. Nervous anticipation filled Hollis.

"You have a tattoo," Ainsley said with surprise.

"Yeah."

"I did not expect that. What is it?"

"It's my college mascot. The team made it to the college world series in 2009 and we all got matching tattoos. I thought it was dumb, but they were all doing it."

Ainsley continued rubbing her hand between Hollis's thighs. "Do you always give in so easily to peer pressure?"

Hollis gasped as Ainsley pinched her clit. She couldn't think straight. She couldn't see straight.

"No," she sighed. "But I made sure to get it somewhere I could easily cover. My parents would have killed me at the time."

"I feel like he's looking at me. Why would you get a weird guy tattooed there?" Ainsley's voice was hesitant.

"It's technically a Viking," Hollis said between breaths. "This has never come up before."

"What?"

Hollis gasped as Ainsley plunged two fingers forcefully inside her.

Ainsley kept her hand inside her and placed her mouth just above Hollis's ear. "You've never been taken from behind before?"

"No." Hollis could barely get the words out.

Ainsley reached for a pillow from the headboard and positioned it under Hollis's hips.

The new position brought slight relief as Hollis strained to stay upright.

"I'll try to go easy," Ainsley whispered. "I told you my first-timers are usually sore."

"Oh God." Hollis couldn't make any coherent thoughts for the next several minutes. Ainsley was taking her in a way like never before. She was owning her, and as much as Hollis wanted to crest the ledge and fall off it, she also never wanted it to end. She wanted to feel Ainsley inside of her forever. With her other hand, Ainsley reached around and made long strokes over Hollis's clit. The sensation of Ainsley inside her and stimulating her was more than she could handle. At last, Ainsley gave one last thrust and curled her fingers firmly inside her. Her body collapsed to the bed as she came. She lay face down on the pillow for several minutes, catching her breath.

Hollis eventually rolled over, finally able to take a full breath. Ainsley patiently lay next to her. Hollis pulled Ainsley up until she was straddling her and ran her hands from Ainsley's thighs up her rib cage. Cupping her breasts, she pinched both nipples. Ainsley arched her back and moaned.

Hollis raked her fingers gently back down Ainsley's sides and rested both hands on her hips. "God, you look amazing."

She stared up as Ainsley's hair fell slowly in front of her. For the first time, Hollis noticed that Ainsley had a small tattoo on her upper thigh just below her hip. "You have a tattoo?"

"You're not the only one with surprises," Ainsley said.

Hollis ran her thumb over it lovingly. It was a small bird. It was hard to tell in the light, but Hollis thought it was a bird just starting to fly. "What is it?"

"It's a bluebird," Ainsley replied. "My mother's favorite."

"Your mother likes birds?"

Ainsley bent down until her face was so close her hair tickled Hollis's bare skin. "Turns out we do need sex rules."

Hollis gave a small laugh. "What's that?"

"No talking about our parents during." Ainsley leaned down and kissed Hollis on the lips.

Hollis slid her hand from Ainsley's hip and held her palm against her throbbing clit. She wasn't sure if Ainsley was soaking wet from having her way with her, or from Ainsley finding her attractive, but she didn't care. Hollis slowly inserted her middle finger. Ainsley exhaled and her chest heaved in approval.

Ainsley sat up, and Hollis bent her knees to give her a back rest. Ainsley put her hands just behind Hollis's knees and leaned back on the bed. Hollis, appreciative of the better angle, pulsed her finger freely in and out of her. This was the moment she had been longing for. To fully feel Ainsley at last. She wanted to know her in a way that no one else could. She wanted to be the one to take Ainsley to places only she could. She accelerated her pace and made full strokes. Ainsley threw her head back and her breasts bounced up and down.

Ainsley picked up one hand, keeping her weight on the other, and moved it to Hollis's center. She made full caresses up and down and Hollis tensed slightly.

"Hey now," Hollis said.

"Mmm?" Ainsley closed her eyes.

"You're distracting me," Hollis said between breaths.

"You're telling me you can't multitask?" Ainsley pushed herself hard inside Hollis.

"Is that a challenge?" Hollis pushed further inside and Ainsley threw her neck back.

"Are you always this competitive?" Ainsley said with a gasp.

"Yes." Hollis grunted. It wouldn't take much to get her to climax again. She tried to focus only on what her own hands were doing, but it was difficult. Her breathing went shallow, and she arched her neck, straining to stay in the same place. She focused on Ainsley's motion and matched her pace.

"That's it," Ainsley said. "That's it," Ainsley repeated herself. Hollis blinked twice and willed herself to focus. The pressure continued building inside her. She was ready to burst. Hollis pushed deeper finding the ridges of Ainley's G-spot and didn't let up.

"Right there." Ainsley's voice rose two octaves as she contracted around Hollis's fingers, gripping them with her whole self. She let out a low groan as her body relaxed.

Hollis had never been inside a woman at the same time, let alone orgasmed at the same time. She slowly slipped out and guided Ainsley down until they were cuddling. Ainsley's head rested on Hollis's shoulder like they had lain this way together a million times. And yet, nothing about tonight had been like anything Hollis had ever done before.

CHAPTER THIRTEEN

Hollis stirred, inhaling the scent of Ainsley's perfume in her bed. Her right arm tingled from falling asleep under Ainsley's small frame, but she didn't care. She would have stayed in this moment, entangled with Ainsley, all morning if she could.

Ainsley must have noticed Hollis staring at her as Ainsley blinked herself awake.

"Good morning," Hollis said, barely above a whisper. She slowly leaned over and kissed Ainsley on the forehead.

Ainsley stretched her arms overhead. "Good morning." She lifted herself slightly to deepen the stretch.

Hollis discreetly opened and shut her hand to regain feeling in her arm. She had a brief fear that it had all been a dream. That Ainsley had never come over. That last night had never happened. But now that she saw that silky smooth skin lying in her bed, she knew it had all been real. Hollis didn't know what time it was, and she didn't care. "I can make coffee," she said.

Ainsley reached out her hand and stroked Hollis's cheek. "Coffee sounds great." Her sleep-filled voice was just as sexy as the night before.

Hollis held Ainsley's hand against her own cheek. "You are so beautiful." She couldn't help herself. Seeing her there, her auburn hair a mess, all she could think about was kissing those lips again.

Ainsley softly pushed her away. "Go. Make coffee."

Hollis hesitated. "You are really hard to leave."

"You aren't going far." The smile hadn't left Ainsley's face yet.

Hollis took her hand and kissed it. "Okay. I won't be long."

She pulled the covers off and stepped out of bed, suddenly feeling self-conscious. She couldn't explain it. Ainsley had seen her naked the night before, but it was dark and in the throes of passion. Now that it was the clear light of day, she needed to cover up fast. She found her T-shirt and sweats on the ground and quickly threw them on.

Sleep still in her eyes, Hollis poured water into her coffee maker. Her dinners from the night before sat in the takeout bag on the counter. She'd need to deal with that later, but first, coffee. She held her head in her hands on the counter as she waited for the coffee maker to brew.

Ainsley was unlike any woman Hollis had ever been with. She thought about how she was normally drawn to women who were more or less her opposite. Ainsley was the first woman she had more in common with than not. They were both hardworking and career-driven. She knew Ainsley was into fitness and clearly understood running. She certainly wasn't opposed to it, and the chemistry in the bedroom was off the charts. Hollis had never experienced sex like that before. She had never let someone else take control, and she had a hard time admitting that she, in fact, liked it. Yes, she had it bad for Ainsley Jones. It wasn't part of the plan by any means, but that was okay.

Hollis rubbed her face a few more times, willing the coffee machine to work its magic faster. A warm pair of arms enveloped her waist from behind. Ainsley leaned into her and pressed her cheek onto her back. Hollis put her hands over hers and inhaled. She slowly turned around. Ainsley took a small step back but didn't break contact.

"I missed you," Ainsley said softly.

Hollis appreciated the sentiment. She smiled when she saw that Ainsley had found one of her T-shirts to put on. God, there was something sexy about a woman wearing just her shirt.

"Jeans seemed too uncomfortable. I hope you don't mind. I went through your drawers."

"Not at all. I actually really like the shirt on you." She pulled her in and rested her chin on top of her head. They were a perfect fit. The coffee maker beeped, signaling it was ready. "How do you take your coffee?"

"Just black," Ainsley said.

"A girl after my own heart." She pulled away and reached for two black coffee mugs in the cupboard. She poured two cups and handed one to Ainsley.

Ainsley took the mug in both hands and inhaled. She took a long sip. "This might be the best coffee I've ever had."

Hollis shook her head. "You're just saying that."

Ainsley leaned her shoulder into her to nudge her. "I don't just say things."

Hollis nudged her back. It was odd how comfortable it already was. Saturday morning coffee. Waking up together. It had just been one night but seemed like a lifetime. She took a sip from her own mug and the coffee dancing across her lips awakened her sleep filled brain. Hollis jumped at a knock at the door. "Shit."

"What?"

"It's Miranda." She shook her head. "I forgot she's bringing that stupid box by this morning."

"Oh shit." Ainsley sounded panicked. "She can't find out about us."

"Go hide in the bedroom or something."

"What is this, high school?"

"Do you have any better ideas?" The knock at the door became louder.

"Can you make this quick?"

"I promise. The last thing I want to do is talk to Miranda right now."

Ainsley retreated to the bedroom. Hollis made sure to hear the door click shut before opening the front door. "Miranda."

"Took you long enough." Miranda pushed past Hollis inside her apartment.

"Please come in," Hollis said to the empty hallway.

"Well, this should be it." Miranda placed a small box on the kitchen island.

"Thanks for bringing it by." Hollis opened the box, relieved to see the running jacket at the top.

"So, how have you been?"

Seriously? Miranda wanted to talk? "Good."

"That's good. Jaydee asked about you at her party last weekend."

"She has my number. If she's all that interested, she can call." The only way to deal with Miranda was bluntness.

"You don't have to be so rude, you know. Could we at least try to be civil?"

Hollis needed Miranda to leave. The longer she stayed in her kitchen, the longer she wasn't enjoying her time with Ainsley. "I am being civil. It's not like we're friends or anything."

"I'm not asking for much here, Hollis. Maybe you can stop avoiding me at work? Is that too much to ask?"

"I'm not avoiding you," Hollis lied.

"Well, whatever you are or aren't doing, it's awkward as hell."

"Hollis?" Ainsley's voice sounded from the bedroom.

Miranda noticed the two coffee mugs on the counter, then shot Hollis a look. "Oh my God, do you have someone over?"

"Hollis, are you coming back to bed?"

"I take it that's my cue to leave," Miranda said. "I guess we really are done here."

"Miranda, don't do this."

"I'm glad you've moved on. I guess it's time for me to do the same." Miranda shut the door behind her.

Hollis was glad she was gone, but definitely didn't like the energy wafting from the hallway. That was beside the point. Miranda was the past. Ainsley was the present, maybe even the future. The shower turning on brought her back to the here and now and what might be waiting for her in the next room.

She opened the bathroom door to see steam rising and Ainsley standing naked in front of the shower. "Took you long enough."

"Sorry about that."

"I thought I was going to have to come out there in a towel and drag you back or something."

"That really wouldn't help us keep things quiet at work, now would it?"

"True."

"Hold on." Hollis sounded more panicked than she meant.

"Okay?" Ainsley looked Hollis in the eyes.

"I just needed to save this image in my mind for later."

Ainsley let out a laugh. "Later, huh?" She opened the shower door and stepped in. "You joining me?"

Hollis tried not to stare blatantly but Ainsley was just as breathtaking in the daylight with her smooth, olive-toned skin and sculpted muscles. Ainsley was the most attractive woman Hollis had ever seen and she happily followed her into the shower.

"I'm a little offended," Ainsley said as she stepped under the steaming water.

"That I took so long?"

Ainsley reached for Hollis and pushed her back against the shower wall. Hollis shuddered at the shock of the cold tile. Ainsley kissed her neck, working her way up. She slid one hand between Hollis's thighs, and all traces of cold disappeared.

"I'm offended that I have left you so unsatisfied this weekend that you'll need to take care of yourself later."

She pushed a finger easily inside Hollis, and Hollis let out a sharp breath. She leaned her head back against the wet shower wall and her eyes rolled back into her head at the pressure building inside her. She managed to form words. "I meant much, much, later," she said between deep breaths.

"Mm-hmm," Ainsley hummed, not convinced. She increased the pressure of her hand and started moving in and out of Hollis. She kept her other hand firmly on her hip, gripping her tight.

Hollis knees buckled underneath her as she struggled to stand upright. Ainsley must have sensed this as she shifted her hand from Hollis's hip to her ass. She squeezed it tight and then grasped her leg, holding her in place. She was pinned and she had never done anything like this before. Hollis was normally against shower sex. It always looked better on TV than it actually was. The reality of it was that one partner stood freezing cold while the other tried to find the right angle. She had only tried it with other women a handful of times, and it had never been enjoyable. However, like with most things, Ainsley was different. She was imposing, domineering, and knew exactly what she was doing.

"My goal," Ainsley said into her ear, "is that you are never going to need those images."

Hollis would have collapsed if Ainsley wasn't holding her up. Between the talking and the sensations, it was too much. She could have melted into a puddle right then and there. Ainsley drove herself in deeper. "Oh God," Hollis barely made out.

Ainsley stepped closer until there was little space between them. "I've got you."

Hollis relaxed her legs ever so slightly and let Ainsley hold her up. She dug her hands into Ainsley's shoulders, gripping them tightly. She needed something to hold on to. Ainsley had picked up her rhythm, and Hollis was right on the edge. She could feel the orgasm building inside her. She was so close.

"That's it," Ainsley said again.

Hollis held her breath. She shut her eyes tight and saw stars behind her eyelids again. A low moan escaped as she finally released her breath her whole body tensed and then relaxed. Ainsley held her in place as she recovered. Hollis could feel her chest heaving up and down as she worked to regain her composure. She opened her eyes to a mischievous grin looking back at her. Ainsley slowly removed herself, placed Hollis's leg back on the ground, and pulled her in for a hug. Hollis took deep breaths. She put her chin on top of Ainsley's head, the mist from the shower tickling her nose. "Holy shit, that was good."

"That should tide you over for a while." Ainsley ran her hands up Hollis's back and pulled her in close.

Chapter Fourteen

"Morning," Hollis said when Harrison came in behind her.

"Wait a minute." Harrison paused as he put his bag down.

Hollis looked up from her computer. "What?"

"You had sex this weekend." Harrison narrowed his gaze.

Hollis coughed. "What's that?"

Harrison pointed at her. "You had sex this weekend."

Hollis stammered. "How could you possibly know that?"

"It's like a sixth sense. So, who's the lucky lady? Was it Jo from the country bar? I'm assuming you haven't changed teams?" He waggled his eyebrows.

Hollis knew she was going to have to tell Harrison something eventually, but she thought she'd have more time to come up with a cover story. She didn't think he would be able to tell within three seconds of seeing her. "I haven't switched teams."

"That's it." Harrison sat down. "You're taking me to happy hour tonight. I'm calling it."

Hollis gave a half laugh. "I guess I did say I owed you this week."

"And you are going to tell me every detail." Harrison sat in his desk chair. "Except for the gross parts, that is."

"You got it."

"So, what's her name?"

Hollis was thankful that Harrison's desk phone rang at that exact moment. She resumed browsing her emails.

"Saved by the bell," Harrison said. He picked up the receiver. "This is Harrison. Oh, hey you. What? No, I haven't seen it yet." Harrison snapped his fingers at Hollis.

Harrison covered the end of his phone and mouthed. "Check your email."

Hollis turned to her laptop and as Harrison continued his conversation. "No, I'm sure it's fine," he said with slight panic to his voice. "We'll talk about it later tonight. Yes, tonight."

The sound of dull ringing in her ears replaced Harrison's voice as she scanned the memo. Just that morning, HR sent a companywide memorandum regarding interoffice relationships. The memo explained that relationships between employees, while they may be consensual, were strongly discouraged. It created unnecessary distractions, and the company needed everyone focused on their job performance. Furthermore, romantic relationships between managers and direct reports were strictly prohibited. Hollis reread that last line four times.

While Hollis had read the employee handbook and knew all the company rules regarding office relationships, she had never seen a policy spelled out so clearly. She knew it was a bad idea to go any further with Ainsley, but how could she stop? How could she go back to viewing her as just her boss? There had to be a way around this.

"Can you believe this?" Harrison said as he hung up the phone.

"Why do you think they sent this out now?" Certainly it couldn't have anything to do with Ainsley so soon.

"I think HR guy found out about Parker."

"Are you serious?" Hollis struggled not to curse. She had met a beautiful, smart, funny woman who happened to be her boss and now she couldn't see her because Harrison couldn't control himself? She wanted to scream at him. She pictured herself grabbing the lapel of his jacket and shaking him senseless. The sound of a phone ringing interrupted her vison.

"This is Hollis," she said.

"Ms. Reed, it's Parker." She could hear the smile in Ainsley's assistant's voice.

"Oh. Parker. I didn't recognize the number."

"Corporate IT is still getting everything set up," he explained. "Ms. Jones would like to see you this morning. Now, if possible."

"Is everything okay?" Hollis could only assume that this was regarding the memo that came out. Her heart sank at the idea of Ainsley calling things off just as they had gotten started.

"I just know that she asked for you as soon as possible. Can I tell her you're on your way?"

"Yes, of course."

"What's that all about?" Harrison asked.

"I have no idea." She headed down the hallway with knots in her stomach. Was Ainsley going to end things? Should she try to end things first? As much as she wanted to pursue a relationship with Ainsley, how could they continue after an edict like that? She let out a long breath as she rounded the corner and saw Parker typing away at his computer.

"Good morning, Ms. Reed," Parker said with a professional tone.

"You can call me Hollis." Hollis was slightly uncomfortable with Parker's formality.

Parker flashed his plastered-on assistant's smile. "No, thank you. You can go on in. Ms. Jones is expecting you."

"Thanks."

Ainsley sat behind the desk as Hollis entered into the large corner office. "Hi." Ainsley's voice was soft and welcoming.

Hollis couldn't help but smile. "Hi."

Ainsley stood up. "Grab the door."

Hollis turned to shut the door and when she turned back around Ainsley had made her away across the office and stopped a few steps away. "What—?

Ainsley cupped her face and kissed her. This surprised Hollis, but didn't stop her from kissing back. They had just come up with rules for work, and Ainsley was throwing them out the window the first chance she got. But Hollis decided she didn't care. The door was shut. No one would know. If Ainsley Jones wanted to kiss her, who was she to stop her?

It took Hollis several moments to figure out what was different about this kiss. The passion and intensity were still there. Ainsley's same soft lips and firm hands were strong on her face. Then it struck her that Ainsley was wearing heels, and they were essentially the same height. It was a small difference, but one that Hollis noticed.

After several moments, Ainsley pulled back. "I'm sorry," she said, just above a whisper.

"I'm not."

Ainsley moved her hands from Hollis's face to the top of her shoulders. "It's just that I see you, and I can't stop myself from kissing you."

Hollis placed her hands on Ainsley's hips. "I'm okay with that."

Ainsley rubbed her hands up and down Hollis's shoulders. "Have dinner with me tonight."

Hollis sighed and rolled her eyes. "I literally just made plans with Harrison." She could see the disappointment in Ainsley's eyes. She braced herself for an argument.

"I guess I have to get to you early to get on your calendar?" One corner of Ainsley's mouth turned up.

Relief flooded Hollis. Miranda would have started a fight over her being busy. Even though they weren't officially anything, Hollis wasn't used to anyone taking news that she already had plans this well. The fact was, she couldn't do anything tonight, and Ainsley was okay with that. "Not usually," Hollis said. "But I've been blowing him off for a few weeks. Plus, the first thing he said this morning was that I had sex this weekend, so apparently my good mood is obvious."

Ainsley stroked her hands over the top of Hollis's blue button-up blouse. "Good mood, huh?"

"That's an understatement. Don't worry, I won't tell him about us." As much as Hollis didn't want to, she needed to bring up that memo. She couldn't pretend that it wasn't out there any longer. She hated how much of a rule follower she was, but how could she not mention it? "I thought maybe you were calling me in here to talk about that memo that just came out," she said with a shaky voice.

"The HR one?"

"The one saying that relationships between managers and direct reports are strictly prohibited?" Hollis squeezed her hips tighter.

Ainsley ran her fingers up from Hollis's chest to her shoulder. "That does make things complicated."

"I don't think I can go back to you just being my boss." Hollis didn't intend to be this honest, but something about Ainsley made her speak exactly what was on her mind.

"I don't want to go back to just being the boss," Ainsley said, just above a whisper.

"So, what now?" Hollis knew what she wanted to do. She wanted to say screw it. She didn't care who knew or who found out. They were consenting adults. It was one thing for the company to track how often she went to the gym, but could they really track who she slept with too?

"Well, the memo said that relationships between managers and direct reports are strictly prohibited. They didn't say anything about friendships."

Hollis took the news like a sucker punch to gut. Friendship? This was so far past friendship, whatever it was. Her face must have shown her disgust as Ainsley quickly cut in.

"As in friendship with certain benefits," Ainsley said tentatively. "I know it's kind of a technicality, but we are basically in a gray area here."

"You can say that again." She couldn't stop thinking of Ainsley as more than a friend, but a relationship was off the table. Ignoring the twinge of disappointment, she said, "Friends with benefits it is, then."

"Do you think you can stick to the rules we came up with?" Ainsley asked.

"The ones about work or the ones about talking about parents during sex?" Hollis joked.

"Both."

"I can agree to that," Hollis said. She could have agreed to anything.

"Well." Ainsley let out a long breath. "I think as long as we keep things professional, then we should see where things go."

Hollis would do whatever needed to make sure she could keep seeing Ainsley, even if that meant trying to dial back her feelings for the time being.

"Seriously." Ainsley intensified her tone. "No one can find out. Especially not Harrison."

"I'll tell him I met a cute girl at the gym or something."

"Don't make her too cute," Ainsley said. "I might get jealous."

"You have nothing to worry about." Hollis wondered what a jealous Ainsley would be like.

"Can I get on your calendar for tomorrow?"

Hollis looked up like she was thinking. "I think I can pencil you in."

"Seven. My house. I'm going to cook for you."

Hollis eyed her questioningly.

"Yes, I can cook." Ainsley nodded.

"I didn't say you couldn't." Was there anything she couldn't do? "That sounds great. What can I bring?"

"Well, my place is a bit of a drive from here."

Hollis laughed. "I can drive."

"So maybe…" Ainsley drew her words out, still playing with her fingers on Hollis's shoulder. "You should bring an overnight bag in case you have a few drinks and don't want to drive home."

Hollis swallowed hard. Ainsley spoke to her in a way that no other woman had in her life. "I can do that," she managed to say after a long pause.

"Do me a favor?"

Hollis nodded. "Okay."

"Remember that mental picture you took on Saturday?" She paused and looked Hollis directly in the eyes.

"You mean the one of you looking sexy as hell in my bathroom?"

"Mm-hmm." Ainsley inched closer.

"What about it?"

"Don't use it tonight."

Hollis let out a long breath. "Are you asking me what I think you are?"

"Mm-hmm," Ainsley hummed. "I'm going to more than take care of you tomorrow and it will be ten times better if you," she paused, searching for the right words, "save yourself."

"Holy shit." Hollis tried to compose herself. It took everything she had not to push Ainsley back against her desk. Her face flushed warm and desire permeated her. She closed her eyes as Ainsley played with her hands on her shoulder again.

"I would have done it tonight," Ainsley said playfully. "But one of us is busy."

Hollis let out a quick breath. "Okay. We're going to have to get a whole lot better at following our work rules." She pushed Ainsley back a step to give some space between them.

Ainsley cocked her head.

"You are getting me all worked up and then I'm just supposed to what," she paused. "Go back to my desk and focus on actual work? It's not going to happen."

"You're right. I'm sorry," she said. "I did actually call you in for a work reason. I just got distracted." Ainsley motioned to the small conference table next to them.

Hollis went to take a seat and Ainsley grabbed a stack of papers off her desk. Her ass swayed ever so slightly, and Hollis didn't know if it was natural or if she was doing it on purpose. Either way, seeing her toned ass in tight black slacks was taking her mind far away from work.

Ainsley put her blue-framed reading glasses on as she took a seat at the table.

"God damn it," Hollis said.

"What?" Ainsley asked, concerned.

"Is there anything you don't look sexy in?"

"What are you talking about?" She scrunched her forehead.

"The glasses." Hollis pointed to the reading glasses. "They are sexy as hell."

Ainsley pulled them off her face and looked at them. "Really?"

"Yes."

"I just started wearing them. I'd be lying if I said I wasn't a little self-conscious."

"Don't be."

"They make me feel old."

Hollis sensed the genuine concern in Ainsley's voice. "I like them." She held her gaze. "I'm going to close my eyes and count to ten. When I open them, we are going to go back to work mode, okay?"

"Okay." Ainsley gave an exaggerated eye roll.

Hollis looked at her lap and then closed her eyes. She breathed in and counted to five. She slowly released her breath as she counted to five again. She took one more quick breath in and then looked up.

Ainsley straightened the stack of papers in her hand and put them on the table. "I sent an email on the brick-and-mortar idea to Andrew. He wants to hear more. They're forming a task force to see if they can make this a reality. I know we're still waiting on your prelim numbers, but it was too good an idea to keep quiet."

"That's great." It surprised Hollis that the idea was actually getting traction.

"It is. The goal will be a West Coast launch in time for the spring line next year. That gives the team eleven months to go from concept to first sale. It's a little aggressive, but if everything is in place, it should be achievable."

Hollis beamed with pride.

"It will be a great win for HQ II. If we can show great ideas coming out of this side of the country, that will help the team back in Raleigh to take us more seriously."

"No doubt that it will be great for you as well."

"Well, yes." Ainsley nodded. "But it will help the two sides of the country work better together. I just wanted you to know that your suggestion was a great one."

"Thank you."

"So, if you have any other great concepts, don't hold out on me." Ainsley was only half kidding. "Can I ask you a question?"

"Of course." Hollis couldn't think of a thing she wouldn't divulge for her.

"Why don't you want to be a part of this? It's a great idea."

"It's not part of the plan." Hollis thought that would be enough of an explanation for someone like Ainsley. Surely Ainsley Jones knew the importance of plans and ensuring that your career stuck to a certain path. Hollis always worked with plans. It helped keep her focused on the days she wanted to up and quit at the drop of a hat. Ainsley's raised eyebrow suggested she needed more of an explanation than that. "My three-year plan. I'm one year in. We rolled out all the SOPs ahead of schedule. This year will be finishing the network rollout of all the additional procedures. Then year three will be training someone on the team to take over for me."

"And then what's after year three?"

"I have all of next year to figure that out." Hollis needed a good plan, but also knew she couldn't get too far ahead of herself. Three years was usually her max.

"Well, I do respect a good plan. But maybe you should keep your mind open. You never know when a great opportunity might come along and change your strategy."

Hollis wasn't one for surprises. She liked having a goal and working toward it. No matter how great the opportunity, she wasn't interested. "Do me a favor?"

"Anything."

"Don't look at me at the ten a.m. meeting." Hollis's tone stayed flat.

"What?"

"If we're going to keep it together at work, then you need to not look at me. Not even a glance. I'll lose it."

"That's not going to be easy."

"I'm serious."

"Okay, but…" She paused. "You can't use the image of me in the glasses tonight either."

❖

Hollis struggled with conflicting emotions on the way back to her office. Ainsley wanting to see where things went excited her. But the rule follower in her was torn. She didn't see how she could ever view Ainsley as just a boss. A friend with benefits didn't feel right either, but if that's what it took to keep pursuing Ainsley, she would do it. The closed office door signaled something was off. She and Harrison touted their open-door policy and never sat behind closed doors.

As she opened the door, Harrison was mid-conversation, "I agree with you, but I don't think I can get Hollis on board."

Hollis stood in the doorframe and stared at Harrison. "Get Hollis on board with what?"

"Hol, come in and shut the door." He pointed to the two sharply dressed men standing in their office. "You remember Steve and Jake from sales?"

"Hi," Hollis said, not wanting anything to do with whatever this conversation was.

"We're just saying, enough is enough." Steve's dark black suit and purple tie probably played well out in the field but didn't blend in at HQ II. The gold Rolex on his wrist probably cost more than her rent.

"Enough of what?" Hollis asked.

"This micromanagement," Jake blurted. Steve had taken him under his wing and was teaching him the world of sales. It wouldn't be long until they had matching Rolexes, since Steve was all about first impressions.

"What am I missing?" Hollis asked.

Harrison took a breath. "Some of the other departments aren't a fan of our new boss." He looked up at Hollis, who still stood in the doorframe.

Hollis stiffened at Harrison's comment. She couldn't go against her coworkers, but she also couldn't let on that she and Ainsley were anything more than boss and employee. "Are things really that different?"

"The damn weekly report." Steve flared his arms. "We aren't doing it. And we talked to the finance guys and they aren't doing it either. It's a level of oversight we don't need."

"Oh, come on." Hollis couldn't help herself. She didn't want to do the report either, but it wasn't a big change. "She's not asking much."

Steve turned to Harrison and motioned to Hollis with his thumb. "Typical vags always sticking together."

Anger flared up inside of her, and she glared at Steve. "Excuse me?"

Harrison raised his hands defensively. "Let's all take a step back."

"Plus, she's sticking her nose places it don't belong. Do you know that she asked Jake why we had two people in our department? I heard that she cut six different teams at corporate in half in the last year." Steve flailed his arms.

"She asked us the same thing," Harrison said. "And I did hear that downsizing departments is one of her specialties."

"None of us like the changes," Hollis started. "But there's not a lot we can do."

"Oh, there's a lot we can do." Steve crossed his arms.

"Like what?" Hollis couldn't mask her disgust for this guy.

"We'll stop selling." He nodded to Jake. "If we shrink the footprint in this market, it'll be a direct reflection on her, and she'll be out before we know it."

Hollis scoffed. "Your paycheck is seventy-five percent commission. You hate this weekly report so much you would give up seventy-five percent of your check?"

Steve swallowed and looked at the ceiling. Hollis realized he hadn't thought that far.

"If you shrink the sales footprint, she'll have no choice but to downsize the department."

"We aren't doing the report," Steve said definitively.

"We'll talk about it," Harrison said.

"We'll see you guys at the meeting." Steve rolled his eyes and motioned for Jake to follow him.

Hollis shut the door behind them. "What's with Tweedledee and Tweedledum?"

"Tweedledumber is more like it," Harrison replied.

"But seriously? What's that about?"

"They don't like the changes."

"It's just one report." Hollis looked Harrison in the eyes.

"That's how it starts. First, it's the meeting, then it's the report. Before you know it, everything is different. If she's asking about their headcount and ours, that can only be a sign that restructuring is coming."

"Steve is dumber than he looks if he thinks selling less is the answer." Hollis sat in her office chair.

"Most straight guys are dumber than they look."

"I know you don't like the changes, but we're still sending the report. Like it or not, it's what the boss wants, and we're doing it."

"I know," Harrison said. "But one of these days, I'm going to get you to break a rule."

Chapter Fifteen

"Thanks, Trevor," Hollis said as she grabbed a beer for her and a martini for Harrison. She joined Harrison at a high-top table.

Harrison scrolled through his phone as he took the drink that Hollis handed to him. "What's with lesbians and sports bars?" He didn't look up from his phone.

"This isn't a sports bar." Hollis shook her head. "It's just a bar."

Harrison's eyes narrowed on the TV behind Trevor. "What's that over there?"

Hollis turned around and saw the pre-season baseball game on the flat-screen TV.

"Looks like some kind of sports to me," Harrison said.

"This bar is close to home and work, has a great happy hour menu, and you know you like looking at Trevor."

Harrison looked at the bartender wearing his signature black T-shirt. "I'm not sure I could do tattoos."

"My experience is you have no problem doing anything."

Harrison feigned offense.

"You know that they don't actually have martinis on the menu, right? Trevor only started making them because he got tired of your complaints."

Harrison took a sip of his drink and played with the olive on the toothpick. "He still has a lot to learn."

Hollis shook her head.

"So." Harrison slipped the olive off the toothpick and into his mouth. "Spill it."

Hollis held her beer glass in both hands. "There isn't much to spill."

"Hollister Jezebel Reed." Harrison slapped the table.

"Where do you come up with these names?"

"Same place you meet your dates."

Hollis had had all day to come up with a story, but she'd been too distracted by Ainsley to invent anything. All she could think about was that kiss. Did she really have to wait until tomorrow to feel her soft lips again? She decided to be as vague as possible. "I met her at the gym." Which turned out to be technically true. She could have lied and said she hooked up with Jo, but that seemed a step too far.

Harrison narrowed his eyes. "When?"

"Saturday." Hollis saw the look on Harrison's face. He would have been at the gym Saturday morning for spin class. "Afternoon," she quickly corrected herself. "I finished my run and then decided to lift weights."

Harrison didn't look fully convinced, but let her keep talking.

"Turns out the gym is pretty empty Saturday afternoons. I saw her across the way and one thing led to another."

"What, did you meet her in the sauna or something?" Harrison joked.

Hollis decided to roll with it. "Actually, yes."

"Really?" Harrison gave her his full attention now.

"Yeah." Hollis stared at the ceiling, trying to find words. "She was in the sauna, and then I joined her. We were alone. Her towel slipped and…"

"That doesn't really seem like you."

"Well, you know I have a thing for blondes." Hollis hoped this would throw him off any trail of Ainsley. "Plus, I think you're finally rubbing off on me."

"It's about damn time." Harrison took another sip of his martini. "So, what now?"

"What do you mean?"

"Are you going to see her again? Are you going to move in with her? I know how you lesbians are."

"I haven't thought that far." Hollis didn't know where things were going with Ainsley. She knew she wanted to see as much of her as possible. But they were just friends. That's all the relationship could be.

"Keep it to just sex as long as you can." Harrison's face turned serious. "I mean it."

"It always goes there with you."

"I'm relieved to hear it's a girl at the gym. After the way you defended Ainsley today, I was afraid you started screwing her."

Hollis spit out her drink and coughed. "What are you talking about?"

Harrison narrowed his eyes. "Just the way you said the changes weren't that bad." He made a sweeping motion with his hand. "You know this is just the start. We're going to be an entirely new division before we know it."

"First of all." Hollis made a one with her hand. "I would never be so bold as to ask my boss out. And second of all…" She paused and made a two. "The new corporate guidelines, which are your fault by the way, make it so that I couldn't see Ainsley even if I wanted to." She looked at Harrison. "Which I don't."

"They say you aren't doing your job until you have at least one rule named after you."

"Who says that?"

"They."

"What are you going to do? Are you going back to picking up baristas?"

"Gosh no." Harrison played with the toothpick in his glass. "They just said that relationships are strongly discouraged. So as long as Parker isn't directly under me, he can still be directly under me." He flashed an evil grin. "You know what I mean?"

"Good lord." Hollis downed the beer left in her glass. She pointed to Harrison's almost empty glass. "Another one? You know I'm buying."

"Damn right you are." Harrison finished his drink and slid the glass toward Hollis.

Chapter Sixteen

Hollis willed time to move faster. After looking at the ceiling for what must be hours, she looked back at her laptop to see that only one minute had passed. The small screen displayed 3:34 p.m. She had made it this far, she could make it to 7:00 p.m. Why did it have to be so late? She didn't question Ainsley when she gave a time; she was just happy at the prospect of seeing her again. Not to mention the fact that she had instructed her to pack an overnight bag.

Hollis had done the best job she could at focusing on work, but she was distracted. As much as she hoped for a fire or a small emergency, nothing popped up and it had been an easy day. She stretched her hands over her head. "That's it. I'm calling it."

"A little early for a Tuesday, don't you think?" Harrison didn't turn around.

"I have passed the point of being productive. I brought my gym bag and I'm going for a run." Hollis noticed the sideways rain out their office window. As much as she hated the treadmill, she needed to get a run in, and this was the best option.

"See you tomorrow, Hol," Harrison didn't even turn around.

At 6:54 p.m., Hollis sat in the parking lot to Ainsley's apartment complex. It was a newly built high-rise building about twenty minutes east of HQ II. She didn't want to be too early and seem overeager, but the next six minutes would be brutal.

She scrolled through her phone and noticed a few unanswered messages from the group text with her sisters The text string often turned into parenting woes and pictures of her nieces and nephews. She loved her sisters, and she loved being an aunt, but the texts got out of control at times. She liked a few pictures and gave a generic, "can't wait to see everyone at Sunday dinner," text.

Finally the clock in her car read 7:00 p.m. She jogged slightly from the parking lot to the entryway to avoid the rain. She stood at the apartment door with her black gym bag in one hand. She knocked once, and the door opened instantly. Had Ainsley been on the other side of door waiting?

Ainsley stood there, looking gorgeous. She changed from her work attire to skinny jeans and a light purple quarter-zip top. The zipper undone just enough to draw Hollis's attention to her cleavage.

Ainsley gave a small wave. "Hi."

"Hi." At last she was alone with Ainsley.

"Please come in." Ainsley opened the door wider and motioned for Hollis to enter.

Hollis stepped in and looked around the large apartment. The vaulted ceilings and exposed wood beams filled the apartment with light. It was three times larger than Hollis's apartment. Hollis turned to speak and was met by Ainsley's soft lips. Ainsley was barefoot and back to her normal height. She stretched onto her tiptoes to meet Hollis's lips. Hollis leaned down and kissed her back. She still had the gym bag in one hand, but with the other she reached around to the small of Ainsley's back and pulled her in close. Ainsley smelled amazing and Hollis breathed her in.

After a moment, Ainsley pulled back. "I'm sorry," she said sheepishly.

"Don't be."

"I just can't help it. I see you and have to kiss you." Ainsley looked down at her bare feet. "It's actually kind of a curse."

Hollis set her bag on the ground and bent to unzip it. "I brought you something," she said. She pulled a bottle of wine out of her bag and handed it to Ainsley as she stood up. "Here."

Ainsley took the bottle and studied the label. "Is there anything better than Oregon Pinot?"

"I can think of a few things."

Ainsley gave a faint laugh. "Thank you. And I see you brought the other thing I asked for." She motioned with her head to the overnight bag.

"I'm good at following directions."

"Oh, I know." Ainsley turned and headed toward the kitchen. "We're having white with dinner, but I will save this for later." Ainsley went to the kitchen island and placed the bottle in the built-in wine rack. It was mostly full.

Ainsley stirred the pot on the stainless-steel stove.

"It smells amazing," Hollis said.

"I'm sorry it's so late." Ainsley furrowed her brow slightly. "Andrew scheduled a call, and I needed to take it from the office."

"Isn't he on East Coast time?"

"He's in Tokyo looking at swatches or something." Ainsley waved the spoon in her hand. "He has no concept of time zones. I feel bad for the guys in Raleigh."

"Well, I needed to get a run in, so it all worked out."

"Oh, perfect." Ainsley sounded relieved. "How was your run?"

Hollis paused to think. She wasn't used to anyone taking interest at all in her running. "It was okay," she said. "I don't like the treadmill, but I didn't want to run in the rain, so I made the best of it."

Ainsley nodded and continued her attention to the stove.

"Sorry we couldn't meet yesterday. I was telling Harrison about the cute blonde I've been seeing."

Ainsley turned around to face her now. "Cute blonde, huh?"

"Yeah." Hollis let out a slow breath. "Apparently, we hooked up in the sauna at the gym."

"Oh, really?"

"That's the story." Hollis leaned back on the kitchen island slightly.

Ainsley moved toward her and put her hands on either side of Hollis, blocking her in. "So." She looked at Hollis. She licked her bottom lip. "This cute blonde. Are you still seeing her?"

Hollis's heart rate picked up. It was impossible to keep her composure around Ainsley. Her mouth went dry. "That depends on who you ask."

"I'm asking." Ainsley's voice was low and full of desire.

"I'm not seeing any blondes."

Ainsley leaned in and kissed her cheek. "Good."

Hollis's stomach gurgled and an audible, low growl emanated from her. She grabbed her stomach, trying to mask her embarrassment. "Sorry," she said quickly.

"Don't be," Ainsley said. "I'm sure you're hungry. It's almost ready."

"Is there anything I can do to help?" Hollis said it out of reflex. She didn't know why she asked. She was terrible in the kitchen. "I'm not sure why I offered that."

Ainsley shot her a look.

"I'm horrible at cooking."

"Really?"

Hollis held her palms up. "Yes," she admitted.

"Can you handle grating cheese?" Ainsley motioned to the cheese sitting on the counter.

"That I can do."

"So, you don't cook, and you don't drive," Ainsley joked.

"I drive. I don't cook. My mom and my sisters have that handled."

"You have sisters?"

"I'm the oldest of three." Hollis picked up the brick of parmesan and started grating.

"Your poor dad," Ainsley said.

"The man is a saint." Hollis didn't look up from her task. "What about you? Any siblings?"

"Nope. Only child." Ainsley nodded. "My dad still lives in Vancouver. I need to get up to see him more. It's just been a whirlwind getting settled in."

Hollis wanted to ask about her mom but thought that if she hadn't brought it up, maybe it was something she didn't want to talk about. "This place is great."

"Oh." Ainsley laughed. "This is still my temporary place."

Hollis looked around. "Really?" She figured that Ainsley made a lot of money. If this was the type of place that corporate was housing her in temporarily, she must make more than Hollis had thought.

"Greg and I went and looked at houses on Sunday." Ainsley stirred a pot on the stove.

"Really?" Hollis sounded more confused than she intended. She liked the idea of Ainsley in a house. That meant she planned to stay a while.

"Yeah." Ainsley nodded. "I actually put an offer in on Sunday night."

"You did?"

"I did." Ainsley nodded.

"That's so adult." Hollis regretted the words as soon as they came out of her mouth. She sounded childish. Of course Ainsley was an adult. She had a real career, a wine rack, and probably washed her towels every week.

"Yes. We are adults." Her tone was condescending.

"I'm sorry." Hollis shook her head and her hands trembled. Her heartbeat picked up. Hollis stopped to find the right words. "I'm just so nervous I'm going to say something dumb around you that then I say dumb things around you." She had finished grating the cheese and found a paper towel to wipe her hands off. "I haven't really dated in a while, and it all feels so foreign."

Hollis normally wouldn't be this vulnerable, but Ainsley had a way of making her want to open up.

Ainsley reached for her hand. "I'm nervous, too."

"You are?"

"Oh my God," she sighed. "I only changed my outfit three times before you got here."

"You did?"

"I wanted to look nice, but not too nice. Casual, but not too casual and slightly sexy without trying too hard." Ainsley buried her face with her free hand.

"Well, you nailed it." Hollis grabbed the hand over her face and looked her in the eyes. "The nice, casual, sexy look suits you."

They held each other's eyes for a beat. "Okay." Ainsley broke the silence. "Since we've both admitted we're nervous, let's get over it and enjoy each other's company."

"I can do that." Hollis nodded.

A timer went off and Ainsley jolted her head around. "If you have any issues with butter, I suggest you look away." Ainsley set a large skillet on the stove.

"Issues with butter?"

"You know? Because it's all fat. I'm about to make Alfredo and it's basically all butter."

"Make it? Like from scratch? I have never seen it anywhere but from a jar."

"Nothing like that in my kitchen." She grabbed a whole cube of butter and set it in the skillet. It sizzled in the heat as it began to melt. "Grab the cream out of the fridge?" She stirred the butter and motioned to the stainless-steel fridge.

Hollis opened the fridge and returned with the cream.

"You do follow directions well. Can you get the cheese?" Ainsley motioned to the pile Hollis had made.

Hollis returned and helped to pour it into the pan while Ainsley kept stirring. Ainsley grabbed a few spices and added them to the pan. She let it sit for a few more minutes, keeping a close eye on it. She grabbed a spoon from the drawer and put some of the sauce on it. "Here." She put one hand under the spoon in case it spilled and motioned it toward Hollis.

"Oh my God." Hollis swallowed. "That's amazing."

"Right?" Ainsley beamed with pride.

"I can't wait to try the rest of it."

Ainsley plated two plates with chicken, Alfredo, and vegetables and carried them to the small oak table just off of the kitchen. "Grab two wine glasses?"

Ainsley had put their plates next to each other instead of across the table from each other. Hollis was happy to be as close to Ainsley as possible. Hollis raised her now full wine glass. "To finding time on our calendars?"

Ainsley toasted Hollis's glass. She took a small sip of her wine and set the glass back down.

Hollis took a bite and the combination of flavors danced over her tongue. "This is amazing."

"You're just hungry," Ainsley said.

"No." Hollis shook her head. "This is amazing. What other hidden talents do you have?"

"I can think of a few."

Her stomach did a somersault. Ainsley had that effect on her. She thought that the more time she spent with her, the more normal things would feel. That eventually, she wouldn't still be turned on by little things like the way her eyes lit up when she got excited, but she was not yet at that point.

Ainsley brushed the back of Hollis's hand on the table. She played with her fingers on the back of her hand and then rested her hand over hers. "Was it just me, or was the meeting yesterday really weird?"

Hollis sat up in her chair. "I thought we agreed not to talk about work." Her voice was timid. She didn't want to disappoint Ainsley, but she really didn't want to have this conversation.

"You're right." Ainsley took her hand and put it in her lap. "I'm sorry."

"It's okay." Hollis picked up her wine glass and took a long drink.

"It's just all I've been able to think about. Something was different about yesterday, and I don't know what." Ainsley stared at the wall on the other side of the kitchen.

If Hollis was in Ainsley's position, she would want to know what her employees thought. However, she didn't want it getting back to Harrison or anyone else that she was feeding information to the boss.

Ainsley turned and looked Hollis directly in the eyes.

Dammit. She couldn't say no to those eyes. "It's just." Hollis let out a long breath. "Some of the guys are not happy with all of the changes."

"What changes?"

Hollis let out another breath. "The weekly report."

"Are you kidding me?"

"I tried to tell them they were being ridiculous."

"What? You all got together to talk shit about me?" Ainsley raised her voice.

"No." Hollis shook her head. "No, it wasn't like that." Hollis paused. She needed to tread lightly. The last thing she wanted to do was upset Ainsley in her own home. "You have to understand, we basically didn't have a boss for the last year. I don't even know the person that gave me my review."

"Right, but—"

Hollis raised a hand to cut her off. "Let me finish. The team feels like we did a great job on our own and now there is unnecessary oversight." She paused when she saw the look in Ainsley's eyes. "I'm not saying I feel that way, but some of these guys are very resistant to change." She thought back to Steve's comment about women sticking together. If only he knew.

"I didn't think asking for a report would be like pulling teeth." Ainsley swirled the wine glass in her hand.

"They're convinced the report is just the start of changes to come."

"Even if that was the case, it's not a huge ask."

"The rumor is you are here to lay off a bunch of people."

"And you believe that?"

"You aren't denying it."

"Sometimes rumors are just that."

"Sometimes rumors have some truth behind them." Hollis had hoped Ainsley would set the record straight. The fact that she wasn't spoke volumes. "Did you really cut six departments in Raleigh last year?"

"No."

Thank God.

"It was only four."

Shit. "We really need to get better at following our rules." Hollis looked Ainsley in the eyes. She didn't know what to believe. Just because she had downsized in the past it didn't mean that's what her job was now.

"You're right. I'm sorry I brought it up." Ainsley didn't break eye contact.

There was stiff silence between them for longer than Hollis wanted. How were they going to keep this up and not bring work into the equation? So much of their lives centered around work, it was bound to come up eventually. She thought of anything to change the subject. "Where did you learn how to cook?"

Ainsley's face softened slightly. "I taught myself." A hint of a smile came across her lips, but didn't reach her eyes.

"What do you mean, you taught yourself?"

"My dad could only make PB&J and frozen lasagna. I finally decided enough was enough and taught myself how to cook. I think I was six when I first made box mac and cheese."

"Really?" Hollis could barely boil water now, let alone figure out how to make mac and cheese as a child.

"If you want things to change, sometimes you have to make them happen." Ainsley said it like she had repeated it to herself a hundred times.

"Well, you are a fantastic teacher, because this was amazing." Hollis set her fork down and pushed her plate back. She tried to picture a young Ainsley standing on a chair in the kitchen, barely able to reach the stove. The image made her smile and tugged at her heart at the same time.

"I have dessert, but it's not in here." The tone of Ainsley's voice changed.

"Want me to get the dishes first?" A certain warmth started encroaching her center at the thought of Ainsley's dessert plan.

"No." Ainsley reached for Hollis's hand and led her to the bedroom.

[illegible] change the subject. [illegible]

[illegible]

[illegible]

[illegible] them happen. [illegible] said [illegible] hundred times.

[illegible]

[illegible] changed.

[illegible] thought of [illegible]

[illegible] reason.

CHAPTER SEVENTEEN

Ainsley pinned Hollis's wrists above her head and rocked her naked body back and forth on top of her. It had taken no time at all to get their clothes off the second they reached Ainsley's bedroom. Hollis hadn't even had time to look around before she was naked and writhing on the bed.

Ainsley prodded Hollis's thighs further apart and slowly started rubbing between her legs with her knee. Hollis gasped as Ainsley stroked her clit with her leg.

"Someone's ready for dessert," Ainsley said in her ear, not slowing the motion with her leg.

"I've always been a sucker for dessert."

"Oh really?" Ainsley drove her knee deeper into Hollis's body and Hollis squirmed at the pressure. "Well, I will not be one to disappoint. Don't move." Ainsley rolled off Hollis and reached for her bedside table.

Hollis tilted her head to watch, but made sure not to move the rest of her body.

"I thought I said not to move," Ainsley said, as she opened one of her drawers.

"Sorry." Hollis turned her gaze back to the ceiling, not wanting to spoil whatever surprise Ainsley had in store. Ainsley's weight shifted on the bed and the sheets moved underneath her. She couldn't help herself as she looked up at Ainsley. "Is that?" Hollis eyed the six-inch black dildo hanging from a harness in Ainsley's hand.

"Dessert? Why, yes it is." Ainsley messed with the straps, working it onto her body.

"I've never actually seen one of those before." Hollis swallowed hard. While she clearly wasn't a stranger to sex, she had never had a partner willing to be any kind of adventurous in the bedroom.

"You're kidding." Ainsley chuckled as she tightened the black straps over her thighs, securing everything in place. "What thirty-year-old lesbian hasn't seen a strap-on?"

"Uh…" Hollis said, while staring as the dildo stood at attention from Ainsley's center. While she had imagined using toys in the bedroom, she had never thought that she would be on the receiving end.

"Oh, you're serious." Ainsley's tone softened. "Oh my God. I am so sorry." She shifted herself and sat on the end of the bed. "I should have asked first. I got ahead of myself. I just assumed that since things went so well our first time, you would be into this."

"I didn't say I wasn't into it." Now that Hollis was in this situation, she couldn't think of anything other than Ainsley on top of her. No, it wasn't something she had ever pictured before, but that didn't mean she wasn't interested now.

"We don't have to do anything you aren't comfortable with."

Hollis sat up and joined Ainsley on the side of the bed, their naked shoulders rubbing together. "I'm comfortable."

Ainsley turned to look Hollis in the eyes, "Are you sure? I don't want you to feel like I'm pressuring you, or were moving too fast or—"

Hollis cut her off with a kiss. She appreciated what Ainsley was doing, but now was not the time for conversations. She broke the kiss. "I'm sure."

"Alright." Ainsley's grin returned. "But I have warned you that my first-timers are always sore." She pushed Hollis back onto the bed and held her wrists at the top of the headboard. "We'll go slow."

Just because she was excited, didn't mean she still wasn't nervous.

Ainsley slowly rubbed the toy up and down Hollis's slit covering it in her wetness. Hollis had been ready to burst since before dinner, and the buildup now just made her that much more ready. Ainsley peppered Hollis's face with kisses as she rocked up and down her body.

"You're killing me," Hollis let out between labored breaths. She needed Ainsley and she needed her now. Ainsley sat up and reached for something again. Hollis heard her open a bottle and squeeze something onto the toy. She watched as she spread lube over it, making it ready.

Ainsley lay back on Hollis and guided the tip of the toy to Hollis's opening. Hollis sucked in a breath as Ainsley entered her.

"Relax," Ainsley said sweetly into her ear.

Hollis tried to relax her muscles and allow Ainsley full entry into her. The feeling was cold and warm at the same time, and she felt her body being stretched further than she ever had before.

"I've got you, relax," Ainsley said.

Hollis relaxed her whole body and gave in to the sensation. Ainsley pushed in deeper, then slowly pulled out. The more she pushed, the more Hollis wanted her. She wanted all of her. Every time she pulled back, Hollis wanted Ainsley deeper, further inside her than anyone had ever been. Ainsley quickened her pace and dug her hands into Hollis's hipbones as she continued to drive herself deeper in.

"Yes, right there." Hollis tensed around the toy inside her. Ainsley continued to push just the right spot, and Hollis's breathing went shallow as she was brought right to the edge. With one final thrust, Hollis relaxed completely as the orgasm ripped through her body.

Hours later, satisfied from both dinner and lovemaking, the two lay in bed, their naked bodies intertwined with each other. Hollis held Ainsley close, with Ainsley's head nestled into her shoulder.

Ainsley slowly rubbed her hand up and down Hollis's bare skin. "I've been thinking," Ainsley said.

"Oh no." Hollis tensed slightly. Her experience was that when a conversation started this way, it was never good news.

"About your running," Ainsley said.

Hollis relaxed slightly but was perplexed as to where this was going. She was still not used to anyone taking an interest in her hobby.

"I think you're in a slump." Ainsley sat up slightly on her elbow.

Hollis went defensive at the accusation.

"Here me out. Every time I ask you how your runs are, you say slow, or sluggish, or not great. It seems like you aren't enjoying it a whole lot right now."

She wasn't wrong. Things had seemed like more of a struggle lately. She had chalked it up to a rough winter and not logging enough miles. "I have a love-hate relationship with running."

"And I get that." Ainsley's voice was soft. "But you still have to have the love part sometimes."

Hollis stayed quiet. She still wasn't sure where this conversation was going.

"When is your next twenty-mile run?"

"Sunday, actually."

"Let me go with you."

Hollis shot her a questioning glance. She didn't think Ainsley could run that far.

"On the bike. I'll just help pace you."

Hollis scrunched her face. "I don't know." Running had always been a solo activity for Hollis. She took it as her time to be completely alone with her thoughts. She had never understood running clubs or people who enjoyed running in large groups.

"I know you're a solo runner. And I get that. But I think I can help you get out of this rut."

"Why?" Hollis was still skeptical.

Ainsley's face softened. "Because I know that this is important to you, and I want to help."

"I don't know." She still didn't think she could let someone into her sacred space.

"Think about it." Ainsley brushed her hand up and down Hollis. "We'll stay in on Saturday night, eat a light, carb-filled dinner, go to bed early, and get a full eight hours of sleep."

"Is it weird that that's turning me on?"

"Oh, really?" Ainsley slowly slid her hand past her belly button and between her thighs. "What do you know?" she said. She spread Hollis's lips and played with her wetness.

"Now that's not fair." Hollis's breathing became short.

"What's not fair?" Ainsley played dumb.

"I would agree to anything right now."

Ainsley moved her head until her mouth was at Hollis's ear. "Anything?"

"Okay." Hollis sat up and pushed Ainsley slightly over. She ran her hands over her face. "Let me think."

"Worst-case scenario, it's a few hours of your life. If you absolutely hate it, I will never mention anything about it again."

Hollis clasped her hands over her head and leaned back against the headboard. "This isn't something you ever did with Rachel McCreedy, is it?" Hollis didn't want to be a repeat of a previous relationship.

"Oh God no." Ainsley laughed. "Rachel was just a fling. And honestly, not that great of one."

Hollis knew it was silly to compare herself to people in Ainsley's past, but she couldn't help herself. "You're just saying that to make me feel better."

"I'm not." Ainsley rested her head on Hollis's shoulder. "I told you." She put one hand on her waist. "I don't just say things."

Hollis decided she didn't care if she was just saying it or not. She liked the idea of her being a better lover than Rachel McCreedy. "Okay."

"Really?" Ainsley sat up, eyes wide.

"Yes." Hollis let out a quick breath as Ainsley's hand wandered back down her body. Ainsley easily slid one finger inside her.

She whispered in her ear. "And since you have to run Sunday, I'll make sure I'm gentle on Saturday night."

"Oh God," Hollis breathed out as Ainsley slowly entered her.

"But tonight isn't Saturday." Ainsley kept her mouth right at Hollis's ear. "And I don't have to be gentle."

Hollis whimpered as her eyes rolled back into her head as Ainsley plunged two fingers forcefully inside her.

Chapter Eighteen

The smell of coffee woke Hollis on Sunday morning. She blinked until Ainsley's room came into focus. The sun shone through the bamboo blinds and Hollis hoped the sun might actually make an appearance today. The blue down comforter lay in a crumpled mess at the end of the bed. While Ainsley had kept her promise to be gentle, that didn't mean that things hadn't gotten a little wild the night before.

It hit her that the bed was empty, and this realization made her a little sad. She knew Ainsley wasn't far, but she liked seeing her first thing when she woke up. She found her shorts under the pillow but couldn't find her T-shirt. She searched through the sheets, then looked around the room. She wasn't ready to walk into the kitchen topless, so she found her overnight bag on the floor by Ainsley's dresser. She slid on the shirt she had brought for her run.

Ainsley poured coffee in the kitchen when Hollis joined her.

"So that's why I couldn't find my shirt." Ainsley wore her gray T-shirt.

Ainsley set two white coffee mugs on the table. "I like wearing it."

"I like you wearing it." Hollis took a seat and grabbed a coffee mug with both hands.

Ainsley sat across from her. "I was just coming to wake you up." Ainsley took a sip of her coffee and closed her eyes. "I love that first sip."

"Me too."

"So." Ainsley set her mug down and clapped her hands. "Are you excited?"

"If you go bubbly spin instructor on me, I'm out."

"I didn't realize you were an angry runner."

"I told you it was a love-hate relationship." Hollis set her mug down and looked at Ainsley. She couldn't get over how sexy it was having her wear her T-shirt.

"Apparently." The toaster popped, and Ainsley stood.

"It's like brushing your teeth. No one actually likes brushing their teeth, but you have to do it."

"Mm-hmm." Ainsley nodded as she grabbed the bread from the toaster and spread peanut butter on it.

"I love race day, and I love the feeling when I'm done. The twenty miles is just something that has to be done to get to that."

Ainsley shook her head and sighed. "Runners." She brought the plates of toast back to the table and set one in front of Hollis.

Hollis grabbed her and pulled her down until she sat sideways on top of her lap. "Hey now." Ainsley pretended to struggle.

Hollis took the other plate out of her hand and set it down. She pulled Ainsley in as close as she could. She rested her forehead on Ainsley's shoulder. It was odd smelling her own shirt that now somehow smelled like Ainsley after only a few minutes of wear. Her mind flooded with thoughts and emotions. She loved waking up in Ainsley's apartment. She loved waking up anywhere Ainsley was. She loved that they were spending the day together. She loved all of it. How could things be so new and yet be so comfortable and familiar? Hollis took a deep breath. "I like you."

Ainsley laughed. "I like you too." She grabbed Hollis's face in her hands and kissed her forehead. "Now eat." She pointed to the plate. "We have a schedule."

"How did you know I liked crunchy peanut butter? Most people think it's gross." Hollis took a large bite.

"Lucky guess." Ainsley winked.

Once outside, goose bumps formed on Hollis's arms. She'd warm up once she started running, but she danced back and forth from foot to foot, trying to keep warm before they started.

Ainsley was getting her bike situated. She wore tight black leggings and a long pink-and-black fitted top.

"How the hell am I supposed to focus on running when you look so good?" Hollis wasn't joking. Ainsley looked fantastic.

"Guess you'll just have to try to keep up." Ainsley held out her hand. "Give me your phone."

Hollis squinted, unsure.

"Come on." Ainsley motioned with her hand. "I'll hold it for you. Plus, I made you a playlist. Your headphones are Bluetooth, right?"

"Yes." Hollis reluctantly handed her phone over.

Ainsley took the phone and opened the music app.

Hollis tensed as Ainsley went through her phone. What the hell was she hiding? She shook her head. This was silly. *You'll let her see every part of you, yet handing your phone over is difficult?*

"And your Garmin." Ainsley pointed to the GPS watch on Hollis's wrist.

Hollis violently shook her head. "I don't think so. I'm going to have to draw the line there."

"To get you out of this rut, we need to do things differently today. You can't be so focused on time and distance."

"Right, but if I don't wear it, then I don't get credit for the miles. I'm not going to run twenty miles and not get credit online." Hollis knew it sounded ridiculous, but she had been logging her miles online for almost ten years.

"Runners." She sighed and rolled her eyes. "At least let me see it?"

Hollis thought about the request longer than she should. When she saw Ainsley grow impatient, she took off her watch and handed it over. The Garmin beeped several times as Ainsley clicked through the buttons.

"Here." Ainsley handed it back.

"Thanks." The display looked completely different.

"I changed it to kilometers and the language to French. Plus it will only display heart rate on the main screen. You'll still get credit, but you're going to have to do a lot of math and scrolling to figure out how far you've gone." Ainsley smiled, proud of her solution.

Hollis shook her head.

"I'm going to stay a few feet ahead of you. Just follow my path, got it?"

"I'm good at following directions."

"Good." Ainsley stepped onto her bike and started pedaling.

Hollis started her watch and ran after her. The sun warmed her arms as it shone through the trees. She noticed Ainsley's neighborhood for the first time. Old-growth trees and spring flowers lined the streets. For being an urban area, there was a lot of green.

She looked up and didn't see Ainsley. Shit, she must have taken a turn. She tried not to panic, but was annoyed that she had just touted her direction following skills and had lost Ainsley not even three minutes in. She picked up her pace and saw Ainsley up and around the corner. Ainsley looked over her shoulder, auburn hair pulled into a ponytail under her helmet. Hollis hurried to catch up.

Ainsley hadn't tried to talk much, and Hollis was thankful for that. Part of her hesitation was that she didn't want to hold a conversation while she was running. She wanted to just run. The playlist Ainsley made was surprisingly decent. It was a mix of songs she knew and some she didn't. All of them were upbeat and helped her keep her pace by matching her footsteps to the music. Long runs were counterintuitive. She was supposed to keep her pace two minutes slower than her goal. The concept always made her panic. If she couldn't run twenty miles at her goal speed, how could she go a full marathon? But there were years of science she needed to trust.

Hollis wasn't sure how long she'd been running. She could check her watch, but the kilometers to miles math was a lot, and the setting Ainsley had it on wouldn't give her a total time. It seemed like a good run. Her legs felt strong. Her breathing was even. It was the kind of run where she could run all day. She couldn't tell her pace. It seemed fast, but she had no way of knowing. Some days she thought she ran fast as lightning only to find out she had run her slowest mile ever.

An annoying song that Hollis only knew from clubs with Harrison played in her ear buds. "Oh, come on!" she yelled as she pulled the headphones out of her ears. Ainsley burst into laughter just ahead of her.

Ainsley circled around on the bike until she was in line with Hollis. "I was wondering when you'd get to that one."

"That's just mean," Hollis said between breaths.

"Just listen to the beat, trust me," Ainsley said.

Hollis shook her head in disbelief.

"There's a hill coming up." Ainsley looked ahead. "I want you to push it up the hill."

"What?" Hollis said nastier than she meant.

Ainsley shot her a look.

"Who puts a hill on a twenty-mile run?"

"I studied the racecourse and there's a hill at mile fourteen. You need to be ready for it."

"Does this mean we're at mile fourteen?" Hollis snapped.

The hill looked grueling, and she didn't want it to only be mile six.

"That I can't say." Ainsley had a mischievous grin. "But push the hill." Ainsley took off ahead of Hollis, and Hollis did her best to catch her.

While she hated the hill, and this ridiculous song, she loved the idea of Ainsley studying her racecourse. She appreciated the fact that she cared about her so much she would think about her in her free time. *This is intimacy.* She never understood the difference between sex and intimacy. She always assumed that being intimate with someone was strictly in the bedroom. Strictly when you were naked and intertwined with someone. She never stopped to think that intimacy was letting someone else into your whole life. Letting someone see all of you and be a part of the you you kept just for yourself. She admitted to herself that she was enjoying this run much more than she was planning to. Long runs were a necessary evil, but with Ainsley, it was almost fun. Almost.

Her eyes came into focus on another hill in front of her. One was pushing it, but two? "Are you kidding me?" She didn't mean to say it loud enough for Ainsley to hear, but with the headphones in, her volume was more than expected.

"Push it."

Hollis kicked it into high gear. She put one foot in front of the other. She remembered that when going up hills to breathe every third foot strike. It was a tip she'd picked up in a running magazine years ago. Probably from Rachel McCreedy. It seemed silly to think of things as simple as breathing, but running came down to mechanics and focus. She kept counting, breathing every third step. The hill was long but not incredibly steep. She turned around and thought she was halfway up it. Ainsley was pulling farther ahead of her. She turned up her speed and powered to the top.

As she crested the hill, she knew she could recover on the way back down. Her chest heaved and her lungs strained to keep up with her body. The downhill brought relief at first, but her knees started to ache. Each step on the pavement sent a shock wave through her joints, growing stronger with each step. The last two miles were always difficult for her, no matter how long the distance was. She hoped she was close to done, but had no concept of how long they'd been out there.

The sun had risen in the sky, and sweat formed along her hairline. The neckline of her shirt was wet, and salt crystallized where the sweat dried. Her ponytail was more like a rat's nest than hair. A few wisps had managed to break free and whipped against her face in the wind. Ainsley turned and circled around until she was even with her again.

Hollis pulled the ear bud closer to Ainsley out of her ear.

"See that tree up there?" Ainsley took one hand off the handlebar and pointed.

Hollis nodded—unable to form words. Her body was at the point of tired where all she could think about was the sensation she would feel when it was over.

"That's the end."

Hollis squinted trying to bring the tree into focus.

"I'll see you at the end." Ainsley took off, pedaling faster.

Hollis thought maybe the tree was a quarter mile away. It always amazed her that she could run so much and still have no concept of distance. She thought at some point she would learn how to eyeball a tenth of a mile, but it had never happened. She picked up her pace and pushed herself to the end.

She lengthened her stride. She ran faster than the beats of the music in her ears, but she didn't care. Her ab muscles expanded and contracted as her chest heaved through strained breath. The tree didn't seem to be getting any closer, even though she knew it was. Then it happened. Her cheeks began to tingle. She couldn't feel her face at all, but it wasn't a bad sensation. The pain in her knees subsided. Her feet no longer struggled with each step. Her stride was smooth, like she was gliding, no, floating toward the finish. She had reached it. The elusive runner's high. *God, how long has it been since I felt this?* This was it. This was the reason people ran. This feeling. The sense of pride. The accomplishment. That feeling that she could do anything with her two feet. She ran past the tree and slowed her pace.

She had passed Ainsley by ten feet or so and turned around to meet her. Ainsley straddled her bike and clapped her hands. "Great job!"

Hollis worked hard to catch her breath. "Thanks," she managed. She took the watch off of her wrist and handed it to Ainsley. "What was my time?"

Ainsley fiddled with the watch and then grinned.

"What?" Hollis asked nervously.

"Your time was 2:59:46." Ainsley kept the proud grin on her face.

"Are you serious?" Hollis reached for the watch to see for herself. "That's a minute off race pace. That's the fastest twenty I've ever run."

"I know it's a little fast for a long run, but you still have eight weeks to recover, so I figured we could push it."

"Damn." She couldn't believe she had just run that fast. "Okay." She still struggled to catch her breath. "Maybe I didn't hate running with you."

"Even though you didn't like my playlist." Ainsley stepped off the bike nudged Hollis with her shoulder.

"A few songs were questionable." Hollis nudged her back.

Ainsley reached for the water bottle on her bike and handed it to Hollis. "Here."

"Thanks." Hollis took a long drink and took in her surroundings. Cherry blossom trees enveloped the street, and the neighborhood was a mix of new and old homes. "Where are we?"

"Actually, only a few blocks from my apartment." Ainsley pointed toward her house. Hollis's phone vibrated in Ainsley's pocket. She reached for it to hand it back.

As Hollis took the phone, something shifted in Ainsley. Her face filled with worry. "What's wrong?"

"It's nothing." Ainsley shook her head and brushed off the comment.

"I'm not buying that for one second. What's wrong?"

"It's probably not even my place to ask, but you're right, there is something bothering me."

Hollis didn't know what to think. Between the exhaustion of the run, then the elation of her time, her mind was filled with happy thoughts. How had things turned so quickly? She didn't like whatever look this was on Ainsley's face and wanted to do anything to rid her of it. "Whatever it is, you can ask me."

Ainsley looked at the ground. "Who's Bobby?"

"What?"

"I know it's not my place, but your phone kept going off. You have ten texts from Bobby. I didn't look at them or anything." Ainsley's confident self disappeared.

Hollis reached for Ainsley's chin and tipped her head up. "Bobby is my old boss."

Ainsley's eyes narrowed into confusion.

"He's trying really hard to get me to come back."

Ainsley crossed her arms but didn't say anything.

"Texting on a Sunday is a little much, even for him, but it sounds like they're getting desperate."

"Are you considering it?"

"Going back to work for him?"

"Yes."

"God no." Hollis barked out a laugh. "I love my job. I honestly don't think they could pay me enough to go back."

"I don't know if I'm more jealous when I thought it was a girl or now that I know it's your old boss."

"Jealous, huh?" Hollis tried to lighten the mood.

"Maybe just a little." Ainsley held out her thumb and forefinger.

"My new boss is a total pain in the ass, but I still have no intentions of leaving."

Ainsley rolled her eyes. "You really know how to make a girl feel better."

"I am beyond exhausted. You'll have to forgive me if I'm just slightly off my game."

"I suppose I can do that."

"Now, can we go home? Or are there any other contacts in my phone you want to know about?"

"I wasn't being a snoop or anything. He was just insistent."

"That's Bobby for you. Now, which way?"

"Actually, first we have to head up this street." Ainsley pushed her bike.

"What's up this street?" Hollis wanted to collapse onto the couch and not move the rest of the day.

"Only the best pancakes you've ever had." Ainsley said.

At the mention of pancakes, Hollis's stomach let out a low rumble, as hunger caught up to her.

"I don't know about you," Ainsley said. "But I worked up a hell of an appetite."

Chapter Nineteen

A frantic call from Harrison cut Hollis's next Sunday long run short. She had intended to run for a few hours and then hibernate on her couch alone. Ainsley had to take care of things with her new house and see her dad, so Hollis was going to try to enjoy a few hours alone. Yes, it would have been more fun to cuddle on the couch with Ainsley, but she was busy, and they technically weren't in a relationship. She needed to try to remind herself of that more and more. Life happened.

Harrison had a way of quickly ruining her plans. On the phone he said there was a "major fire" and "no, it couldn't wait until Monday." She needed to drop what she was doing and help—now.

Hollis opened the door to her apartment when her phone rang again. A warmth grew in her chest as she saw the display. "Hi," she said, trying to play it cool.

"Hey, babe." Ainsley's voice was soft and warm.

Her heart fluttered at the sound of Ainsley calling her "babe."

Ainsley let out a sigh. "So I was absurd for saying I couldn't hang out this weekend."

"Yeah?" The words delighted Hollis. While they were both independent people, she missed being around Ainsley more than she cared to admit.

"Yeah." Ainsley let out another sigh. "I miss you. What are you doing?"

"Well, I just got back from my run." Hollis held the phone between her ear and shoulder as she bent down to unlace her shoe.

"That's right. It's Sunday. How was it? How far did you go?"

"Just eight today." Hollis switched the phone from one shoulder to another and removed her other shoe.

"Eight?"

She still couldn't believe that Ainsley got it. "I got sidetracked by a work thing. I just have to take care of it real fast."

"Work thing, huh?" Ainsley's voice turned husky. "Do you need me to talk to your boss again about working weekends?"

Hollis let out a slight laugh as she stood up. "First of all, if you keep doing that, people are going to accuse you of playing favorites." Hollis pulled sweats out of the drawer. She had cooled off on the way back to her apartment. She needed to shower, but Harrison had made it clear that this needed to be dealt with now. "And second of all, if I don't get this sorted out, my boss will be in trouble." Hollis flinched as soon as the words left her mouth. She had said too much. A momentary lapse and she forgot that she wasn't just flirting with a pretty girl, but talking to her boss.

"What's going on?" Ainsley switched to work mode instantly.

"It's nothing."

"Hollis, what's going on?" Ainsley didn't change her tone.

"It's just a small issue. I'm fixing it."

"That's it. I'm coming over," Ainsley said flatly.

"No. It's fine. Really. I've got this."

"I can either come to your apartment and you can tell me what's going on, or you can meet me at the office and tell me there. You choose."

Hollis grimaced. She let out a sigh. "Fine. Come over. But I'm not putting on real pants." The phone went dead, and she wasn't sure if Ainsley had caught that last part.

Not even twenty minutes later, there was a knock at the door. She stood and took a long breath as she opened it.

Ainsley stormed into the apartment. She wore dark skinny jeans and a white button-down blouse. Hollis was underdressed in her own home. Ainsley blew past Hollis and threw her bag on a chair like she had done it a hundred times.

She stepped toward Hollis, grabbed her face with both hands, and kissed her. Hollis started to step back in surprise, but Ainsley tightened her grip, slid one hand around the back of her neck, and held her in place. Commanding her attention. Ainsley's tongue entered Hollis's mouth and swirled forcefully for several moments. Ainsley slowly pulled back and kissed Hollis on the cheek.

Hollis tried to catch her breath. She was expecting Ainsley to come in yelling or angry or accusatory, basically anything but that.

Ainsley let out a breath. "I'm sorry." She smoothed her shirt tails. "I just can't not kiss you." She sounded angry about it.

Hollis was truly speechless.

"So, what's going on?" Ainsley was the boss now.

"Step into my office." Hollis motioned to the small desk in the corner between the wing-back chair and couch. Hollis tried to joke, but Ainsley didn't laugh.

Hollis sat down at the wooden chair at her desk. "There was a small problem with one of the buyers, but we're handling it."

"How small?" Ainsley furrowed her brow.

"There was an issue with one of the orders."

"Jesus, Hollis. Just get to the point and tell me what the hell is going on."

Hollis took a steadying breath. "One of the buyers on the procurement team messed up the order on the burnt orange fabric."

"Burnt orange?" Ainsley looked at the ceiling, clearly thinking. "That's our number one seller for the summer line. We've already sold out in pre-sales."

"I know."

"How badly is the order messed up?"

Hollis tilted her head back and forth. She was stalling. "Well." Ainsley stared daggers at her. "It wasn't ordered at all."

Ainsley stood up reflexively. "Are you kidding me? Our number one seller wasn't ordered at all? What are we going to tell all the customers that have already paid?"

"We aren't going to have to do that. We're handling it."

"When were you going to tell me?" Ainsley looked her in the eyes.

Hollis shrugged. "I wasn't."

Ainsley sat back down in the chair. "What do you mean you weren't going to tell me?"

"I was going to fix the problem and then there would be nothing to tell you."

Ainsley held up a hand. "We are going to come back to that. Where are we at with fixing this?"

"That's where the hang-up is." Hollis took another breath. "We can place an order with the manufacturer, but the owner of the plant has changed since the initial order. If we get the order in today, there will be no disruption whatsoever, but we're having a difficult time getting the contact information. The plant is in Malaysia. Harrison has five different calls in, but with the language barrier and the time change, it's getting messy."

"Send me the information you have." Ainsley reached for her bag and pulled out her laptop.

Hollis emailed the information and tried hard to mask her annoyance at Ainsley showing up as the silence stretched on. Finally, Ainsley placed a call.

"Johnny, it's me, Ainsley Jones. I have a situation I need your help with." Ainsley stood up. Hollis figured it wasn't so much that Ainsley didn't want her to hear what she was saying, but she needed to pace back and forth. Hollis probably would have done the same thing. Hollis heard a lot of "Yeses" and "Mm-hhms" come from Ainsley's side of the conversation, but she wasn't completely following.

After several minutes on the phone, Ainsley sat back down into the wing-back chair and released a sigh of relief. "Well, Johnny was able to get everything squared away and the order was placed."

"I had it under control," Hollis said flatly.

Ainsley gave her a questioning look. "No need to thank me or anything."

"I didn't need your help," Hollis snapped.

Ainsley opened her mouth to speak and then shut it. "I didn't say you did."

"Harrison and I would have had the order placed in time." Hollis could feel her heart beating in her throat.

"Hey." Ainsley softened her tone. "I'm not the bad guy here."

"I didn't say you were." Hollis tried to keep herself calm. She didn't want to get into a screaming match with her boss, or the woman she was sleeping with. God, this was getting messy.

"We're on the same team." Ainsley stared into Hollis's eyes. "It doesn't matter how the problem got fixed, just that it got fixed."

"Okay." Hollis couldn't control her tone as her frustration set in. She didn't need Ainsley sweeping in to save the day. She would have had it handled without issue, just like she'd handled every other problem before.

"Look." Ainsley's tone changed. "I know you don't like asking for help or admitting that you need it, and I get that, but we're on the same team here. We both needed that order to go through."

"Okay." Hollis nodded and started to stand.

"Sit back down." Ainsley pointed to the chair. "We aren't done."

Annoyed at the admonishment, Hollis sat back down. "What else?"

"Let's go back to the part where you said you weren't going to tell me about this."

Hollis turned her palms up. "I wasn't going to tell you. I was going to fix the problem and then there was going to be nothing to tell. No point in bothering you with something that isn't an issue." She clasped her hands together and set them in her lap. "I handle issues every day that you never know about. In fact, I solved all kinds of problems last year without your help."

"And that's part of the problem." Ainsley's tone was oddly flat.

"What are you talking about?"

"This whole Wild West thing. Why do you think I was actually brought in?"

Hollis's mind swirled. Did corporate really think this side of the country wasn't in line with what corporate wanted? "Andrew said himself we're outperforming."

"Of course he said that. Come on, Hollis. The CEO can't say I think you are all overstaffed and acting like your own company. You know as well as I do, they don't bring people in to run well performing teams."

"But we are performing!" What more did Fitwear want from her?

"Yes, you're hitting the metrics, but it's not repeatable or scalable. What good is it if only one half of the country can hit numbers?"

"So you really are coming in to dismantle the team." Hollis sunk into the realization. It all made sense. How much longer did she and Harrison have together?

"I didn't say that."

"You didn't *not* say that."

"I've probably said too much. But the only hope I have of keeping everyone is if I show a unified front. I can't give the impression that I don't know what's going on in my own building. I don't know how he does it or who tells him what, but Andrew has his hands in everything. So, at some point, a week from now, a month from now, six months from now, he'd say something like, 'we really dodged a bullet with that burnt orange situation' and I would have no idea what he was talking about." Ainsley paused, gathering her thoughts or reining in her temper. Hollis couldn't tell. "So, no matter how big or small the problem is, you have to tell me."

Hollis sat and listened, taking in Ainsley's words. Could a top performing department be spared? She hated that Ainsley was making sense. She hated that she had showed up and solved the problem so quickly, but mostly she hated admitting to the fact that she needed her. "I didn't think of it like that."

"I know. You think that admitting problems is showing weakness or something. But again, I am not the enemy here. You have to stop viewing your career as a boss versus an employee. We both need each other."

She had always viewed her boss as an enemy. It was probably due to the string of awful bosses she had previously had. The corporate world was so competitive that bosses and employees were always crawling over each other for credit. She had never viewed her boss as an asset, as a person who could actually help her get ahead instead of trying to cut her down.

"The more successful the team is, the better it is for the both of us," Ainsley said. "Once they stop seeing us as being out in left field and on our own, we will get more autonomy, more funding, all of it. But we have to show that this team is all on the same page. So, you have to keep me in the loop, okay?"

"Okay, I will work on it." She hesitated. She wasn't sure she could fully commit to telling Ainsley every little problem that arose, but she would try.

"Thank you." Ainsley patted her palms on her thighs. "Now, is there any other work stuff you have to do today?"

"Nope." Hollis shook her head. "That was it."

"So, you can get back to your weekend then?"

"I can."

Ainsley took the three steps toward Hollis. She sat sideways on her lap. Hollis pulled her in and held her for a moment. She breathed in Ainsley's scent.

Ainsley kissed her forehead. "You okay?" she asked softly. She was out of work mode.

Hollis nodded. "Yeah. Still reeling from getting my ass chewed by my boss, but I'll be okay."

Ainsley laughed. "Oh, sweetheart, that was nothing."

"That was nothing?" Hollis said disbelievingly.

"I wasn't even mad. You didn't get to see me flare my nostrils or hear me yell or anything fun."

Hollis buried her head in Ainsley's shoulder. "Well then, I hope I never see you mad."

"Me too." Ainsley lifted Hollis's chin with her hand and leaned in to kiss her. It was a soft kiss, gentle, forgiving.

"Come to Sunday dinner with me." Hollis didn't know she was going to ask the question, but it came out of her mouth before she could stop it.

Ainsley pulled back slightly. "Today?"

"Yeah." Hollis held her breath. Now that she had asked the question, she really wanted Ainsley to say yes. *Friends could meet each other's parents right?* "I want you to meet my family, and I want them to meet you."

"Okay."

"Yeah?" It surprised Hollis it hadn't taken more convincing. This certainly seemed like a step past just friends, but one she was happy to take.

"Yeah."

"It's in a few hours. So, we'll have to kill some time before we head out."

Ainsley kissed Hollis again and pulled back slowly, "I can think of a few things we can do."

Chapter Twenty

Ainsley offered to drive to Hollis's parents' and Hollis was happy to let her. She realized that the more she didn't drive, the more she enjoyed not driving. Sitting in the passenger seat of Ainsley's SUV, holding her hand, it brought a level of comfort she hadn't had in a long time. They didn't go places together very often. Yes, they would go to dinner and the occasional outing, but for the most part, they were either at Hollis's apartment or at Ainsley's place to avoid being seen.

Hollis liked driving places with Ainsley. She wanted to drive more places with her; she didn't even care where. "We should take a road trip," she said out of nowhere.

"Okay. Where do you want to go?"

"I don't care." Hollis spoke the words fast and looked over at Ainsley. "Anywhere."

"Well, I'm going to need a few more details than that, but I don't see why we can't make that happen." Ainsley briefly took her eyes off the road and smiled at Hollis.

Hollis loved that smile. She looked out the window of the familiar drive. Her parents were only twenty-five minutes away, but the scenery changed from suburban to rural quickly. They drove down a two-lane highway lined with barns and horse stables. The grassy fields had reached a new level of green with the recent rain. The sun shone highlighting the spring colors reminding Hollis how beautiful Oregon was this time of year.

Hollis pictured her and Ainsley at her parents' home together. She was excited to share this part of her life with her family. Then it hit her. Who was Ainsley to her? How would she introduce her to her parents? She couldn't introduce Ainsley as her boss, as that would cause a lot of questions. She certainly couldn't say she was her friend with benefits. If she just said she was a work friend, that would lead to more questions. At the end of the day Ainsley was her boss and their relationship was against company policy.

As if Ainsley could sense her rising anxiety levels, she squeezed her hand and asked. "Is everything okay?"

"I'm not seeing anyone else," Hollis blurted.

"Well, that's good." Ainsley kept her eyes on the road.

"And I don't want to see anyone else." Hollis turned and faced Ainsley.

"Where is this coming from?" Ainsley only briefly looked away from the road.

Hollis rubbed her temples. "I put the cart before the horse."

"Hey." Ainsley squeezed her hand. "What's going on?"

"I don't know how to introduce you to my parents."

"We're friends."

"Right. But it's a little more than that. I don't want to be friends with anyone else." Hollis looked forward out the windshield. "And I don't want to get into a lengthy conversation about what that means, so I just need you to know that I'm not seeing anyone else, and I don't want to see anyone else."

"I see. So you want us to be exclusive friends?"

"Yes." She wanted more than that, but would settle for now.

"And you want me to stop seeing all the other girls I've been seeing?" Ainsley's tone stayed flat.

"Wait, what?" Hollis's head whipped around, and she stared at Ainsley.

"There's this cute blonde at the gym," Ainsley said straight-faced.

"Are you being serious right now?" Hollis said, panicked. Her heart raced. She assumed that since she didn't want to see anyone else that Ainsley didn't either. If Ainsley had been seeing other people, she didn't know what she would do. They hadn't had this conversation before; Hollis had assumed it wasn't necessary. Now she feared that she had been wrong in a big way.

"I mean, we never talked about being exclusive." Ainsley kept her eyes on the road.

Hollis didn't know if she wanted to will the car to turn around or jump out of it.

Ainsley's face finally broke and she couldn't contain her laughter. "I almost got through it with a straight face."

"Oh my God." Hollis rubbed her hand over her head again. "So, you're not serious?" She knew the answer, but she needed to hear it.

"I'm not seeing anyone else, and not just because I barely have time to see you, I don't want to see anyone else." She let go of Hollis's hand and reached for her chin. She turned her face until they were able to hold eye contact for a brief moment. "Only you."

Hollis relaxed her shoulders, which she didn't realize she had been holding tight. "That's enough for now."

"You sure?"

"It has to be." Hollis appreciated the mention that Ainsley hadn't had enough time for her. She hadn't said anything about it and it was nice to be on the same page.

Ainsley followed the GPS instructions and turned off the two-lane highway. The road narrowed with farms and open fields on either side.

"The GPS gets a little glitchy up here." Hollis pointed. "It's this road up on the right."

Ainsley slowed the car to turn. "You didn't tell me there would be a gravel road."

"Why do you think I let you drive?"

"Well, lucky for you, I bought a membership to the carwash by my house. I can't pull into the parking garage at work with a muddy car."

Hollis looked down the familiar road. Moss-covered oak trees lined either side of the gravel road. It hadn't rained all day, but the road was still muddy, and Hollis knew Ainsley's car would have mud splatter up the running boards.

"I didn't know you were taking me to the boonies," Ainsley said.

"Yeah. They are kind of out of the way, aren't they?"

"You grew up out here?"

"I did." Hollis nodded. "It's not really a surprise that I focused so much on school and sports. There's nothing else to do and nowhere to go." She motioned to the trees on either side of her. "Even if I wanted to sneak out, where would I go? Up here on the left. Park anywhere."

The remnants of daffodils lined the long driveway, and dark purple and red tulips sprang up in bunches. Ainsley parked, and they entered through the large wooden front door.

"Hello!" Hollis yelled. The smells of home cooking greeted them.

"In here, sweetheart," Hollis's mother called from the kitchen.

Hollis's mother stood at her normal post at the farm sink, washing vegetables for dinner.

"Hi, Mom," Hollis said.

Her mom turned off the water and turned to face them. "Oh, hi."

Hollis pulled back and motioned to Ainsley. "This is Ainsley."

"Hi there." Hollis's mom stuck out her hand. "Nancy."

"Thanks so much for having me," Ainsley said. "You have a wonderful home."

Her mom blushed. "Why thank you." She looked directly at Hollis. "No Harrison today?"

Hollis caught the look of surprise on Ainsley's face. She knew that Ainsley knew they were work friends, but it must not have registered just how close the two of them had become. "No, not today, Mom. He said if he keeps eating your delicious cooking, he'll have to go to spin class every day. Not that he would mind…"

"He sure is charming," Her mom said in a dreamy tone.

Ainsley mouthed. "Harrison?"

"What?" Hollis whispered. "He's charming."

Her mom motioned to a tray of brownies on the counter. "I made those special for him. Will you take them to him from me?"

"Of course I will, Mom. And you can feel free to make me brownies."

Her mom laughed.

"Hey, Nance!" a booming voice yelled from down the hall.

"In here!" Her mom yelled back.

Hollis's father joined them in the kitchen, his blond hair slightly tousled from being outside. "Well, hello."

"Dad, this is Ainsley." Hollis motioned to her.

"Todd Reed." He stuck out his hand, and Ainsley shook it in return. "This is actually perfect timing," he said. "We need one more for croquet. Ainsley?"

"Dad, we just got here. Give us a minute," Hollis said, annoyed.

"Well, you aren't allowed to play anymore, so…" he rocked back and forth on his heels.

"You aren't allowed to play?" Ainsley asked.

"It's nothing." Hollis tried to move the conversation along.

Her dad put his arm around Hollis. "My daughter here gets a little too competitive, and she has been banned."

"Banned?" Ainsley gave a slight chuckle.

"You throw a croquet mallet one time," she said under her breath.

"You throw a croquet mallet and almost hit your grandmother, and yes, you are banned for life. House rules," her mom explained.

"So, Ainsley?" her dad turned to face her.

"You don't have to say yes." Hollis shook her head.

"It's okay," Ainsley said. "I love croquet."

"Perfect." Her dad placed his large hand on her shoulder. "We need someone to be blue."

"You sure?" Hollis didn't want Ainsley to be overwhelmed so soon.

"I'm always blue." She followed down the hallway and out the back door.

Her mom went back to the sink.

"So, Mom," Hollis started.

"Mm-hmm?" Her mom didn't look up.

"Don't make a big deal or anything, but Ainsley and I are kind of seeing each other."

Her mom turned off the water and looked at her. "Oh, really? This is the woman Harrison was mentioning, yes?"

"Don't make a big thing." The last thing Hollis needed was her mother giving Ainsley the fifth degree. "It's still new, and I don't know what we are, but I just wanted you to know."

"She's very pretty," her mother said.

"I know."

"She's older." She said it as a comment, but Hollis thought she sounded judgmental.

"She's a little older, yes," Hollis replied.

"You don't normally date older women."

It was true, and Hollis knew it. She didn't know how to explain it to her mother. "Things are different this time."

"She must be important to you if you brought her here."

"She is. I just don't know where things are going. They are good, we just…It's complicated and we're figuring it out. So, don't give her a bad time or embarrass me or anything."

"I would never do such a thing."

"Right."

"Why don't you grab a drink and head outside? I know it must be killing you that she's out there alone with your father."

Her mother was right. It was killing her. Had her dad shared embarrassing stories of her youth already? Hollis pulled open the door of the fridge and grabbed two water bottles.

The French doors off the living room opened into a large grassy backyard. Her dad took pride in his perfectly kept yard never having a brown spot. The large patio was home to a long wooden table, perfect for outdoor family dinners when the weather cooperated.

The croquet game had been paused and Ainsley was standing directly behind her father, who struggled to maintain warrior pose.

"That's it," Ainsley said. "Now just release your breath slowly and bring your arms back down."

He listened attentively. "Wow."

"What's going on?" Hollis asked.

"Ainsley is a miracle worker." Her dad rotated his neck.

"Your dad here was just complaining about a stiff neck."

Her chest swelled at seeing Ainsley getting along with her dad so well. She wasn't sure if Ainsley was putting on a show or not, but either way, she loved it. She handed a water to Ainsley.

"Thanks." Ainsley brushed her fingers as she took it.

A small hand tugged on Hollis's shirt. "Auntie Hollis, you're in the way," her nephew Lyle said.

"Hi to you too." Hollis ruffled his hair, and he recoiled.

"Grandpa, it's your turn," Lyle whined.

"You're right. Let's get this game moving."

Hollis stepped out of the grass as her dad, Ainsley, and her four nieces and nephews resumed their game. She took a seat at the table bench..

"Hey there, Hol." Madison took a seat next to Hollis.

"Well, hello, little sister," Hollis said and nudged her.

"Who's your friend?" Madison pointed toward Ainsley.

"That's Ainsley. I'll introduce you once this game is over." Hollis took a drink of her water.

"I already got her name," Madison said, annoyed. "I meant who is she?"

"Just a friend," Hollis said flatly.

"A friend or a spin instructor with benefits?" Madison nudged her shoulder into hers. Madison was the middle child and clearly resembled her mother. Madison and their youngest sister looked so much alike that they were often mistaken for twins. The girls were all two years apart, yet Hollis looked nothing like either of them.

Hollis shook her head, not ready to get into the details with her sister. "Just a friend."

"Mm-hmm." Madison was clearly not convinced. "Well, I like her."

"I'll be sure to pass that on."

Her mom carried a hot pan of mac and cheese out the double doors "Alright, dinner is ready."

Lyle protested, but her dad quickly interrupted him. "We'll finish after we eat," He reassured him and steered him to the table.

Her mom dished up the hot food onto plates and passed it around. Everyone took a seat at the long table. Her dad sat at the head of the table. "I know we aren't a religious family," he said. "But few things bring me greater joy than seeing this table grow." He motioned to everyone at the table. "I am a blessed man."

"We get it, Dad." Amy rolled her eyes. "Can we eat?"

"Hey, I'm trying to have a nice moment," he said. "I don't get you all together very often."

"Yes, you can eat," her mom butted in. "If we keep waiting for your father to be over his sentimental moments, the food will get cold." She shot him a loving, albeit annoyed, look.

"Nancy, this is amazing," Ainsley said. "Hollis told me you were a great cook, but this is heavenly."

Her mom beamed with pride. "Thank you."

Ainsley complimenting her mom was the greatest thing she could have done in that moment. She knew that her family was going to take to Ainsley, but she'd still been nervous.

"Ainsley, where are you from?" her mom asked.

"Vancouver, actually. Born and raised. My dad still lives up there." Ainsley set her fork down.

"And your mother?"

"Mom," Hollis interjected. "Easy with the questions."

"No, it's okay." Ainsley rubbed her hands on her thighs. "She passed when I was four. So, it's just been me and my dad. He never remarried."

"How awful." Her mom sounded genuine.

Hollis's heart sank. She knew Ainsley didn't talk about her mother, and now she knew why. She ached for the little girl who had to grow up without a mom. It explained a lot about Ainsley and why she was so independent.

"It's okay," Ainsley said. "It was a long time ago."

The meal continued, and they all chatted into the evening. It capped off with her mom's famous berry pie. Ainsley and Hollis gave hugs and said their good-byes, and made their way back into Ainsley's SUV.

"I couldn't possibly eat another bite," Ainsley said as she started the car.

"That's the main reason I have to run long runs on Sunday."

"Your family is very nice," Ainsley said.

"I'm sorry about all the questions. I told my mom to go easy on you, but she can't help herself."

"It's okay. I didn't mind." Ainsley shifted the car into drive and the SUV crawled back down the gravel road.

"Thank you for coming," Hollis said, and she meant it.

"I had a great time." Ainsley reached for Hollis's hand and squeezed it. "Really."

They sat in silence as they made the drive back to civilization.

"I was just wondering, how come you never told me about your mom?" Ainsley's posture tensed.

"You never asked," she replied.

"That must have been difficult, growing up."

"It was." Ainsley kept her eyes forward.

"I can't even imagine." Hollis shook her head.

Ainsley let out a breath. "Let's talk about something else."

Hollis didn't want to talk about something else. She wanted to hear more about Ainsley growing up and what she must have had to go through. But Ainsley was keeping her at arm's length. She wanted to be let in all the way, to fully understand her, but every time they got close to breaking through, Ainsley threw that wall up. This was the downside of being "just friends."

Ainsley took a left turn instead of a right, and Hollis wasn't following where she was going. "I think you missed the turn," Hollis said.

"No, I didn't," Ainsley said, matter-of-fact.

"Okay?"

Ainsley pulled her car into the car wash line, paid at the machine, and pulled forward. As she put the car in neutral, her eyes glinted with desire. "Ever made out in a car wash?"

Chapter Twenty-one

Hollis basked in the kind of relief that only comes from changing into comfy clothes after a long day at work. Ainsley had to stay late for a conference call with Andrew, so Hollis knew she'd spend the night alone. However, that didn't stop Hollis from making sure she gave Ainsley something to miss. She'd worn her blue, form-fitting blouse that she knew drew Ainsley's attention. Hollis wondered if Ainsley had the same strategy. She'd worn a black dress with white stitching that highlighted her slight, but sensual curves. Hollis would be imagining that dress on her floor later tonight.

Hollis placed an ice cream order on her phone, deciding to treat herself since she couldn't have the dessert she'd been growing so used to over the last several weeks.

It had been so long since Hollis was in a healthy relationship that she'd forgotten what it was like to miss someone when she was gone. She wanted to spend every second with Ainsley. She tried her hardest to not be overly clingy or needy, but Ainsley drew her in like a magnet.

It was difficult for her to have this budding relationship in her life and not be able to share it with anyone. She'd lost most of her friends in the breakup. This was news she'd normally share with JayDee and Margo, but since they were Miranda's friends first, it didn't feel right. She definitely couldn't talk to Harrison and risk him running his big mouth. Her phone rang and her heart skipped a beat. A flurry of butterflies filled her stomach as she looked at the caller ID. Then her heart sank. Of course it wouldn't be Ainsley. Ainsley had to work. She knew this. Why had she gotten her hopes up?

"Hi, Mom." A disappointed Hollis flopped onto the wing-back chair facing the TV.

"Hi, sweetheart." Her mom started every call the same way. "Did you give Harrison those brownies?"

"I did." Hollis nodded to the empty apartment. "He appreciated them, as always."

"I sure do love him," her mom gushed. "I really like Ainsley too, dear."

"Oh yeah?" Hollis sat up a little straighter at the mention of Ainsley's name.

"Yes. She's great. And you two are great together."

Were they great together? Hollis pondered how her mother could know after one night if someone was good for her or not.

"Maybe next time you can bring Harrison and Ainsley."

Hollis snapped back to reality. How could she tell her mom she couldn't bring them both because Ainsley was her boss and no one at work could find out? She didn't know how to tell her parents she was sleeping with the boss. Is that what this is? Hollis tried to calm her spiraling brain. She had real feelings for Ainsley. This was so far past just a fling. Realizing she'd been silent a long time, Hollis responded. "I don't know, Mom, we'll see."

"Well, if Harrison can't get along with your new girlfriend, that's a huge red flag."

"She's not my girlfriend."

"You know what I mean."

Her mom was right, but she couldn't divulge all the details. "It's just that we are still figuring out what we are, Mom."

"I know. I know. I tend to get ahead of myself. I just love seeing you with someone who makes you happy."

The sound of a knock at the door jolted Hollis. "Mom, that's my dinner. I have to go."

"I can't believe you're ordering out every night. I can teach you to cook."

"Mom." Hollis turned into a whiny teenager. "It's fine, really. Plus, it's my money and if I want to treat myself, I will."

"Whatever you say, dear. I love you."

"Love you too, Mom." Hollis ended the call and checked her app to make sure she had already paid. She still couldn't remember which apps took prepayment and which required cash. She opened the door, still looking at her phone. "Thanks so much." She stuck her hand out.

"Please tell me you weren't having ice cream for dinner." Ainsley held out the ice cream with both hands and stepped into the apartment.

"Ainsley," Hollis said in surprise. "How did you end up with my ice cream?"

Ainsley shut the door behind her and stepped closer to Hollis. "I saw the delivery kid in the lobby, assumed it was for you, since I've noticed you never actually have real food at your place. Although if I'd known it was ice cream and not actual food, I might have turned him away."

"There's no rule that says you can't have ice cream for dinner."

"Mm-hmm." Ainsley closed the space between.

"I'm serious. It's not written anywhere."

"Stop talking," Ainsley said just above a whisper as she met Hollis's mouth with hers. Ice cream in one hand, she took her free hand and wrapped it around the back of Hollis's neck, pulling her in close. Hollis shuddered slightly at the cool touch of her hand. Ainsley was such an amazing kisser that all other thoughts floated away. Hollis didn't care why Ainsley was here or what had happened. She was just glad it was her on the other side of the door.

Ainsley slowly pulled back, and Hollis kept her eyes closed a second, savoring the kiss. "I thought you were working late."

"My call just ended. Not that I could give it my full attention." Ainsley played with her fingers on Hollis's shoulder.

"Why's that?"

"Someone dressed extra sexy today and had my mind thinking incredibly dirty thoughts." She ran her fingers up Hollis's shoulder and rested her hand on the back of Hollis's neck. Hollis's body warmed to Ainsley's touch.

"Was it Harrison?"

"The red tie really does it for me." Ainsley's eyes looked her up and down. "I see you've changed into something a little more comfortable."

"In my defense, I didn't think I was going to see you tonight."

"Even if you are all alone, that tank top needs to be burned." Ainsley let out a small laugh. "But I was hot and bothered going into my call, and then I got my ass kicked every which way from Andrew. My head is spinning, and I don't know if I just need to come or find a punching bag to take out my anger."

"The call was that bad?" Hollis didn't know much about Andrew but couldn't imagine being on the receiving end of a difficult call with him would be a good thing.

"Let's just say that HQ II is still viewed as the wild west."

"Okay, I have just the solution." She turned toward the kitchen and put the lid on the island while she pulled a spoon from the drawer. Hollis dipped the spoon in the container and held a bite out.

"Is that chocolate with gummy bears?"

"Is that judgment?"

Ainsley let out a small laugh and fell back against the front door. She leaned her head against the door and let out a sigh. "My girlfriend is such a child."

"Wait. What?" Hollis dropped the spoon back into the container. They had agreed to be just friends. Yes, lines had been blurred, but the deal was no relationship. There was no way Hollis could continue with Ainsley as an official girlfriend.

"Sorry. Slip of the tongue."

"You sure? Because if this is getting too messy, we can stop?" Could they though? In what world could Hollis send Ainsley away in this state? She should send her home, but with Ainsley in her apartment wearing that dress, begging for release, could she really say no? A real friend would help, right?

"I'm sure. It's just been a long day. Like I said, I don't know which way is up and down right now."

Was that disappointment in Ainsley's voice? Was she hoping for something more? How could that even work? Besides the fact that relationships with superiors were forbidden, Hollis didn't want to be attached to someone she worked with every day. A certain amount of healthy separation was natural. Hollis decided to focus on the here and now and the fact that Ainsley was backed against her front door.

"I have just the thing to take your mind off of work." Hollis held the spoon up again and Ainsley slowly took a bite. Ainsley's eyes rolled back into her head slightly. "Oh my God, that's good," Ainsley said through a full mouth.

"I know." Hollis took her own bite before putting the rest of the carton into the freezer for later. "Now, I believe you said something about being distracted all day?"

Ainsley stayed leaning against the front door. "So distracted."

Hollis placed one hand on the door and the other on Ainsley's thigh, pinning her in place. She grazed her fingers from her knee to the top of her thigh feeling her smooth skin. She touched between Ainsley's legs and slowly worked up under the black dress. Ainsley's breath hitched and she prided herself on being the one to make her feel this way. She continued working her hand up her inner thigh. She placed her foot between Ainsley's and nudged her stance wider.

"Hollis." Ainsley's voice was breathy. "I need you."

Hollis continued stroking smooth skin. She paused when nothing but skin met her hands all the way up the back of her leg and on her ass. She started patting her ass frantically, finding only bare skin. "Ainsley?"

"Mmm?"

"Please tell me you didn't go all day without underwear?"

"You don't like?"

"No, I like." Hollis took a deep breath. "But I will never be able to focus at work again if I know you're going around commando."

"I took them off in the car," Ainsley admitted. "Call me presumptuous."

Is there anything hotter than Ainsley Jones? She surprised her in her apartment and made certain Hollis knew she wanted her. "I'm okay with presumptuous." Hollis brushed her hand along Ainsley's wet slit and paused to feel Ainsley throb under her touch. Ainsley hadn't been kidding when she said she was distracted all day. Hollis knew not to make her wait any longer. She hiked her dress up to give her better access and plunged a finger inside her.

"Oh God," Ainsley breathed out. She lifted one leg and wrapped it around Hollis and pulled her in closer. Hollis quivered slightly as Ainsley's right hand was still cold from holding the ice cream.

"Harder," Ainsley breathed out.

Hollis quickly added a second finger and picked up her pace. Ainsley arched her back and leaned her weight into the door.

"Right there," Ainsley said between pants. She tightened her grip on Hollis's back, digging her fingers in slightly. "I'm so close."

Hollis picked up her pace, making long, full strokes. Ainsley's wetness and the fact that she glided in and out of her so easily amazed her. Ainsley tensed around her. She touched her thumb to Ainsley's clit as she continued thrusting in and out. She clamped down her own desire and focused solely on Ainsley.

"Oh God yes." Ainsley shifted from words to groans and dug her hands deeper into Hollis's skin. She let out one last high-pitched moan and relaxed her body against the door. "I needed that," she breathed out.

"I can tell."

Ainsley slowly put her leg back on the ground and raised her hands over her head, catching her breath.

"Now." Hollis gave Ainsley a satisfied smile. "I have an idea for how you can take out the rest of your frustrations."

"What's that?" Ainsley's shoulders heaved as she continued to catch her breath.

"I kind of have this hot boss fantasy."

"Is that so?" Ainsley looked Hollis up and down.

"Yeah." Hollis's confidence dwindled now that she said the words aloud. Sharing her bedroom fantasies was a level of vulnerability she wasn't expecting.

"Tell me more." Ainsley's voice lowered and her tone turned husky.

"Um…" Hollis could feel her heartbeat in her chest. *Why am I so nervous?* She had already had sex with Ainsley. She had already committed to her. Why was she panicking now?

"Let me guess. You've missed a deadline or something and you're in big trouble." Ainsley leaned in until she was whispering in Hollis's ear. "So you go to see the boss and tell her you'll do anything to keep your job."

Hollis swallowed hard. She was already aroused from earlier, but she grew even wetter at Ainsley's words. "Something like that," she said, trying to keep her breath even.

Ainsley pulled back slightly and gave a devilish grin. "I can work with that."

"Really?"

"Really." Ainsley nodded. She leaned in closer. "If there's something you want to try, all you have to do is ask." She whispered into Hollis's ear and a warm tingling sensation started in her stomach and then traveled further south.

"I'm just not used to—"

"Being in an adult relationship?" Ainsley cut her off.

"Um?"

"Jesus, not like that okay? I just meant like a relationship where people openly talk about their wants."

"Right." Adult situationship? What was the term for what this was? With the way Ainsley eyed Hollis, it didn't matter. Whatever term for whatever they were was fine as long as Ainsley kept looking at her like that.

Ainsley's eyes raked over Hollis again. "This won't work with you dressed like this. Go change back into your outfit from earlier."

Hollis snorted slightly. "Seriously?"

"You want this to happen or not?"

"Okay." Hollis turned toward the bedroom and Ainsley grabbed her hand.

"Wait." She pulled Hollis back. "Give me the tank top now."

Hollis shot her a questioning look.

"I'm serious. I'm throwing it out. No one should be caught wearing something like that, alone or not."

"So that's how it's going to be?" Hollis only half joked.

"Mm-hmm." Ainsley held her hand out for the tank top.

"Do I get any say?"

"Not really." Ainsley waved her fingers toward the tank top.

Hollis slipped it off her head and gave it over. It did need to be donated. She just hadn't brought herself to do it yet.

"Thank you. Now go change," Ainsley commanded.

Hollis quickly switched back into her work outfit. She tried to put herself together as best she could, but replicating her look from earlier in the day proved difficult with an already worn outfit. She looked herself over in the mirror, making sure her shirt was tucked in straight.

Ainsley sat at Hollis's small desk in the living room. Ainsley turned the chair around and nodded, clearly approving the wardrobe change. "Hollis, have a seat." She motioned to the chair.

Hollis sat and worked through the combination of nerves and excitement coursing through her.

"I supposed you're wondering why I called you in here." Ainsley played her character perfectly.

Hollis didn't know if she should answer or not. She opted to stay quiet.

"It seems you missed the deadline on the weekly report, again." Ainsley crossed her arms and glared at Hollis.

"I can explain—"

Ainsley put her arms up. "There will be no need for that. This is the final straw. You can clean up your things and be gone by the end of the day."

"Wait. Please." Hollis tried her best to sound desperate.

"There isn't anything to discuss."

"I need this job. I'll do anything to keep it."

Ainsley sat up a little straighter. "Anything?"

"Anything." Desperation clear in Hollis's voice.

Ainsley nodded. "Stand up."

Reluctantly, Hollis stood.

"Take your shirt off." Ainsley's voice held firm.

"What?" Hollis wasn't expecting that.

"You heard me."

"I don't know." Hollis's self-conscious side appeared.

"Unless you don't really *need* this job."

"No. I do." Hollis started unbuttoning the blue blouse. She got all the buttons undone, slid the shirt off of her shoulders, and laid it on the back of the chair.

"Good." Ainsley crossed her arms. "Now your pants."

Hollis's cheeks heated. On the one hand, she couldn't believe that Ainsley was playing along. She'd never experienced a partner willing to try things like this in the bedroom. It was thrilling. She told Ainsley something she wanted to try, and Ainsley went along with it. This kind of communication was definitely new. On the other hand, it made her nervous, but in a good way. An excited kind of nervous. The kind of nervous where she knew something great was about to happen. The kind of nervous like stepping up to bat with two outs already. She undid the button and zipper to her pants and stepped out of them. She folded them slightly and put them over the blouse on the chair.

Hollis didn't know what to do with her hands. Standing in her living room in just her bra and underwear made her feel exposed. Ainsley stood up and grabbed Hollis, pulling her in close. She tightened her hands on her hipbones and whispered in her ear, "I'm going to make sure you never miss a deadline again."

Goose bumps formed on Hollis's arm from the slight chill in the room and the suggestiveness of what was about to happen. With her hands still on her hips, Ainsley pushed her backward until she was at the arm of the couch.

"Turn around," she said quietly but forcefully.

Hollis turned around so the arm of the couch stood at her mid-thigh. With one hand, Ainsley undid the clasp on her bra and the straps fell loose. Ainsley reached her arm around and pulled it off. "We won't be needing this."

Hollis felt ready to burst. She needed Ainsley to touch her. She needed to feel her. Be taken by her. She didn't know how much longer she could wait. Ainsley ran her hand on the waistband of Hollis's underwear, teasing her. She continued her hand down Hollis's front and paused when at her throbbing clit already slick with wetness. "You will do anything," Ainsley joked. She placed her hand on Hollis's back.

"Just real quick." Ainsley sounded different—panicked even. "You did turn the weekly report in, right?"

Hollis turned her head around and faced Ainsley. "Of course, I did."

"Okay." Ainsley let out a sigh of relief. "You're positive?"

"Of course, I'm positive. Do I need to show you?"

Ainsley paused and seemed to think about that. Hollis didn't want to, but she would pull her laptop out right now to prove that as usual, she turned in all her reports on time.

"No." Ainsley shook her head. "No, it's okay."

"I have it set to auto send every Monday at 3:59 p.m."

"What?"

"Every Monday, I finish the report first thing, and then I set my email to send it at 3:59."

"Why don't you just send it when it's finished?"

"Because it isn't due until four," Hollis said matter-of-fact.

"Oh my God, are you serious? You sit on it all day because it isn't technically due until four?"

"Yes." Hollis didn't understand what was confusing about this. "If you want it sooner, you should move the deadline up." Hollis said. Ainsley stared at her with a confused expression. Hollis turned the rest of her body around and faced her. "This was a bad idea."

"No, I'm sorry. I shouldn't have brought that up now, of all times."

Hollis sat on the edge of the couch. "It's okay. It's hard enough keeping work and us separate." Hollis motioned a hand back and forth between them. "I shouldn't have tried to combine them."

"Part of my ass-chewing today was on deadlines. So, it was top of mind. That's all. I had a brief second where I couldn't shut my brain off."

"It's fine."

"Let me finish what I started." Ainsley leaned in and kissed Hollis. She ran her hands up Hollis's arms and gripped them tight.

Hollis broke the kiss. "Do you want to talk about your meeting?"

"Not really." Ainsley leaned back in to resume kissing, but Hollis pushed her back.

Hollis reached for her shirt on the chair. "If we're going to be in an adult relationship, or whatever this is, then we need to be able to talk to each other." She slid the blouse on and buttoned a few buttons.

"We do talk." Ainsley crossed her arms and sat on the edge of the couch.

"You clearly had a rough day, and you just want to clam up on me?"

"I'm not great at talking about my feelings."

"You don't have to be great at it."

"And there are some things at work I can't share with you," Ainsley snapped.

"I know that. I'm not saying you have to share confidential secrets or anything, but if you had a rough meeting, you can talk about it. That's what friends do."

Ainsley let out a long breath and sat on one of the couch cushions. Hollis followed suit and sat next to her.

"Andrew doesn't think things are moving fast enough."

"What? How can that be? We're outperforming in every metric in this market."

"I know. You don't have to tell me that. But Andrew doesn't like that our reporting isn't standard."

"Are you fucking serious?"

"Can you understand why I didn't want to share this?"

"I'm sorry. This isn't about me. Keep going."

"He says if I can't get everyone to get the reporting the same, how can I take on bigger projects?"

Hollis bit her tongue. There was a lot she wanted to say about what Andrew thought, but remembered this wasn't about her.

"So that's why I was hung up on deadlines."

"Are you sure it's just about deadlines?" Not that Hollis didn't believe Ainsley, but was the CEO really this upset about a report?

"He's making it into so much more than it is. But at the same time, it's his company and if he wants everyone using the same font and letterhead, then he gets to make those choices. He wants to expand internationally, and I have some difficult decisions to make."

Hollis's stomach churned. Difficult decisions in business almost always meant restructuring. "What kind of difficult decisions?"

"Personnel decisions."

"Like layoffs?"

"Not exactly."

Hollis stayed quiet, unsure of how much she was supposed to know.

"I'm trying to avoid layoffs, but Andrew thinks there is redundancy on the West Coast. He thinks we have too many people doing exactly what employees on the East Coast are doing, and he'd rather redeploy resources elsewhere."

Hollis shuddered at Ainsley's word choice. Those resources were people with families and lives, not just chess pieces Ainsley and Andrew could move wherever they wanted.

"I'm trying to get him to see the full picture and understand why all of these roles are needed, but he only sees dollar signs. He keeps coming back to the fact that I can't even get the team to send the report out correctly."

"I can start sending the report early," Hollis said sheepishly. It was a little ridiculous for her to hang on to it all day out of principle.

Ainsley gave a half laugh. "Babe, you are the least of my problems. At least your department actually turns it in."

"There are departments not turning it in?" She could never in a million years not turn in something her boss asked for, whether she found it useful or not.

Ainsley nodded.

Hollis wanted to know who, but again, didn't press.

Ainsley put a hand on Hollis's thigh. "I'm sorry for getting distracted earlier."

"You have nothing to apologize for."

"As much as it pains me to admit it, it did feel nice to talk about my meeting. Thank you for listening."

"Of course. Thank you for sharing." Although she could have done without the part about layoffs, but she didn't get to pick and choose what parts Ainsley shared.

"I really do want to finish what I started." Ainsley's playful tone returned.

"How about we keep going, but with you *not* as my boss?"

A sparkle filled Ainsley's eyes. "I can work with that." She leaned in and kissed her on the cheek. "Stand up." She kissed Hollis and moved her until she was sitting on the end of the couch like before. "Turn around," she said softly.

Hollis hesitated for a beat, then turned around, facing the couch. Ainsley put her hands on her waistband again. She didn't waste any time and pulled her underwear down to Hollis's ankles. She stepped out of them and kicked them across the room. Ainsley placed a gentle hand between her shoulder blades and pushed her forward. "Bend over," she whispered.

Hollis tingled with anticipation. After all the emotions of today, she needed this. Ainsley put her feet between Hollis's and made her stance wider. Hollis shifted her weight until she leaned completely on the arm of the couch. Her stomach did a complete somersault when Ainsley whispered "relax," into her ear. Hollis gave in. She let go of whatever tension she was holding and eased into the couch.

Ainsley ran her hand up the inside of one thigh and down the other. After Hollis thought she couldn't stand another second, Ainsley entered her with two fingers. Hollis let out a sharp breath as Ainsley started moving in and out of her. Her voice turned to a whimper as Ainsley hit the perfect spot. It was a combination of pleasure and pain and vulnerability that she had only experienced with her. Ainsley kept her rhythm going and continued pushing deeper and deeper. "You're close," she said as Hollis tightened around Ainsley.

Hollis didn't know what sound came from her mouth at that moment, but it was some form of yes. She clamped her eyes shut wanting to focus only on this feeling. Ainsley gave one last, forceful thrust and Hollis fell onto the couch as she rode out her orgasm.

CHAPTER TWENTY-TWO

Hollis needed a distraction. The numbers on the spreadsheet were not adding up no matter how many ways she changed the data. She knew better than to visit Ainsley at work, but what harm would five minutes do? Just a quick break to get her mind off of forecasts and then she could refocus on the job at hand. Really, Ainsley should want to distract her to be able to get her to focus again. Hollis stood outside Ainsley's office, not knowing what she was going to say. She just wanted to see her. Parker's chair was empty and the door slightly cracked. If she was busy, it would be shut, right? Hollis knocked slightly and opened the door. "So I was thinking for dinner—"

"Hollis," Ainsley cut her off and shot her a surprised look. Hollis noticed that there was a man sitting across from Ainsley's desk.

"I'm so sorry," she stammered. "I didn't know you were busy."

"Oh, no, it's fine." The man turned around. "We were just wrapping up."

Hollis's stomach dropped when she recognized the man as Andrew Williams, the CEO. He wore a light purple Fitwear polo and black slacks. Hollis's mouth went dry. She could not believe she had interrupted the CEO.

"Andrew, this is Hollis Reed." Ainsley motioned from Andrew to Hollis.

Andrew stood up and stretched out his hand. "Pleasure to meet you, Hollis."

Hollis noted the firm handshake.

"Now tell me." Andrew squinted slightly. "Do you two go to dinner often?"

Hollis saw the panic in Ainsley's eyes.

"I was just trying to help Ainsley get acquainted with her new town." Hollis hoped it sounded like a reasonable explanation. Ainsley gave her a slight nod.

"Oh, I like that." Andrew snapped his fingers. "It's important to understand the communities we support. So where are we going?"

"Sir, I could never," Hollis said.

"Nonsense," Andrew said.

Hollis searched her memory bank for any restaurant she could think of. "There are these new food trucks I was looking into. But I could never take you there."

"I'm a man of the people." He made a sweeping motion with his hands. "It seems like lately all I have is fancy restaurants or room service. A food truck sounds phenomenal." He patted his stomach. "And I'm still on East Coast time. What do you say we go now?"

"You're the boss," Ainsley said.

Andrew looked at his watch. "Actually, I have that three thirty call coming up. But we can head out after that?"

"Sounds great. Why don't you use my office, and I'll step into the conference room."

Andrew's phone buzzed. "Sounds good." He nodded in Ainsley's direction as he answered it.

Ainsley ushered Hollis into the vacant conference room across the hall. "I am so sorry." Hollis's head was still spinning.

"It's fine." Ainsley brushed it off.

"I didn't know Andrew Williams was coming to the office today."

"Surprise visit. Turns out the over-the-phone ass-chewing wasn't enough."

"Is everything okay?" Hollis ran through everything she knew about the company in her mind. They were hitting their numbers. Morale was good. Could Ainsley really be getting yelled at for that damn report?

"It's okay. Really it is."

Hollis wasn't convinced but decided now was not the time to push the subject.

"So what food truck are we going to?"

"I don't know."

"What do you mean, you don't know?"

"I just said that."

Ainsley shot her a confused look.

"I was going to say that I was thinking for dinner we could order in and watch trashy reality TV."

Ainsley rolled her head back and stared at the ceiling. She let out a slow breath. "That sounds amazing."

"I know."

"Okay, takeout and trashy reality TV tomorrow. Can you find us a food truck for tonight?"

"Deal."

❖

Ainsley parked next to the food court sign a few miles from HQ II. Hollis didn't drive to work, so it didn't seem too odd that they would ride together. Hollis tried to behave, but Ainsley riding with her hand on her thigh made it difficult. She had to remind herself repeatedly she was going to dinner with the CEO. They met up with Andrew at the fenced area lined with various food trucks and multiple picnic tables in the middle.

"They change the trucks out here all the time," Hollis explained.

Andrew looked around, taking it all in. "This is really something."

"Yeah, the food trucks are really taking off out here."

"A beer truck?" Andrew pointed to a yellow truck in the corner. "Now I've seen everything."

They made their way back to an open picnic table with various foods and beverages in hand.

"I don't think I understand half the ingredients in this thing." Andrew eyed the gyro in front of him. "What is an organic, handspun lentil?"

"I try not to ask too many questions," Hollis joked as she eyed her own dinner.

"Well, whatever it is, it's delicious," Andrew said through a full bite of food. He set the gyro down. "So Hollis, why is your name so familiar?"

Ainsley answered before Hollis could. "Hollis is the one who came up with the storefront idea."

Andrew snapped his fingers. "That's right. That was a great idea."

"Thank you."

"And I hear we're ahead of schedule?" He eyed Ainsley.

She nodded timidly.

"Great. Hollis, how long have you been with Fitwear?"

"I just hit the one-year mark," she responded. "I was part of the group that opened HQ II."

"Fantastic. And where were you before here?"

"I was with the other guys," Hollis admitted.

"Ah. Well. I'm glad we could steal you from the competition. Are you from around here?"

"Yes." Hollis didn't realize she would be the center of conversation tonight. Not that she minded the CEO knowing who she was, she just didn't expect the interrogation. "I grew up not very far from here and went to school at Portland State."

"Hollis played softball for Portland State," Ainsley interjected, and Hollis thought she detected a hint of pride in her voice.

"Oh really? What position?" Andrew asked.

"Third base."

"Good." Andrew nodded. "You need quick reflexes for third base."

"You do." Hollis didn't know what he meant by any of that, however a small part of her liked that he approved of her playing third base. Her phone buzzed on top of the table. She reached to silence it quickly.

"You can take that if you need to," Andrew said.

Hollis read the texts quickly and shook her head. "It's just Bobby." She rolled her eyes and looked to Ainsley. "He's being quite persistent."

"Most guys are when they want something. The competitors do a much better job at team sports than we do. That's an area we just haven't been able to break into." Andrew looked off into space as he spoke.

"I think we need to think smaller." Hollis said it without thinking.

"What do you mean?" Andrew turned his attention to her.

"Nothing. I'm sorry. I overstepped." She forgot she was at dinner with the CEO and shouldn't be making business suggestions.

"Nonsense. If you have a good idea, I want to hear it."

"Okay." Hollis took a breath and steadied her voice. "I think we need to think about local high schools. Easier sports to outfit. Things like cross-country and track. It'll be a long time until we can compete with the football teams because most schools have gear and uniform contracts, and we just aren't there yet."

Andrew pressed a finger to his lips in thought, seeming to take it all in.

"But if Fitwear could sponsor more running-based sports, I think we have an excellent shot at making it in. We could even outfit golf teams if we wanted." Hollis could hear the excitement in her voice as she pictured her old high school golf team in Fitwear polos.

"That's a great idea." Andrew looked to Ainsley. "We should have her sit down with Mark. See if we can get some legs behind this."

"Of course," Ainsley said.

Andrew put both hands on the table and pushed himself up. "Alright, ladies, I have to go. Early flight and all." He reached his hand across the table, and Hollis stood to shake it. "Hollis, keep those great ideas coming."

"I will," she said, pleased the CEO took her ideas seriously, especially with Ainsley there.

"Ainsley." He shook her hand and put an arm around her shoulder. "Whatever you do, don't let this one get away." He motioned with his head to Hollis.

"I won't," Ainsley said.

They both sat back down, and Ainsley visibly relaxed for the first time all night. "That was good," Ainsley said.

"Yeah?" Hollis wasn't sure if she had overstepped too much today with the impromptu dinner invitation and then business ideas.

"Yeah, it showed that I have a great team and not everyone out here hates me."

"Who hates you?"

"Oh everyone hates the new boss."

"Are you sure everything's okay?" Ainsley threw her wall up again, and she so badly wanted her to take it down.

"I'm sure." Ainsley reached for Hollis's hand across the table and gave it a squeeze. "What's going on with Bobby?" She exaggerated his name.

"Nothing. He's just getting desperate."

"Are you sure that's all?"

"What can I say? I'm a sought-after employee."

"I don't disagree." Ainsley lifted their joined hands and placed a kiss on the back of Hollis's palm.

Hollis eyed their hands. "We should probably be careful in public. We aren't that far from work."

"You're right." Ainsley slowly brought her hand back.

"I just don't want you to get in trouble."

"It's okay." Ainsley looked at her watch. "It's getting late. I should get you home. I can't be responsible for keeping my employees out late on a work night."

That's right. Employee. Hollis would be wise to remember that.

Chapter Twenty-three

Hollis looked up from her desk to see Harrison with two coffee cups. "Is one of those for me?" She stretched her hand out, hoping so. She needed the extra caffeine today.

"Coffee is for friends only." Harrison held the cup just out of reach.

"Are we not friends anymore?" Hollis didn't know what she could have possibly done to upset Harrison this time.

"That depends," Harrison snapped back.

"On?" Hollis wasn't in the mood for Harrison's antics this morning.

"On what you were doing with the CEO at dinner last night." Harrison used his best accusatory voice.

"Wait, how did you know I was at dinner with the CEO last night?" Hollis didn't think anyone would have known.

"Parker told me."

"That's still going on?"

"Don't change the subject," Harrison said, actually sounding angry. "What were you doing at dinner? Were you trying to get promoted and leave me behind? Are you going behind my back?"

"Whoa." Hollis held her hands up. "Slow down. It was a complete misunderstanding."

"How do you misunderstand your way into dinner with Andrew Williams?"

"I went to go see Ainsley—"

Harrison cut her off.. "Why were you going to see Ainsley? Is this about the layoffs that I hear are coming?"

"Dammit, Harrison, listen. Wait. What? Where did you hear about layoffs?" If Harrison knew about it, then it must be true. Was Ainsley just trying to make her feel better the other night?

"HR guy told me. Said something about needing to look into all the personnel here and look at what severance packages might look like."

"That's still going on?"

"It pays to have connections in various departments."

Hollis tried to focus. If HR was calculating severance packages, then this was closer than she thought.

"So back to why you were going around behind my back last night?" Harrison held the coffee just out of reach.

"I went to talk to her about that new project she has me working on," Hollis lied, but she knew it was a good cover.

"The storefront project?"

"Yes."

"That's actually a really good idea," Harrison admitted.

"I know. Anyways, I went to talk to her, and Andrew happened to be in her office. Somehow food trucks came up, and he wanted to go to dinner."

"You took the CEO to a food truck?" Disgust clearly marked Harrison's face.

"He's a man of the people," Hollis mocked Andrew.

"Okay. We can be friends." Harrison handed her the hot coffee and made his way to his chair.

"What a relief." Hollis took a sip.

"What's going on with sauna girl?" Harrison asked out of nowhere.

"What do you mean?" Hollis didn't know who sauna girl was. What was he talking about?

"You know, the girl from the gym? Or was the sex so unremarkable that you forgot?"

"Right." Hollis nodded slightly. "That fizzled out."

"Damn. I was just starting to like her."

"Like her? You never met her."

"No, but I like you better when you're having sex."

"Whatever."

"Besides, I didn't think you'd ever get over Ainsley."

"What?"

"Oh, you had it bad for her and you know it."

Hollis didn't know how to play this off. First the lie about dinner, now this. The lies were adding up. How she wished she could just come clean about everything. "That was then—before I knew…everything."

Vague and not exactly accurate, but adding lies to lies would just make things worse eventually.

"Thank God. Now maybe you can go back to coming out with me."

"Whatever." Both of their laptops chimed at the same time, signaling an urgent email from corporate. It was an annoying feature, but corporate wanted the ability to get employees' attention from time to time.

"Online training? What's this?" Harrison asked.

Hollis quickly scanned the email and her heart rate took off. "Online sexual harassment training? What or who did you do?"

He held both hands up. "It wasn't me this time."

Hollis knew that. She knew exactly what this email was about. The question was, how did Andrew know? Her phone rang, and Parker's name popped up. She steadied herself for the call. "Hollis Reed," she answered.

"Ms. Reed. Ms. Jones would like to see you. Now, if you are available?" Parker's cheery yet professional tone made Hollis want to vomit.

"I'm on my way."

Hollis left before Harrison could ask questions. She didn't know how to lie her way out of this one. Parker signaled for her to enter Ainsley's office, and she let out a sigh as she opened the door, bracing herself for whatever was coming.

"Hi." Ainsley said.

"Hi." Hollis turned around and shut the door behind her. When she turned back around, there Ainsley was. In her space, pressing her mouth onto hers. Ainsley intertwined her fingers in the belt loops of Hollis's slacks and pulled her in close.

Ainsley backed up as she ended the kiss. "I'm sorry. I know we're supposed to be better at work. I just see you, and I have to kiss you."

That made Hollis feel better about where this conversation might be going. "It's okay."

"I'm sorry we didn't get to do more last night. Andrew kind of highjacked our evening."

"He did. But I'm hoping you'll make it up to me tonight."

"I will." Ainsley flashed her devilish grin.

"Parker said you wanted to see me?" Hollis was trying to get back on to the safer topic of work.

"I just didn't want you to worry about the email that just came out. The training one."

"You mean the online sexual harassment training that is now required?"

"That's the one. Anyway, don't read too much into it. It isn't a big deal."

"Any idea why it came out?" Hollis knew Ainsley didn't want to answer the question, but she wouldn't let her off the hook.

"I got a little talking-to this morning," Ainsley admitted. "Andrew just reminded me to stay focused, blah blah blah."

Hollis couldn't comprehend how Ainsley was acting nonchalant about this. If the CEO had given her any kind of talking to, she wouldn't be able to focus. "What does that even mean?"

"Oh, you know, corporate stuff."

"No, I don't know." Hollis stiffened her tone. She couldn't just let this go.

"Andrew wants to make sure I stay objective. If there are changes coming, I need to make sure I stay impartial to that kind of thing."

"So you need to make sure you aren't just keeping me around because you're sleeping with me?"

Ainsley looked down, embarrassed. "Your work performance speaks for itself. If Andrew didn't know that before, he certainly knows that from meeting you last night."

A perk that Hollis only got because she was sleeping with the boss. This wasn't how she wanted to get ahead in her career. "The word about the layoffs is out."

Ainsley looked up. "What do you mean?"

"It didn't come from me. I heard it from someone else. But people are definitely starting to talk." Hollis didn't want to give Harrison up but also needed Ainsley to know that her secrets were safe.

"I'm still hoping to avoid that. I think I have a plan."

"Ainsley, we can't keep this up if you're going to be getting in trouble. If some big changes happen, I don't want people thinking that I'm just here because I'm with you. It isn't worth it."

"First of all." Ainsley held up a one with her finger. "I'm not in trouble, and everyone in this building knows how great you are. So don't think for a minute that that would change. And second of all, it is worth it. You are worth it." She placed a kiss on Hollis's cheek and Hollis went weak in the knees. "Plus, we just have to keep things quiet until I can figure something out."

"You can't just figure things out on your own. It's my career here, too."

"I meant to say until we figure something out."

But it wasn't just until they could figure something out. Unless Hollis found another job, she'd still be dating her coworker. She wanted to believe that there was a solution to this. She wanted to believe that Ainsley could find a way to make it work, she just couldn't see it. But she also couldn't see a life without Ainsley at this point either. Things were so far past the point of no return. "Okay."

"Seriously, babe, don't worry about the email. We're good."

Hollis relaxed slightly. She would just keep seeing where this relationship led.

"We're still on for tonight?"

"Unless you barge in here and offer to take someone else to dinner."

Chapter Twenty-four

Hollis did her best to keep boundaries at work, but having a sexy woman working only a few doors down was damn near impossible. One night, Hollis really couldn't control herself. Ainsley had yet to say good night on her way home, signaling that Hollis should wait a few minutes and then follow. Hollis finished her work for the day and would much rather wait for Ainsley somewhere else than at her desk.

Hollis saw that Parker's chair was empty, which made sense since it was after normal working hours. Light peeked under the crack on Ainsley's shut office door. She knocked softly as she opened it.

Ainsley sat behind the wooden desk, staring at her computer screen, her head in her hands. Papers were strewn on the credenza desk behind her, which Hollis knew was unlike Ainsley. Something was up.

"Hi," Hollis said as she closed the door.

Ainsley looked up from her computer screen and her brown eyes lit up. "Hi."

"You're here late."

Ainsley stood up. "Budget season. I have to have my first draft in tomorrow, and things just aren't adding up." She motioned to the papers behind her. "I can't figure it out, but I'm off by over a million dollars."

Hollis went behind the desk and pulled Ainsley in for a kiss. Ainsley rubbed her hands up Hollis's back, pulling her in close. Hollis pulled back slightly. "I think you need a break."

Ainsley took a step back and put some space between them. "I really have to get this finished."

Hollis looked down and noticed Ainsley's bare feet, her nylons and heels in a pile by the trash can.

"I don't know what I'm missing."

"I think." Hollis pulled her back in. "You've been staring at screens too long and you need a break." She leaned in and kissed her. Ainsley was hesitant, but Hollis persisted. Ainsley relaxed as Hollis swirled her tongue into her mouth.

She guided Ainsley until she was leaning on the credenza desk. She was careful to find a section that was cleared off to not disrupt any filing system that Ainsley had in place. She placed one hand behind her and leaned down as she continued kissing her. She pulled back and said in her ear, "Trust me, you need a break."

"I think you might be right."

Hollis ran one hand up Ainsley's thigh and under her black skirt. She was happy that Ainsley had already taken off her nylons, as that made her job that much easier. She slowly teased her outer thigh. She spread Ainsley's thong to the side pleased by Ainsley's wetness. "Please tell me it isn't the budget that has you this excited?"

"It isn't," Ainsley groaned as Hollis easily slid her finger through her folds. Hollis held a steadying hand on Ainsley's back as Ainsley writhed under her touch. Hollis kissed her deeply as she inserted a finger inside of her. Ainsley gasped and Hollis kept going. She went slowly at first. She dug her hand into the small of her back, keeping her in place. She pushed Ainsley's skirt up and spread her thighs apart with her legs. She stood in between her legs now. She didn't break the kiss. She pulled her finger out slowly.

Ainsley started to protest, but before she could, Hollis returned two fingers inside her forcefully.

"Oh God," Ainsley moaned.

Hollis kissed her neck and kept moving herself in and out. One hand firmly on her back, the other hand finding just the right rhythm.

"Yes," Ainsley breathed out. "Right there."

Hollis kept going. She could feel the orgasm building inside Ainsley and she pressed on.

"Right there," Ainsley repeated.

Hollis felt her tense around her curled fingers and then relax. She held herself there for a moment, careful to bring Ainsley back down. "Damn," Ainsley said.

Hollis slowly exited her and kissed Ainsley on the cheek. "Don't work too late."

❖

The phone ringing shook Hollis from her daydream. She squinted at the display; it was a friend she hadn't talked to in months. She looked out the window from her desk as she answered. "Hello."

"You know you didn't lose us in the breakup," JayDee responded without any pleasantries.

"Okay?"

"I'm just saying. We're your friends too. Just because you and Miranda broke up, it doesn't mean we aren't friends." There was an intensity to JayDee's voice.

"I guess I just assumed since you were Miranda's friend first."

JayDee interrupted. "Lesbians are all friends with everyone. Get with it already. You didn't even come to my birthday party."

"Right. Because of the whole my ex was going to be there thing." Hollis had no idea where this conversation was going or why she was getting yelled at.

"You can't date in this town and then be unwilling to see your ex's places. You need to get over that. Margo misses you."

Margo and JayDee had been married for five years. They had known Miranda since middle school, and when Hollis and Miranda had been together, they had done a lot of couple things. Picnics, hikes, wine tasting. The tough part of breaking up with Miranda had been losing JayDee's and Margo's friendship.

"We definitely need to hang out, sometime soon." Hollis grew excited at the idea of seeing them.

"I'm glad you said that. How about Thursday?"

"This Thursday?"

"Brenda and Margaret got married and they're on their honeymoon."

"And that means what?" Hollis wasn't following.

"I told them this is the worst possible time to get married, but no one takes the softball team into account anymore. I'm short two players for Thursday's game, and you are the best third base I know."

Of course there was an ulterior motive, but it was true that she was the best third base player JayDee knew. They had played together last year, but Hollis had decided to sit this season out, mostly because she didn't want to run into Miranda.

"I wouldn't ask if it wasn't important," JayDee pleaded now. "If we win, we make it to the championship." JayDee had always taken rec league softball way too seriously. Yes, she was competitive, but JayDee's intensity for her team had almost landed Hollis in multiple fistfights as tensions ran high. "If we don't get two more players, we have to forfeit. You wouldn't do that to me, would you?"

Hollis contemplated the offer. It would be nice to play again. She regretted saying no this year and realized she was missing softball more than she thought she would. This was the first spring in almost twenty years that she hadn't played.

"Beers on me after we win," JayDee offered, trying hard to convince her.

"Okay. I'm in."

"Great! Is there any chance you know anyone else that might want to play? We have to find one more."

"You know what?" Hollis looked out her office door. "I might."

"Really?" JayDee sounded hopeful.

"Yeah, maybe. Put me down as a yes and I'll text you later today if I can find one more."

"Perfect. I'll see you Thursday."

Hollis hung up the phone and headed down the hallway. She turned the corner and saw that Parker wasn't sitting at his desk. It was too early for lunch. He must be making copies or something. No matter the reason, it worked out because she didn't want to ask permission.

Hollis knocked and opened the door to Ainsley's office. She saw Ainsley sitting at her desk with her head in her hands. Hollis had never seen Ainsley like this at work before.

Ainsley looked up slowly as the door opened. "Oh, hi." Ainsley started to stand up.

"No." Hollis said. "Don't get up."

Ainsley sat back down.

"We need to keep this nice large desk between us." Hollis sat across from Ainsley. "I have actual work to do today."

"Okay." Ainsley rolled her eyes.

"You okay? You looked stressed out just now."

Ainsley breathed deep. "Just giving myself a moment to be overwhelmed."

Hollis made eye contact and nodded, urging Ainsley to go on.

"Andrew has given me full oversight over the storefront project. Which is great because I will get full credit if it goes well. But—"

"You'll get all the blame if it doesn't."

"Exactly." Ainsley nodded. "And the paranoid side of me feels like it's a setup."

"What do you mean?" Hollis couldn't comprehend who would want Ainsley to fail.

"Let's just say that not everyone was thrilled about me taking this job." Ainsley ran her hands through her auburn hair. "Andrew has always been supportive. But the board," she paused, "they said I was too young, too female, too gay."

For the first time, Hollis comprehended the weight of Ainsley's position. Being a female in an executive position was difficult enough, but being gay on top of that added another layer. There were always going to be people who refused to judge Ainsley solely on her accomplishments.

"Not to mention I'm still having issues getting everyone here on the same page. How are we supposed to expand when I can't even get everyone to send me a damn report every week?" Ainsley paused and rubbed her hands over her face. "It'll all be fine," Ainsley said, and Hollis thought she was reassuring herself more than anything. "I just had a moment."

Hollis hated to see Ainsley like this. She could only imagine the pressure that she was under, and she hated that she couldn't do anything about it. "Can I make a suggestion?"

Ainsley looked up and waved her palms. "Of course."

"Again, this isn't my wheelhouse, and I want nothing to do with this project." She looked Ainsley directly in the eyes. "But you should consider tying sales commissions to the new storefront."

"What do you mean?"

"Think about it. In a way, the storefront is competing with the sales team's commission structure. They get paid based on certain markets, online sales, sporting good contracts, and so on. If we set up a new store, then there's nothing for these guys to sell, and there are going to be plenty of sales coming out of the storefront."

Ainsley clasped her fingers together and set her chin on the back of her hands.

"If you tie commissions to the storefront's success, then the sales team is instantly bought in. If you make Steve report his weekly commission, maybe he'll send in the report."

"That's a great idea. Gets traction from the team that's fighting me the most and would actually encourage collaboration."

"Just a thought." Hollis put her hands up. "Again, not my project."

"No, but you keep having great ideas about a project you want nothing to do with."

"You can have great ideas about something you want nothing to do with."

Ainsley took a breath. "You came here to see me for something, not solve my problems. What can I do for you?" She changed her tone to boss mode.

"Actually, I came here for something not work-related."

Ainsley shifted in her seat. "What's up?"

"Do you by chance play softball?"

Ainsley snorted. "I have played softball. But I'm not a former college athlete or anything."

Hollis brushed off the comment. "My friend JayDee needs two people to play in her game Thursday night. I was thinking maybe you would want to?"

"I don't know," Ainsley said hesitantly. "It's been a long time, and I was never that great."

"There are zero expectations, I promise. If she doesn't get two more people, she can't play. You just need to show up and look pretty."

"As long as there are zero expectations."

"None," Hollis lied.

"And I can't play infield, I'm too scared of getting a line drive to the face."

"Right field it is. I'll let JayDee know."

"Are you playing third base?"

"Yes."

"Have her put me in left field then. At least I can look at that cute ass all night." Ainsley winked.

Hollis blushed. She still wasn't used to being spoken to this way. "The game is at seven, so I'll pick you up at six, okay?"

"You're picking me up?" Ainsley didn't sound so sure.

"I drive."

"I've just never seen it."

"I drove to your place this weekend."

"Right, but I've never actually seen you get out of a car. For all I know you're taking an Uber or something."

"Oh my God, this is so dumb," Hollis said, annoyed.

Ainsley stifled her laughter. "I'm looking forward to it. And we're still on for Friday?"

Ainsley had gotten reservations to a hot new restaurant that had just opened. The waiting list was months long, and Ainsley had managed to get them in for Friday. Hollis was looking forward to it, not just because the restaurant was supposed to be amazing, but because she loved having plans made with Ainsley. "Yes." Hollis stood up to leave. "Don't be late Thursday. JayDee yells when I'm late."

"You got it."

Chapter Twenty-five

Hollis leaned on the front of her white car as she waited for Ainsley to come out of her apartment complex. Right at six p.m., Ainsley was ready, gym bag slung over her shoulder.

"This is your car?" Ainsley asked.

"Yes." Hollis opened the passenger door for her. Ainsley got in and Hollis went around to the driver's side.

"This is a Range Rover," Ainsley said.

"Yes." Hollis pushed the start button and headed out of the parking lot.

"I am shocked."

"I told you I have a nice car."

"I know, but I just assumed it would be covered in rust or something. Since you hate driving, I figured you wouldn't have something this nice."

"I hate driving. That doesn't mean I don't have a nice car."

"Fair point. It's just not at all what I pictured."

"Now I have to warn you," Hollis said. "JayDee takes this way too seriously."

"You said there were zero expectations." Ainsley's posture stiffened.

"There are. But JayDee forgets. So just don't mind her."

They pulled into the parking lot of the large sports complex. There were multiple softball fields placed next to of each other, with a large concession stand in the middle.

"Well, hey, stranger." Hollis looked up to see Margo, JayDee's wife, smiling and waving.

Hollis greeted her with a hug. "Hi."

"You know we're still friends." Margo slapped her shoulder.

"I know. I've never been good at keeping in touch."

Margo eyed Ainsley.

"This is Ainsley." Hollis motioned to her. "Ainsley, this is Margo, JayDee's much better half."

Margo let out a laugh and took Ainsley's hand. Margo sported jeans and a red shirt. Her black hair was cropped close to her face, shorter than the last time Hollis had seen her.

"Speaking of," Hollis asked. "Where is your wife?"

"She's running around like a chicken with her head cut off." Margo laughed. "She is stressed out."

"You're not playing?" Ainsley asked.

"God, no," Margo said. "My marriage could not handle that."

JayDee appeared behind them. "You're late," she said flatly. It was rare for Hollis to feel small next to anyone, but JayDee towered over her. Her skin was just a shade lighter than her wife's, and her hair was in long black dreads pulled into a loose ponytail.

"Sorry," Hollis said, "I got distracted by this beautiful woman."

"Flattery will get you nowhere," JayDee said.

"If you're going to be rude, we are going to leave." Hollis knew she had the upper hand.

"No, no. I'm sorry. Where are my manners? I'm JayDee." She stuck her hand out to Ainsley.

"Ainsley," she said as she shook her hand and looked up to JayDee

"Here." JayDee handed them each a red jersey that said "Cats" in block letters on the front.

They put the jerseys on and headed to the dugout where JayDee did quick introductions for the team. Hollis leaned to Ainsley's ear. "I'm not going to remember any of these names."

"I was thinking the same thing," Ainsley said.

A dog barked at the other team's dugout. It wasn't that out of place at a softball field, but this bark was oddly familiar. Hollis's cheeks burned hot as she turned to JayDee. "Are you fucking kidding me?" Jasper's leash was attached to the far end of the visitors' dugout, as the Australian shepherd tried to make friends with everyone.

"I might have left out a few details."

"What's going on?" Ainsley asked.

"Nothing," Hollis answered quickly. She wasn't ready for this level of drama.

Ainsley turned her head toward the other dugout. "Is that?" Ainsley squinted.

"Miranda," Hollis gritted her teeth. "Did you know she was going to be here?" Hollis stared at JayDee.

"I mean," she shrugged, "I knew what team we were playing."

"I can't fucking believe you," Hollis said.

"I owe you one," JayDee said. "Plus, it's like I said, you can't be a lesbian in this town and not get used to seeing your exes places. This will help."

"You owe me more than one," Hollis snapped. She wanted to leave. She didn't want to deal with Miranda. But she couldn't let Miranda control her choices anymore. She loved playing softball and wouldn't let Miranda, of all people, take that from her. Surely they could be adults about this.

The game started, and Cats was the home team. After three easy outs—two pop flies, and one grounder to Hollis—they ended their half of the inning and went to bat. Hollis was first up. The pitcher was a stocky brunette who looked like she had a mean fastball.

Hollis's strategy was to always swing at the first pitch. She hated it when people got into battles with the pitcher, so she would sit back and knock the crap out of the first pitch.

The clouds turned a glorious shade of pink against the setting sun. The weather was perfect. Not too hot, not too cold, with a slight breeze and the wonderful smell of fresh cut grass. Hollis stepped into the batter's box and made eye contact with the pitcher. The yellow ball released from the pitcher's hand. It sailed up and then leveled out. She told herself to be patient. Sit back. Then, when it came within reach, she swung.

The ping of the bat resonated as the ball made contact. The ball sailed just over second base and landed squarely in the grassy outfield. She ran through first base easily. The right fielder grabbed the ball and threw it to first. Hollis jogged the few feet back to the bag when all of the air left her lungs as a glove sucker-punched her stomach.

She keeled over, trying to catch her breath. Unsure of what had just happened, she looked up to see Miranda playing first base.

"What the hell?" Hollis had her hands on her knees and was breathing hard from having the wind knocked out of her. Her stomach throbbed.

"Oh, sorry." Miranda made a show of throwing the ball back to the pitcher. "Was just making sure you weren't off the bag." Miranda took a few steps away from the base.

Apparently, they couldn't act like adults. This was going to be a long game. Hollis muscled through the pain and scored easily after JayDee hit a long ball over the right fielder's head and all the way to the fence.

Hollis jogged into the dugout and winced as she sat down, her stomach still stinging. Ainsley joined her on the bench. "Are you okay?"

"Yeah." Hollis shook her head. "Fucking Miranda."

The overhead lights clicked on as the game went on into the later innings. Playing under the lights was a different feeling altogether. Softball was great on a warm spring afternoon, but playing under the dome lights always made the stakes seem higher. The game had been tied at one for several innings. Miranda was up, and Hollis stared her down from third base.

JayDee took her time at the pitcher's mound. She rocked back and released the ball. It took a long slide away from the plate. Miranda swung and missed. "Nice work, Jay," Hollis yelled in encouragement.

Miranda glared at Hollis.

Hollis stayed focused. She tried not to let Miranda get to her. JayDee rocked back again and released the ball. The crack of the bat sounded and Hollis saw the ball fly into the air. She knew it was going high and judged that it was going over her head. She turned and sprinted. Her cleats slipped slightly as she transitioned from dirt to grass, but she kept sprinting. She didn't lose the ball in the lights and followed it into the outfield. She opened her glove wide, stretched her arm out as far as it would go and leapt. She clasped her glove around the ball as she fell and felt it land in her mitt.

"Nice!" Ainsley yelled from right behind her.

Hollis popped up and fired the ball to second base. The player grabbed the ball and, in a sweeping motion, tagged the runner that had left the base. The umpire called "Out!" and she pumped her fist to herself. The double play ended the inning.

Hollis jogged back to the dugout as something swatted her ass. She turned and saw a smiling Ainsley jogging next to her.

"Impressive."

"Still got it."

At the top of the seventh inning, Cats trailed 2-1. JayDee was not holding her stress in well. Hollis knew how badly she wanted this win, but things just weren't falling their way. There had been a few easy outs that they should have had. A few miscues between shortstop and right field. Then there was Hollis's hitting. After the first hit, she couldn't get anything to land. She was trying too hard to hit it out of the park and kept finding center field. They needed one out and two runs so JayDee could relax.

Miranda was up again. Hollis took a deep breath. Two of her three hits had come down the third base line. She prepared herself for another. The ping of the bat sounded and the yellow ball got closer and closer. The orange stitching came dangerously close, and she reflexively put her glove in front of her face. White-hot searing pain filled her body as the line drive hit Hollis square on the cheek.

She fell to the ground, her glove still against her cheek. Was her face broken? Something must be broken. She tried to take a deep breath but gasped through the pain. She opened her eyes, trying to find her bearings, but all she saw was red. She'd heard of being so mad you see red before, but she didn't think she was that angry. Why would she be that angry? No. Shit. That wasn't anger. That was blood. She closed her eye, not wanting to see anymore.

Hands gently rolled her over onto her back and she soothing words comforted her. She blinked the world into focus the best she could with one eye. Her face throbbed. Something wet and sticky covered her collar. Blood? What could cause that much blood? She had no concept of where she was. She kept blinking, but pain seared the right side of her face with every blink. There were bright lights shining above her, and she saw moths swarming under them. She saw Ainsley's eyes right above her head, full of concern. She saw JayDee standing over her. Then it clicked into place.

"Did I catch it?" was all she could muster.

JayDee let out a long, throaty laugh. "Yes." She pointed to her gloved hand that still had the ball in it.

Hollis started to move. Ainsley, who had been kneeling at her head, put a hand on her shoulder. "Don't try to move just yet," she said softly. She pressed a towel to Hollis's cheek to stop the bleeding. Her right side was covered in blood. The stitching on her glove had caused a deep gash to form on impact, and the thin skin of her face bled uncontrollably.

Hollis thought about protesting, but her face hurt too much to move. She lay back down, her head resting on Ainsley's knees. There was movement on the field as players gathered to see if she was okay.

"Hollis, I am so sorry," Miranda said but Hollis couldn't turn to look.

"Fucking a, Miranda. I know you're mad at me, but did you have to take it out on my face?" She yelled but still didn't turn to look at her.

"Hollis, it was an accident," JayDee chimed in.

Hollis started to sit up, but Ainsley held in her place. "Don't take her side on this too, Jay."

"What the hell are you even talking about?" JayDee said. "I told you I didn't take sides."

"And that's why it took you four months to call me?"

"Where the fuck is this even coming from?"

Miranda inched closer to where Hollis was. "Here, let me help."

Ainsley put a hand up to stop her. "Look, I think we can all agree that this was an accident." Hollis again started to protest, but

Ainsley held her firmly in place. "Miranda, I think you've done enough. Now everybody back up and clear some space for when the ambulance gets here."

"Don't tell me you're on her side too," Hollis said above a whisper.

"You know that I'm not. Plus, I've seen her hit, and her aim isn't that good."

Hollis coughed a laugh and then winced in pain. Ainsley kept pressure on her cut and reassuringly rubbed her shoulder.

The field cleared of all the players and shortly after, an ambulance pulled up to the field. One paramedic got out and approached Hollis. "Emily?" Hollis asked.

"I thought that was you," the red-haired paramedic answered. "What have we got here?" Emily approached Hollis. She had Ainsley move the towel back and looked at her face. "Ya, that's gonna leave a mark," she joked.

"When did you become a paramedic?" Hollis asked.

"Oh, this is just something new I'm trying." Emily brushed her off and reached into her bag for an alcohol wipe.

"Emily was my college roommate," Hollis told Ainsley. The last thing she needed was Ainsley thinking she had more exes on this softball field.

"This is going to sting," Emily said as she wiped blood from the open wound on Hollis's face.

"Holy shit." Hollis writhed in pain, and Ainsley put pressure on her shoulders to keep her in place.

"Sorry about that." Emily reached into her bag for gauze. She put tape across the gauze and took a long look at Hollis's face. "Okay, we got the bleeding stopped. You're going to need to change that out when you get home. You are going to have a hell of a bruise, but near as I can tell, nothing is broken. You don't have signs of a concussion, but stay awake the next few hours just in case."

Hollis breathed out. "Got it."

"Are you sure she doesn't need to go in?" Ainsley asked.

"Well, my boss would want me to take you in." Emily looked over her shoulder at the overweight paramedic still in the ambulance.

"But that's just so we can push fluids and charge the hospital for a transfer. I'm going to give you your night back."

"Thanks." Hollis winced.

"Let's get you up," Emily said. She put her shoulder under Hollis and helped her stand. The few people in the stands clapped as she hobbled toward the dugout feeling dizzy. Emily looked at her face one more time. "Yeah, that's going to be a nice bruise. Don't be surprised if your eye swells shut. Keep ice on it, and if the swelling doesn't go down by Tuesday, see your doctor."

Emily helped ease her down on the wooden bench. "Thanks, Emily," she said.

Emily headed back to the ambulance.

"Let's get you home," Ainsley said as she sat next to Hollis.

Hollis saw the panicked look in JayDee's eyes. If they left, it would be a forfeit. "I think we need to stay," she said hesitantly.

"Are you serious?" Ainsley's eyes went wide.

Hollis looked to JayDee. "You'll have to take an out for me, I can't bat. But it's just one more at bat. I can wait."

Ainsley shook her head.

Hollis put a hand on her thigh. "Please. It's really important. The team was short two players before we showed up, so if we leave now, Miranda wins."

"Fine," Ainsley sighed. "But keep this on your face." She handed her an ice pack.

"Deal," Hollis said. She cringed at the cold as Ainsley put the ice pack on her cheek. She went to pull it off, but Ainsley pushed it back on.

The umpire asked if everyone was ready to resume, and JayDee said yes. Ainsley was the first at bat, and she left for the plate hesitantly.

JayDee took a seat next to Hollis on the bench. "Nice catch."

"Thanks." Hollis shifted to make room and grimaced in pain.

"So, do we need to talk about what happened back there?"

"Shit. Miranda just gets under my skin, you know?"

JayDee let out a small laugh. "I've known that girl a long time. So yes, I do know."

"The whole reason I avoided softball this year was to avoid her, and then tonight she's here and she takes it out on my face? I shouldn't have yelled at you."

"Apology accepted. So." JayDee eyed Ainsley who was taking a few practice swings. "What's the deal with you two?"

"We're just friends," Hollis said. She wanted to scream that she wanted to be more than just friends, but that wasn't the agreement.

"Right," JayDee dragged the words out. "And Margo is about to join the softball team."

"We are figuring out what we are," Hollis admitted.

"Well, she really likes you," JayDee said. "You went down, and she was there in two seconds. I've never seen someone move so fast."

"Really?" Hollis wasn't surprised, but it was nice to hear.

The ball connected with the bat and Hollis saw Ainsley rounding first base. She hit the ball to the perfect spot behind the left fielder and easily got to second base.

"That's our girl." JayDee nudged Hollis.

The next batter hit an immediate out. Unfortunately, Hollis was the next up and they had to take an out. Hollis didn't want to disappoint, but there was no way she could even stand long enough to get to the batter's box. She had played third base as long as she could remember and had taken the brunt of many line drives, but she had never taken one to the face like this. The pain was searing, and she was struggling to even sit upright. With two outs and Ainsley at second, JayDee stepped up to bat. At least it was all on JayDee.

After battling with the pitcher, JayDee quickly racked up a 3-2 count. It all came down to one final pitch. The ball released from the pitcher's hand and JayDee got all of it. She knew it right away. The ball sailed easily into the outfield. Hollis lost it in the lights but saw the excitement on JayDee's face. It flew past the centerfielder, who jumped at the back fence as the ball fell just out of the park.

Ainsley ran to home plate and then waited for JayDee who was flailing her arms excitedly. The rest of the team stormed the plate and congratulated JayDee.

The celebration calmed down, and everyone made their way back to the dugout. "Well, I would ask if you are available next week," JayDee started. "But I think you're riding the pine for a while." She motioned to Hollis's face.

"Yeah, I think I'll have to pass," she replied.

"Come on." Ainsley reached for Hollis's hand. "Let's get you home."

Hollis's face throbbed with each step, and she realized that she had landed hard on her hip and her elbow when she fell. All she wanted to do was curl up and go to bed and forget about the searing pain in her body.

They got to Hollis's car, and Ainsley went to the driver's seat. "If you didn't want to drive, you could have just said so. You didn't have to be so dramatic about it."

Hollis tried to laugh then grimaced, touching her cheek.

Ainsley reached for her hand. "I'm sorry."

"Just take me home," Hollis said.

They got to Hollis's apartment complex and Ainsley carried both of their bags upstairs. Hollis made her way to the bedroom. She went to take her shirt off and couldn't get her arm all the way up because of the stinging pain in her elbow.

"Let me help." Ainsley took the sleeve from her arm and pulled the shirt off of her. She let out a sigh.

"What?" Hollis asked.

"Your side." Ainsley touched her, and Hollis recoiled. "You must have slid when you fell." The skin was rubbed raw on parts of her rib cage and dirt stuck to the dried blood. "We need to get you in the shower. It'll be quick."

Hollis wanted to protest, but knew Ainsley was right. She followed Ainsley into the bathroom and threw her shorts in the hamper in the corner. She looked at her side in the mirror and saw her left butt check covered in red scratches. She was a wreck.

Ainsley had started the shower and warmed the water up. She touched Hollis's shoulder. "Come on."

Hollis arched her back as the water hit her skin. The warm water soothed her but stung all of the raw parts of her body. Ainsley stood fully dressed outside the shower door, white washcloth hand. "We'll make this fast," she said. She wet the cloth and then guided Hollis to turn so she could reach her cuts. She gently patted the area.

Hollis tried to move, but there was nowhere to go.

"I know, babe," Ainsley said. "Almost done."

"God, it stings," Hollis said through gritted teeth.

"Almost there," Ainsley said. "Okay." Ainsley pulled her out of the shower and wrapped her in a gray terrycloth towel. She shut the water off and pulled Hollis into a hug. She held her close for a few moments. She pushed Hollis back and looked up at her. "Don't hate me."

"I don't think I could," Hollis said, confused. Of all the things to feel for Ainsley in that moment, hate was not on the list.

"We need to change the bandage on your cheek."

"Shit."

"I'll be gentle,.

"Just get it over with." Hollis held her breath as Ainsley peeled the taped gauze off her face. It stung as she pulled, and her skin stuck to the tape. She closed her eyes, knowing that it would be over soon.

"There," Ainsley said.

Hollis noticed the panic in Ainsley's eyes.

"What?"

"Nothing." Ainsley shook her head.

"Is it that bad?"

"No," Ainsley lied.

Hollis looked past her and glimpsed herself in the mirror. "Damn," she said and traced her finger along the cut. It ran almost six inches long. It wasn't wide enough to warrant stitches, but Hollis feared it would leave a scar. The right side of her face was swollen to almost double its regular size and she could feel her eye starting to force shut. She had no idea what kind of state she would be in tomorrow.

"This is going to sting." Ainsley dabbed an alcohol pad to Hollis's cheek.

It took everything Hollis had not to punch her out of reflex. Her face was on fire. She gritted her teeth and tried not to call Ainsley unspeakable names.

"There," Ainsley said. "All done." She grabbed a long Band-Aid and covered her cheek. "Let's go to bed."

Ainsley helped her into pajamas, and they made their way into Hollis's bed. Hollis lay on her left side as her face was too swollen to put any pressure on it. Ainsley spooned her and snuggled in close.

"It's a work night," Hollis said.

"It's okay." Ainsley slowly rubbed her side.

"Don't you need to go home?"

"I'm not going anywhere." Her tone left no room for questions.

Hollis breathed deeply, thankful that Ainsley was still there.

"Hollis?"

"Yeah?" Hollis murmured, already half-asleep.

Ainsley whispered, "I think I'm falling in love with you."

Hollis started to sit up, but Ainsley pushed her back down.

"I am so far past just being able to be friends. I've wanted to tell you for some time, but haven't been able to find the words. Then tonight when you fell…I just…I can't keep it in any longer. I know it's not what we agreed to, but I can't deny that I have real feelings for you."

Hollis smiled the best she could, warmth flooding her body. This warranted a longer conversation, but she couldn't focus on anything but Ainsley's words. "I think I'm falling for you too." It was going to get messy, but she didn't care. That was a problem they could sort out later. For now, she would bask in the feeling of Ainsley holding her. Ainsley pulled her closer, and in a matter of seconds, despite the pain in her cheek and the little voice in her head telling her trouble was on the way, she fell asleep.

Chapter Twenty-six

Hollis awoke to an empty bed. Her face throbbed, and she cringed as she touched it. It all came back to her. The softball game, the line drive to the face, and then Ainsley taking care of her. Whispering *I think I'm falling...*

Hollis hoped that she hadn't dreamed it. She slowly got herself out of bed. Her body was stiff and sore from the fall.

She found a yellow sticky note stuck to the coffee pot. She smiled as she pulled it off to look closer.

I had to catch an early call. I hope you're feeling better. I can't wait to see you tonight.

Ainsley had signed her name with a heart, and Hollis grinned. Tonight could not come fast enough.

Hollis had given up on trying to hide how bad her face looked. Thankfully, her eye hadn't swollen shut, but her bruised cheek held varying degrees of purple around the clear imprint of her softball glove. She found the thinnest bandage she could to mask the long cut, but it was still six inches long. After several tear-filled attempts at using concealer to cover her bruises, she gave up. She debated calling off sick, but she wanted to see Ainsley tonight. She couldn't in good conscience call out sick and then go out on a date. Although, she would insist that Ainsley call ahead and seat them somewhere in a dark corner.

Harrison had beaten her in to work. He handed her a coffee. "Who'd you piss off?"

"Miranda." Hollis took a long sip of the coffee.

"Okay?" Harrison clearly wanted more information.

"I took a line drive to the face playing softball last night."

"What is it with you lesbians and softball?" Harrison's voice was full of disgust. "You are like moths to a flame. You can't stay away."

"Thanks for the coffee."

"There's a new cute barista."

"I hope he doesn't get a real job anytime soon."

The day went on and Hollis did her best to think about work, but between the pain in her face and the excitement of her date, she couldn't think of much else. The sun brought an unseasonable seventy degrees with it, and she took a quick stroll around the block to loosen her sore muscles and hopefully help her regain her focus. Moving helped her stiff body. She had made it to noon. She just needed a few more hours to pass and she could start the weekend. Hopefully, one filled with Ainsley.

When she got back to her desk, a white envelope greeted her on her keyboard. She opened it to find a letter with a yellow sticky note stuck to the top with handwriting she was growing to love. It read: *For us to discuss tonight*

She grabbed the note to reveal the body of the letter. She truly had no idea what kind of surprise Ainsley had for her. She scanned the letter. The words swirled on the page. None of it made sense. Her blood pressure rose instantly, and she reread the letter three times. Her heartbeat raced and her breathing went shallow. She shoved the letter back into the envelope and stormed out of her office.

She raced down the hall. Parker stood watch in his normal spot. Hollis blew past him and ignored him when he said that "Ms. Jones was in a meeting."

She threw the door open and held the letter up, blocking her face. "What the hell is this?" She kicked the door shut behind her.

Ainsley quickly put herself on mute and looked up from her computer. "I'm on a call."

"End it." Hollis shocked herself with the force of her words. She didn't know if Ainsley would oblige or not, but they needed to talk. Now.

Ainsley took herself off mute. "Gentlemen, I'm going to have to drop off. Something urgent has come up. I will follow up with you later." She ended the call and stood.

"What the hell is this?" Hollis asked again.

"That's something I thought we could discuss at dinner tonight, and I didn't want to blindside you. Certainly not something worth interrupting my meeting for."

Hollis dropped her arm and saw Ainsley's eyes widen as she got the first look at her face for the day.

"Hollis, your face." She backed away from the desk and started toward her.

"It's fine." She brushed her off. It wasn't fine. It hurt like a pain she hadn't experienced in her life. It stung and with every exaggerated heartbeat, a shot of fire pulsed through her cheek. She tried to take her attention off of her anguish. "You're transferring me?" Hollis held out the letter. It contained a job offer for a position in the marketing department. Project manager for the new storefront initiative.

"It's technically a promotion."

"That I didn't ask for." Hollis knew she was yelling, but she couldn't contain herself. "I told you I want nothing to do with this project!"

Ainsley kept her tone calm. "I thought we could talk about it tonight."

"Talk about it, or you could tell me all the reasons why the decision has already been made?"

"The latter. I kind of figured we'd be celebrating."

"Celebrating the fact that you don't have to lay me off?"

"It's not that simple. This is a great opportunity for your career."

"*My* career, Ainsley, not one you can just play around with to make yourself look better."

"I think it would be best if you take a beat and we can talk about this tonight."

"There's nothing to fucking talk about." Hollis glared.

"Just listen," Ainsley said with exaggerated calmness. "I know we have blurred the lines here, but I'm going to remind you that we are at work, and I am your boss."

Hollis let out a frustrated laugh. "Oh really? Were you my boss when you kissed me in this office? Were you my boss when I fucked you behind your desk?"

Ainsley just held her gaze.

Hollis took a deep breath and gathered herself. "I'm sorry, Ms. Jones," she punctuated her words. "You'll have to forgive me for my outburst. I have recently suffered a head injury, and I'm not myself." She motioned to her cheek. "Since this is a work-related matter, I will schedule time with Parker for us to discuss this during work hours." Hollis turned for the door.

"Hollis, wait," Ainsley pleaded.

"We will discuss this during work hours." She opened the door and stormed out of the office. Hollis was beside herself. Not even twenty-four hours ago, Ainsley was telling her she might be in love with her, and now she was taking advantage of her. Hollis knew that the reason Ainsley wanted her to take the position was due to the pressure she was getting. Hollis had said multiple times that even though it was her idea, she wanted nothing to do with it. Yet Ainsley hadn't listened. She had done what was best for Ainsley, no matter who it might have hurt. Ainsley had known this was about to happen, had to have been part of the decision, and didn't even bother to let Hollis know about it. As if what Hollis felt didn't matter. As if *she* didn't matter.

Ainsley was not the woman she'd thought she was. What a fool she'd been.

Harrison was sitting at his desk when Hollis got back.

"I need a drink," she said.

Harrison turned around. "It's one p.m."

"I need a drink. Are you coming or not?"

"I'm coming." He stood quickly.

"Good. You're driving." They left for the elevator together. "Take us somewhere no one will find us."

"I know just the place."

After the quick car ride, Hollis stormed into the bar and took a seat. She got the bartender's attention and asked for two tequila shots. She pushed one in front of Harrison and downed hers instantly. He was hesitant, but took it. She signaled the bartender for two more. She downed it and went to signal the bartender again.

"That's enough." Harrison cut her off. "She'll have a beer or something." He signaled to the tap behind the bar. "I think you need to slow down. What's going on?"

"I've been seeing Ainsley." She grabbed the beer from the bartender and thanked him.

"You've what?"

"For the last few months, I've been seeing Ainsley."

"As in our boss?"

"Yes." Hollis nodded.

Harrison had a look of shock Hollis had never seen. "Is she good in bed?"

"Seriously? That's the first thing you ask?"

Harrison shrugged.

"Of course she's good in bed." Hollis sighed.

"Actually, I take it back. I don't want to know any of the gross details."

Hollis took a long sip of her beer. For the first time, she looked around the dark bar. It was just past one p.m., but dark as night inside. She noticed the neon signs lighting up all the pictures of shirtless men. "Are we in a gay bar?"

"You told me to take you somewhere no one would find us."

"Good work." She took a long sip of her drink.

"So, what happened? I'm all for leaving work early, but why are we day-drinking?"

"She's transferring me."

"What?" Harrison said, disgusted.

"This whole storefront project. There's a lot of pressure for it to be successful. So, I found out today that I've been transferred. Even though I want nothing to do with it. Plus, if she transfers me and doesn't backfill, she can avoid the whole layoff thing and look like a hero for giving someone up. It almost feels like a setup."

"What do you mean?"

"Well, if it fails, they need someone to blame. Who better than the person in charge?" Hollis pointed to herself.

"Damn." Harrison shook his head. "That's cold. But you know? You don't get to the top without stepping over a few people."

"I guess I just thought she was different, better than that." Hollis held her beer with both hands. "I thought I meant something to her."

Harrison put his hand on her shoulder. "No one in the corporate world is better than that."

Hollis's phone buzzed in her pocket. She pulled it out to see a text from Ainsley. "Great." She rolled her eyes.

Can we talk?

Hollis typed a reply before she could over think it.

Is it work related?

Bubbles appeared and reappeared for a few seconds. She picked up her phone and replied.

Actually, even if it is work related, you can talk to Harrison. It's his department now.

She set her phone back on the bar, satisfied with her snippy response.

"So, what now?" Harrison asked.

"Well, I'm not taking the transfer," Hollis said. "I'm certainly not going to continue working for her." She stared at her reflection in the bar mirror. Her face was atrocious, but there was nothing she could do about it. She had worn her hair down today to try to draw attention away from her cheek, but she was failing.

"Bobby keeps calling me," she finally said.

"The old boss, right?"

"Yeah. I think I might go hear him out. He's been recruiting me pretty hard."

"So that's just it then? You up and leave me over some woman?"

"I thought she was more than just some woman. I don't see how I can stay." As Ainsley had said, the lines had been blurred and after showing her true self today, there was no way Hollis would work for someone like that.

Chapter Twenty-seven

Between the splitting hangover headache and the piercing pain from her face, Hollis spent all of Saturday in bed. She made a few trips to the living room for a change of scenery, but didn't go far. She had gotten several calls and texts from Ainsley but refused to answer any of them. At the bar, before she had too many beers to function, she had emailed Parker to set up a formal meeting time with Ainsley. She would meet with her Tuesday at three p.m. and had no intentions of talking to her any time sooner. While she was buzzed, but not too far gone, she had called Bobby. She tried to mask the sounds of the bar in the background as she agreed to interview with him on Monday.

Saturday rolled into Sunday, and Hollis willed herself out of bed. The swelling in her face had gone down, but the varying shades of purple remained. She looked more like herself than she had since Thursday. She put on her running clothes and left the apartment. The sky was gray, but it wasn't raining. Perfect running weather. She hit start on her GPS and took off.

Each step on the pavement sent searing pain through her face. She thought if she could just keep going, she could power through it. Then her mind wandered to Ainsley and how amazing she had been on that run together. The thought she had put into designing a route and a playlist. It was a connection unlike any other. She swallowed the lump forming in her throat and blinked back tears. No, she was not going to let Ainsley take running from her. This had been her escape for years; she wasn't going to give it up.

She hated to admit that she missed Ainsley, but she ached for her. Just because she was furious with her, it didn't mean she wouldn't have done anything to be able to go back in time. She wanted to go back to the night when Ainsley said she was falling in love with her. She wanted to go back and live in that memory. But that was all it was, a memory. Ainsley had shown that she would put her career before anything else, and that wasn't something Hollis could live with.

Hollis stopped after two miles. It was too painful. All of it. She showered and paced back and forth in her apartment. She turned the TV on and saw the Mariners game had just started. She headed for her car and drove to her parents' house.

"Hello!" Her voice echoed in the empty house. No one was in the kitchen or the living room. She turned down the hall and sounds of the baseball game echoed from the den.

"In here, sweetie," her dad called.

Hollis saw her dad sitting in his black recliner in his den. Somehow, her dad had sheltered his man cave from any upgrades over the last forty years. Dark wood paneling covered the walls, and the carpet was a dark red pattern indistinguishable due to wear.

"Your mom is out with Amy." He sat up in his recliner.

Hollis saw the concern in his eyes as he noticed her face. "Line drive at the game on Thursday."

"Did you catch it?"

"Of course I caught it."

"That's my girl." He smiled the proud smile only a father can. "I thought Sunday dinner was next week."

"It is." Hollis slumped down in the matching recliner. "But the Mariners are playing, and there was no one in my apartment to explain all the mistakes the pitching staff are making."

He leaned back in his recliner. "You've come to the right place. Can I get you a drink?"

Hollis stood up. "I'll get it."

"Sit back down." He motioned with his hand. He opened the armrest of his recliner to reveal a built-in cooler. He handed her an ice cold can.

She laughed as she took it. "I can't believe Mom lets you have that."

Her dad put a finger over his lips. "She doesn't know it's here. And you better not tell her."

She pulled the lever on the recliner and leaned back, kicking up her feet. She opened the beer and set the cold can against her face.

"You know what major league baseball needs?"

"A pitch clock?"

"They already added that. Besides, that's not what I was thinking." He took a sip of his beer.

Hollis turned and looked at him.

"A theme song." He nodded.

"Theme song?"

"You know? Like how Sunday night football got that cute blonde to sing a theme song at the beginning? Not the current one, she's too young, but that other blonde."

"Faith Hill?"

"That's the one." He took a sip of his drink.

Hollis shook her head, astounded that her dad was talking about girls in that way with her. She knew that most people weren't so lucky when they came out, and she tried not to take it for granted. When she finally came out at twenty, she had held her breath, waiting for her parents to respond.

"So, are you seeing anyone?" he had asked.

"Well, no," Hollis replied.

"So, then what's the news?" he scrunched his face.

"That I'm gay." She was clear with her words because she wasn't sure her dad was following.

"That's not news." Her dad shook his head. "Now when you find a nice girl, that will be news."

Hollis could sit in silence with her dad in his den all day.

"That Faith Hill has nice legs," he said.

"Jesus, Dad." Hollis didn't know how to respond.

"What? Speaking of nice legs, how's it going with Ainsley?"

Hollis let out a long sigh.

"What'd you do?" he asked, his tone accusatory.

"What makes you think I did something?"

"Because I know you, sweetheart." He turned and faced her. "There's a reason you're thirty and not married."

"Who says that marriage is the end goal?" She came to see her dad to feel better about things, not be accused of ruining relationships.

"No one. I'm just saying, I've known you a long time and when things go wrong, it's usually you, as much as you don't want to admit it."

Hollis thought about it. Her dad was right. It was usually her. Usually because she wasn't as invested in the relationship as her partner, and she realized it too late. "It wasn't me this time, Dad."

"What happened?"

"Long story short, she betrayed me." Hollis looked at the TV.

"She cheat on you?"

"No." Hollis shook her head.

"That's good. There are a lot of things that people can be forgiven for, but there are some things a person can't come back from."

Hollis nodded.

"You only get one shot at this, sweetheart."

"Shot at what?" Hollis wasn't following.

"Life. You can't waste your time with someone who doesn't make you better. So, if Ainsley isn't making you better, you need to move on."

Hollis thought about her dad's words.

"But I will say this." He sat his recliner up and looked at her. "I have never seen you as happy, calm, and relaxed as I have since you started seeing Ainsley."

"Really?" Hollis didn't think it was that obvious.

"Really." He made eye contact with her. "From what I've seen, Ainsley makes you better. But if you're telling me that she has crossed the line and has done something unforgivable," he paused and looked her in the eyes, "then I never liked her anyway."

Her dad always knew the right thing to say.

"Now," he switched gears quickly. "The problem with the Mariners bullpen is they are spending too much time on left-handers."

Chapter Twenty-eight

Hollis stared at the Global Headquarters sign. She let out a long breath on the path to the main entrance. It was a walk she had made every day for seven years, yet it didn't feel familiar. She had put on her best suit for the occasion. She knew she would be overdressed, but she wanted Bobby to know she was serious about whatever he had to say. She had done her best to cover the remaining blue spots on her face, but she still looked pretty banged up.

Hollis had taken a personal day. She had more saved up than she could count. She checked in at reception and had a seat in the massive lobby. The vaulted ceilings and industrial-grade railings made the lobby seem bigger than it was.

After a few moments, Bobby came through the door behind the reception desk. He was wearing golf pants and a black polo with a white swoosh. "Hollis!" He was in his mid-fifties, and his black hair was more salt than pepper at this point.

"Bobby." Hollis stood to greet him.

He pulled her into a hug. Hollis hated hugs at work. She hated the double standard that men could give handshakes, but women were somehow expected to give hugs. She tried to mask her disgust as she needed this job and didn't have the energy to take on gender politics.

"We'll grab a room." He motioned for her to follow him behind reception and into one of the empty conference rooms nearby.

She took the seat across from him in one of the bright orange chairs. It was an odd contrast to the gray walls, but the company was always trying to be modern in their looks.

"I have to ask." Bobby cocked his head. "Did you join a fight club?" He motioned to her bruised face.

"What's the first rule of fight club?"

Bobby let out a deep belly laugh.

"I took a line drive to the face last Thursday, but I got the out." That last part thrilled her. It would be a much more embarrassing story if she hadn't caught the ball.

Bobby contained his laughter. "I'd be lying if I said that part of the reason we want you back is our third base is really suffering."

Hollis had spent all seven years playing on the company softball team. Her coworkers took it way too seriously, but Hollis was competitive, and it had been a great way for her to network with the executives higher up the food chain. "I think I can help with that."

Bobby slid a piece of paper Hollis's direction. "I'm not going to waste your time. Here's the offer."

Hollis picked up the document. She tried to mask her excitement as she viewed that the salary would be a twenty percent increase.

"You would have complete control of the department. And I want to assure you, things have changed around here."

"You mean you're less of a micromanager now?" Hollis was surprised at her forwardness. However, Ainsley had helped her to realize that she needed to view her boss as an asset and not an enemy. Just because she wasn't speaking to her, it didn't make her advice any less valid. If she was going to start over at this company, she was going to be completely honest.

Bobby gave a slight laugh. "You have to understand the pressure we were under. A lot of that was coming from the top. Now that the C-suite has completely changed over, things are different."

Hollis wanted to believe him. She wanted to believe that she could come back here and make a difference. But more than that, she just needed somewhere else to be. "You've given me a lot to think about."

"Can you get me an answer by Wednesday?"

Hollis could have given him an answer now, but didn't want to seem overeager. "I think I can do that."

"Do me a favor?"

"Okay?"

"Don't haggle me on salary."

Hollis gave a half laugh.

"That's the offer. And it's a good one. I just don't have the energy to go back and forth on this, okay?"

"Got it."

"I really hope you'll take it." Bobby looked sincere.

"I'll let you know Wednesday."

Bobby saw her out, and Hollis started back to her car. She pulled her phone out and saw three missed calls from Harrison. That was unusual. She dialed him back.

"How did it go?" he answered the phone, frantic.

"Great," Hollis said. "It's a really good offer and we had a candid conversation."

"I'm happy for you, Hol." Harrison sounded genuine. He let out a long sigh. "She came by looking for you."

"She did?" Hollis knew he meant Ainsley.

"She did. I told her you took a personal day."

"Did she say anything else?" Hollis didn't know what she was hoping for. She knew she sounded like a teenager, but she was dying to know what Ainsley had said. What had she been wearing? Did she look like she'd slept?

"She asked if I'd talked to you at all and wanted to know how you were doing."

It was comforting that she'd asked about her. "What did you say?"

"That I saw you leave the bar with three different girls on Friday night."

"You did not?" Hollis squeaked. She wanted Ainsley to know that she messed up, but she certainly didn't want her to think she was sleeping around. "What did you say, really?"

"I told her you were upset, and you were figuring out what you were going to do. Then she left, and that was it."

Hollis wondered why she didn't ask any follow-up questions. But then again, Ainsley was an adult. She didn't need to be prying information out of Harrison. Plus, there was still the matter of their relationship at work. Technically, they couldn't be together, and Ainsley wasn't the type to confide in Harrison. Hollis had thought that since she didn't have any missed calls or texts from Ainsley today that maybe she had gotten over her, but maybe not if she had asked about her.

"Thanks for having my back," Hollis said.

"And your front," Harrison joked.

"I'll see you tomorrow."

Chapter Twenty-nine

Hollis had done a good job of avoiding Ainsley. She showed up to work thirty minutes late, which absolutely killed her. She hated to be late anywhere, but she couldn't chance running into Ainsley in the hall, or worse, being stuck in the elevator with her. Harrison played a good sport and agreed to let them have the office door shut and the blinds closed all day. They told the team they were working on a new release for next fall and asked to be left alone.

"So, you're really going to do it?" Harrison asked.

"I'm really going to do it." She needed to keep saying it out loud.

"You could just get her fired." Harrison could be conniving.

"I can't do that." As mad as she was, she wouldn't lie about Ainsley.

"I'm just saying, boss takes advantage of employee, employee reports boss, boss gets fired. It's a tale as old as time."

"She didn't take advantage of me."

"It's not fair," Harrison whined. "You're leaving and she gets to stay and who knows who they'll stick me with."

"Is it not fair because I don't get to keep my job or because you don't know who they'll replace me with?"

"Are they mutually exclusive?"

"You know they won't replace me with anyone, right? There's no way she'll be able to justify it. It kills me to leave. I love working here, but I don't see how I can stay."

"I get it. But that doesn't mean it doesn't suck."

"Yeah." Hollis let out a long breath. She looked at the clock on her laptop. Two fifty-five p.m.

"I'm probably going to duck out of here pretty soon. Might be my last chance for a while, what with you abandoning me and all."

"Here goes nothing."

Parker looked up from his computer as Hollis approached. "She's just finishing up a call, Ms. Reed. Go ahead and have a seat." He motioned to the chair across from his desk.

I can't believe she's making me wait. It was a power move if there ever was one. Hollis tried to take deep breaths to regain her composure. She was going to be in control of this conversation. Yes, Ainsley was the boss, and yes, she was doing petty things to try to have the upper hand, but this was Hollis's meeting.

She bounced her knee up and down. She fidgeted with the envelope in her hand. Her watch read 3:05. *This is ridiculous. It's one thing to make me wait a few minutes, but come on.* After an eternity, Parker said, "I'll send her right in." Parker switched off his Bluetooth. "Ms. Jones will see you now."

"Thanks." Hollis let out a slow, cleansing breath as she slowly opened the door.

Ainsley stood up from her desk. "I'm so sorry about that." She sounded panicked.

"It's fine." Hollis made her way to the conference table.

"Please have a seat."

Hollis tried to mask her eye roll. Of course, she was going to have a seat. She took a long look at Ainsley's face. She wasn't her normal self. Her eyes were bloodshot and sunken into her face. Her cheeks looked ashy, and like she hadn't slept in days. Hollis caught herself from beaming with pride, justified that she had made Ainsley feel that way. She caught herself. As hurt as she was, she didn't want to cause Ainsley harm.

"Hollis, thank you for—"

"This won't take long." Hollis raised a hand and cut her off. She was not here to listen or negotiate. She was going to say what she had to say and then leave.

"Okay?" Ainsley was clearly taken aback.

Hollis slid the envelope across the table toward Ainsley. Ainsley took the envelope and opened it.

"This is my resignation letter." Ainsley scanned the letter. "I wanted to deliver it in person. I put two weeks, but I understand that I'm going to a competitor, so if you need to accept my resignation as of today, I will cooperate." Hollis knew how the corporate world worked. Anytime someone said they were going to a competitor, they were escorted out the door by security. She spent the morning packing up her few things. She had no intention of making a scene, but she also didn't want security over her shoulder while she put her diploma in a box.

Ainsley shook her head, still scanning the letter. "That won't be necessary."

"Fitwear has been good to me. I appreciate all the opportunities it has given me, but I need to move on." She looked Ainsley directly in the eyes as she said that last part.

Ainsley opened her mouth and closed it.

Hollis backed her chair out and stood up. "Thank you."

Hollis grabbed her bag off of her chair and headed home. She would gather her things another day. It was clear she wasn't getting any more work done today. She really didn't have any work to do for the next two weeks, but she couldn't leave Harrison out on a limb. She would ensure that the transition was smooth.

She called Harrison as soon as she was in her apartment.

"And she said nothing?" Harrison asked after she had told him the full story.

"Not a word." She had truly stunned Ainsley, and she didn't think that was possible.

"No counter or anything?"

"No."

"Damn, that's cold."

"Right? If I'm such an asset, shouldn't there be a counteroffer?"

"I still can't believe you're leaving me," Harrison whined.

Someone knocked on her door. "Hang on, my ice cream is here."

"You single-handedly keep that delivery place in business." Harrison was only half kidding.

"Did you ever think growing up that you could have ice cream delivered to your door? If young Hollis could see me now." She opened the door and took the bag from the delivery kid. "What a time to be alive."

She set the carton on the kitchen island and held the phone between her cheek and shoulder as she searched in the drawer for a spoon. There were three quick knocks at the door. "Dammit. I must have forgotten the tip. Hang on a second." She shut the cabinet door with her hip. Harrison mumbled something about her being a cheapskate, but she couldn't make it out. She opened the front door and took a step back when it wasn't the delivery guy. "Harrison, I have to go." He asked, "Why?" as she quickly ended the call.

"Hi," Ainsley said.

"Hi?"

"Can I come in?" Ainsley was tentative.

Hollis opened the door wider and motioned her inside. She shut the door and turned around to Ainsley kissing her. For a moment, she forgot why she was mad and kissed back. It had only been a few days, but she missed those soft lips. She missed her smell, her taste, she missed all of her. Ainsley put her hands on Hollis's face and Hollis recoiled as she touched her cheek. Her feelings of anger came flooding back to her, and she stepped back quickly.

"I'm sorry." Ainsley pulled the white envelope that Hollis had handed her earlier from her back pocket and pushed it into Hollis's chest. "I don't accept this."

Hollis took the letter. Her hand brushed Ainsley's as she took it back. "What?"

"I don't accept your resignation," Ainsley said flatly.

"I don't think it works like that."

"Then go talk to HR about it." She flailed her arms slightly. "But I don't accept it."

"Then what?" Hollis stood stunned. Of all the scenarios she had envisioned, this was not one of them.

"Can we talk?" Ainsley pleaded with her eyes.

"There's nothing to talk about."

"Then can I talk, and you listen?" Ainsley wouldn't let up.

Hollis looked her up and down. She so badly wanted to let go of whatever she was holding on to. She wanted to go to Ainsley, to hold her, but she couldn't bring herself to forgive. There was nothing Ainsley could say. They both just needed to move on.

"After everything, don't I at least get two minutes to explain myself?" Ainsley blinked back what might have been tears.

Hollis let out a short breath. "Okay. I can give you two minutes."

"That would be great." Ainsley sounded relieved. She paused gathering her thoughts. "I had a good reason—" she started.

"For transferring me to a job I never wanted without even asking me all so that you could look good on your budget? I'm sorry. I can't do this. I thought I could, but I can't."

"I love you." Ainsley searched her gaze. "What I said before—that wasn't quite right. I fell for you a long time ago. As much as I wanted us to just stay casual, there's no way I can deny these feelings anymore. When I told you I was falling in love with you, what I meant was I love you."

"I think you should go." As much as Hollis wanted to bring Ainsley into her arms and tell her she loved her back, how could she trust her? Ainsley had put her career on the line just to hit budget. Love wasn't enough. Hollis needed an equal partner. She needed to hear Ainsley say that she was sorry and she would remember her wants and needs in the future. She couldn't stomach staying with someone who didn't view her career as just as important. How could she trust that she would actually listen to her going forward? People didn't change overnight.

"All right." Ainsley stood up and quickly brushed her eyes. "I'll expect you to finish out your two weeks."

"Of course." Hollis followed her to the front door.

"Good-bye, Hollis." Ainsley shut the door firmly behind her as she left.

Chapter Thirty

"Hey!" Hollis called as she entered her parents' house for Sunday dinner. She arrived early, hoping to catch a few minutes with her parents before her sisters arrived.

"In here, sweetheart," her mom called from the kitchen.

"Hi, Mom." Hollis leaned in to give her mom a side hug. Her mom hugged her back with both arms and gave her a final squeeze.

"No Ainsley today?"

Hollis had been dreading this part. Her parents gushed over Ainsley, and now she got to be the bearer of bad news. "No. Just me today."

"I'll make her a plate." Her mom returned to the sink where she was washing vegetables.

"It's fine, Mom. I won't see her tonight."

"Nonsense. She can take it for lunch tomorrow or something."

Hollis took a deep breath. Time to rip off the Band-Aid. "I won't see her tomorrow either. We broke up." There. The news was out.

Her dad looked up from the table, no longer interested in whatever was on his phone.

"Oh, sweetheart. What happened?" Her mom turned around and leaned against the sink.

Hollis looked up and blinked back the tears behind her eyes. The last thing she needed to do was break down in her parents' kitchen. "I don't know." She sounded like a whiny teenager, but being back home, she couldn't help it.

"I thought you two were going to work it out," her dad said.

"You knew there was a problem?" her mom shot him a dirty look.

"I knew Hollis was upset about something."

"And you didn't think to clue me in?"

Hollis was happy to no longer be the center of attention, but didn't care for being caught in her parents' crossfire.

"Conversations between fathers and daughters are sacred." He looked smug.

"Oh, I'll tell you a thing or two about sacred." Her mom wiped her hands on a dish towel and pulled a chair out at the table. She turned to Hollis. "Sit."

Hollis tried to protest, but her mom gave her the glare. The one that meant there was no getting out of this, and she was better off listening. She took a seat in the chair.

"What happened?" her mom interlaced her fingers and set them on the table.

Hollis didn't know where to start. How do you explain why something that seemed so perfect came to an end? "Ainsley is my boss."

"Oh, sweetheart." Her mom let out a long sigh.

Hollis could hear the disappointment in her mother's voice. "Relationships between bosses and employees are prohibited. We thought we could make it work, but…" She didn't know what else to say.

"So they found out and you had to break up?"

"What? No."

"You said she betrayed you. What happened?" her dad asked.

"Betrayed you?" her mom cut in.

Hollis raised both hands. "Not like that, Mom. She was part of a decision to transfer me to another department."

"That's great!" her mom perked up.

"No, it isn't."

"And why not?" her mom asked.

"Because it's a job I told her repeatedly that I didn't want, and she didn't listen. I wanted my current role for three years. I explained that to her. Then she goes out and does whatever she wants to do without so much as asking my opinion just so she can hit budget numbers. As if what was important to me didn't matter!"

"So now what?" She looked concerned.

"I quit."

"You what?" her dad asked.

"Well, I'm certainly not going to work for my ex, and I'm not going to take the job I don't want, so I'm going back to my old job."

Her mom slapped the table. "Hollis Theodosia Reed."

Hollis's stomach soured at the use of her full name. She was about to get her ass handed to her, and she knew it.

"There is a perfectly wonderful woman who is trying to be with you and instead of taking a job you'll probably love at a company you already love, with a woman you love, you up and quit? Because it isn't part of your plan?"

"Well, when you put it like that—"

"You quit when relationships get hard." Her mom's tone remained firm.

"I do not," Hollis whined.

"You do." Her mom nodded. "You did it with Miranda, thank God. You did it with whatshername before that, and you're doing it now."

Hollis stiffened. This was not the conversation she expected to have today. She knew that breaking this news to her parents would be tough, but she thought they would be more comforting than calling her on out on her shortcomings. "Don't you think it's a red flag that she just went about all this without even talking to me?"

"I think it's something you should discuss, but not a reason to throw the whole relationship away," her mom answered.

Hollis sighed. Short of telling her parents they were right, and she would do what they said, there was no winning this. They were making good points, but that didn't change the fact that Ainsley hadn't talked to her first. She needed to know she mattered to Ainsley as someone other than a friend with benefits. Because she was in love with her too, damn it.

"We love and support you no matter what." Her mom reached her hand across the table, and Hollis took it. "But you know there is more to life than work." Hollis started to interject, but her mother cut her off. "I know. I know. I'm not saying marriage is the end goal, I'm just saying Ainsley seemed to make you happy, and I hate for you to throw it all away over something so fixable."

Fixable. Were they fixable? Hollis had been plenty harsh to Ainsley the last few times she'd spoken to her. Even if she did accept the job now, would Ainsley accept her? It didn't matter. She was moving on. Moving on from Fitwear, and moving on from Ainsley Jones.

CHAPTER THIRTY-ONE

Hollis swiveled back and forth in her office chair. The last two excruciating weeks were finally behind her. Now all she had to do was count down a few more hours, eat her good-bye cake, and Fitwear would be a line on her résumé.

"For fuck's sake!" Harrison screamed at his laptop.

"What now?"

"There is another one of these reports. I don't know what's worse, you leaving me, or her attitude now that you're broken up. She's not even here today, and she's micromanaging me."

Hollis wheeled her chair over to his desk to lean over his shoulder. "That's not a new report."

"It's not?"

"No. I've been doing that one every week for a year."

"Seriously?" Harrison let out a low groan. "I can't believe how much you did and I had no idea."

"I'm glad you're finally appreciating me."

There was a knock at the door, and they both turned to face it. "Oh good. You're still here." A frazzled Mark stood in the doorway.

Hollis pushed back in her chair toward her side of the office.

"Did I hear correctly that you hated my job offer so much, you're leaving the company altogether?" Mark asked.

"What's that?" Hollis hadn't asked a single question about the position she had been offered.

"The storefront project. I was overseas, so I figured Ainsley could handle all of the paperwork. I guess I was wrong."

"You were in charge of the new position?"

"Well, it was your idea, but yes. We needed to get this thing up and running, and you are the only one who can get us there fast enough."

Hollis met Mark by the office door. "Let's go find a conference room. I think we'd better talk."

❖

Rain came down in sheets, and Hollis turned the windshield wipers to the highest setting. She gripped the steering wheel as tight as she could. A sedan cut her off, sending an extra spray of water to the front of her car. "Motherfucker!" Hollis screamed to no one. She tried to take a calming breath. She wasn't actually mad at the car in front of her. She was mad at herself. Mad for not listening to Ainsley. Mad for being so hung up on her own plans that she didn't consider anything different. The car put on its brakes suddenly and Hollis slammed on hers, screeching to a halt. She took it all back. She was mad at the car in front of her.

She jogged quickly from the street to Ainsley's house, rain pelting her from all sides. She had only been to Ainsley's new house a handful of times. The blue house sat tucked into an older neighborhood. The outside had been freshly painted and the yard kept neat. She knocked on the door, then danced back and forth from one foot to the next. The wind picked up and rain blasted from all sides.

Finally, the door opened. "Good lord, you live far away," Hollis let out in frustration.

"Hollis." Ainsley's eyebrows shot into her hairline. "Come inside. That rain is awful." Ainsley welcomed her in, and Hollis tried to recover from her embarrassing outburst. Ainsley looked comfortable in her oversized purple sweater and yoga pants. Whatever she was doing, she was in for the night.

"Are you busy?" Hollis asked tentatively.

"Um." Ainsley looked to the living room just off the entry way. The TV was paused on one of her favorite reality shows.

"Ains, who's at the door?" a man called from the living room.

A man's voice? They had never talked about it, but was Ainsley seeing a guy now? Hollis wanted to throw up. This had been a colossal mistake.

Greg appeared in the doorway holding a bowl of popcorn.

Relief coursed through Hollis. Greg. Her best friend. Obviously, her best friend would be over at her new place. "I'm sorry, I didn't mean to interrupt." Hollis turned for the door.

"No. No," Greg said. "I was actually just leaving. I left my oven on, and I need to get home before the whole place explodes." He set the bowl on the table and reached for his coat by the door.

"How could you know your oven is on?" Ainsley wasn't buying it.

"And I left the water running. The whole place is probably flooded by now. It was great to see you, Hollis." Before anyone could say another word, the door shut and Greg was gone.

"I was hoping we could talk."

Ainsley folded her arms across her chest. "I thought we had nothing to talk about."

"Well, maybe I can talk, and you can listen?" Hollis hoped this would lighten the mood and let her through Ainsley's hard exterior.

Thankfully, Ainsley caved. "Come in."

Hollis shed her coat and took a seat on the red couch. The place was so Ainsley. From the bright colors to the framed art, everything about it screamed Ainsley, even if it was an ungodly driving distance. Hollis put her palms on her thighs. She needed to just jump in and do it. "I talked to Mark today."

"I heard he was back from Europe." Hollis couldn't read Ainsley's tone.

"Turns out you didn't create that job for me."

"That's what I tried to tell you. The marketing department doesn't actually report to me. Now that the project has legs, I'm not overseeing it anymore. That's also why I was off budget by over a million dollars."

"He said he asked for me specifically." Hollis remembered her meeting in the conference room with Mark. After talking with him, she had found a renewed energy for her idea. With the right support structure, she could actually bring this idea to life.

"Also what I tried to tell you." Ainsley folded her arms across her chest again. Hollis needed to break through. She needed to get past this force field and get to the woman she loved.

"I think I'm going to take the job." Hollis held her breath.

"You'll be great at it." Ainsley's tone remained flat.

"I think I'm going to take the job, and you and I should go back to being together." There. She'd said it. She'd spilled it all out. Now she just needed Ainsley to take her back, arms wide open.

"Oh, Hollis," Ainsley said. "If the last few weeks have taught us anything, it's that we weren't working great together. I mean, we were good when we were good, but at the first sign of trouble, we self-destructed."

Hollis tried not to be defeated. Ainsley was still talking to her. She hadn't thrown her out or demanded she leave. If they were talking, she still had a chance. "We just need to get better at communicating, and now that you won't be my boss, we can be out in the open. There won't be any more sneaking around or wondering if we are about to get caught. If we could just be one hundred percent honest with each other, and with the world, I think it would make a difference."

Ainsley let out a laugh. Hollis stiffened. What the hell was so funny? Of all the reactions she expected, being laughed at was not one of them. "I should go."

"Wait!" Ainsley grabbed her hand. The mere touch of Ainsley's skin electrified her. God, how she had missed her touch. "I wasn't laughing at you."

"Then what?" Hollis didn't let go of Ainsley's hand.

"Greg was over tonight because he was convinced I needed a plan to get you back. Then you show up out of the blue, and I don't know if I believe in fate or anything, but it just seems like interesting timing."

"Why did Greg think you needed a plan to get me back?" They were so close. Feelings were out in the open. Walls were coming down. She just needed Ainsley to see there was a way to make this work.

"Because I'm miserable without you." Ainsley's eyes connected with Hollis's "He said that I've been the happiest I've been since you and that I needed to learn how to communicate like an adult and beg you to take me back."

"I knew I liked that guy."

"I'm not going to beg."

"I would never want you to." Hollis pushed herself closer on the couch. She looked past Ainsley to the container sitting on the end table. "Is that ice cream? After all the crap you gave me?"

"Yeah, well." Ainsley shrugged. "I just got dumped, and I've been drowning my sorrows in sugar. Turns out, eating your ex's favorite ice cream doesn't help." A slight smile crossed her lips. Ainsley reached for the container and placed a melted bite on the spoon. She held it out for Hollis, who carefully enclosed her lips around it.

"Ice cream delivery might be the greatest invention of our time," she said through a full mouth.

Ainsley laughed.

Hollis took the spoon from Ainsley's hand and reached for another bite. She paused before it got to her mouth. "I don't want a dog."

"Okay?" Ainsley quirked an eyebrow.

"Like, ever." Hollis took a slow bite of ice cream. "I don't want you thinking that someday I will want a dog. I will never want a dog."

"I don't remember asking you about a dog." Ainsley squinted.

"If I'm going to take this job." Hollis stabbed her spoon into the ice cream container and left it there. "Then you need to be serious about being with me for a long time." She looked Ainsley in the eyes. "Are you serious about being with me for a long time?"

"Yes," Ainsley answered quickly, much to Hollis's relief. "Of course. I love you. I don't say that unless I mean…forever."

"I'm not going to completely move career paths and then have you dump me in a month."

Ainsley put her hand on Hollis's thigh and squeezed it. "I'm not going to dump you."

"Then we need to figure some things out. Communication was our issue before, but we are going to fix that going forward. Tonight." Hollis grabbed the spoon and took another bite.

"Whatever you need. No dogs. Got it. How do you feel about cats?" Ainsley took the spoon and dove into the ice cream.

"One cat might be okay, but I'm not cleaning the litter box."

Ainsley laughed. "Deal."

"I don't know if I want kids." Hollis paused as she had given herself a brain freeze. She forced her eyes shut and placed her tongue on the top of her mouth. Ainsley's warm hand rubbed her thigh.

"Okay," Ainsley said softly.

"But I might want kids," Hollis said. "I don't know."

"I'm good either way."

"I'm not going to live farther than walking distance to work."

"We can take my car. You don't have to drive."

"No, no." Hollis violently shook her head and put the spoon back down. "I'm not going to carpool with you and then sit around on the nights where you work late waiting for my girlfriend to finish up just so she can give me a ride home."

Ainsley smiled.

"What?" Hollis was hesitant.

"I like the sound of being your girlfriend." Ainsley's cheeks blushed slightly. "I'll sell my house."

"You can't sell your house." Hollis shook her head. "You just bought it."

"It's just a house."

"You would sell your house for me?" Hollis knew this was a big ask, but she said it anyway.

"You are making the work sacrifices, I will make the life sacrifices." Ainsley was serious. "Plus we can turn this into a rental or something. The market here is actually really great for that. I'll tell you what, I'm sure you still have several months left on your lease. For now, if I have to stay late, which isn't very often," she emphasized, "you can walk to your place, and I'll pick you up when I'm done. That way you don't have to drive or wait around for your girlfriend at work."

Hollis thought about it. "That could work."

"Then, when your lease is up, if you want, we will find a place within walking distance to work." Ainsley paused and looked at Hollis. "Together."

This was a lot for Hollis to take in. The new job, getting Ainsley back, hearing her say she loved her. Yes, it was all she had thought about this afternoon, but now that it was close to becoming a reality, it overwhelmed her. "You know, I could take the other job and we could be together. There are lots of ways for us to make things work."

"I can't let you do that," Ainsley said.

"Why?"

"You'd be miserable. I'm sure they gave you some song and dance about turnover in the C-suite and how things are different now, but you know that deep down, they aren't. Big corporations like that are incapable of cultural change."

Hollis laughed slightly; Ainsley was dead-on.

"Plus I heard your last job turned you into a real grouch. I can't have that." She playfully squeezed her thigh.

Hollis was so close to seeing a world where this could work. The job wouldn't be perfect, but it was with a company she loved with coworkers she loved. There was just one thing missing to complete this puzzle. She took Ainsley's hand. "You have to start letting me in."

"I know." Ainsley nodded slightly.

"Like actually let me in." Hollis didn't break eye contact. "No more telling me things are fine when I know they aren't. I know there are some things you can't share, but you don't have to pretend that everything is okay. Not with me." Hollis rested their joined hands on her thigh. How she'd missed holding her hand.

"I know." Ainsley nodded again.

"Can you do that?"

"I've never actually wanted to let anyone in before," Ainsley admitted. "I've basically been on my own my whole life. My dad was great, don't get me wrong, but he's not the touchy-feely type, and I never learned how to open up. It was always easier to just say that everything's fine."

Hollis listened intently. This was the most Ainsley had shared about her past, and she didn't want to miss any of it.

"My mom died when I was four." Ainsley paused slightly, and Hollis kept her mouth shut. "She went for a bike ride like she had done thousands of times before. A driver veered into the shoulder and hit her in the bike lane. The paramedics say she died on impact." Ainsley let out a slow breath. She met Hollis's eyes. "I've lived my whole life knowing that someone could walk out my front door and never walk back in."

"Oh, Ainsley—"

Ainsley held up a hand to stop her. "I know. I know it doesn't work like that. I have a very good therapist who is helping me work through that." She laughed nervously at this admission. "But you have to understand where I am coming from."

Hollis searched Ainsley's eyes. Her heart broke slightly at the sadness she saw behind them. Her heart broke for the little girl who had grown up motherless and who acted like she had to take on the world by herself. She squeezed Ainsley's hand. "I'm so sorry. That must have been so horrible."

"It's just so much easier to throw the walls up and keep people at a distance. It's my default setting." Ainsley smiled slightly but it didn't reach her eyes. "These last two weeks were horrible."

"Tell me."

"I've never been so broken, so incomplete…" Ainsley paused, and Hollis could tell she was struggling to find the right words. "I pushed you away, and it was completely my fault. I didn't listen. I did what I thought was best. Even when Kayla and I split, I didn't even feel an ounce for her of what I felt these last few weeks."

That revelation made Hollis's competitive side beam.

"I couldn't sleep. I couldn't eat. I wanted to drink to drown my sorrows, but I wanted to stay sober in case you called. I was a complete wreck."

Hollis held her hand tighter.

"I meant it when I said I won't make that mistake again. I care too much about you, about us, to not learn from this. I promise to let you in, completely. I love you."

"I love you too." God, that felt good to finally say. Hollis had never said those words to anyone but her family. It had never been right with anyone else. Hollis held her gaze and Ainsley's eyes bore into her. She couldn't handle any more time not touching her, feeling her, being connected to her. Ainsley's lips parted slightly, and Hollis leaned in, tilting her head. Much to her pleasure, Ainsley returned the kiss. This time, the gentleness faded, and Ainsley kissed her in a way that Hollis knew was an apology. The kiss told her she knew she would never make a mistake like this again. It told her she loved her.

Hollis pulled her on top of her lap; she needed to be closer. She reached her hands up Ainsley's sweatshirt and ran her hands up her bare frame. She missed her skin. How could she miss someone so much after only a few days? Ainsley planted soft kisses on Hollis's cheek, then down her neck. Ainsley grabbed Hollis's breasts with both hands, squeezing and kneading. Hollis's nipples hardened under her touch. Ainsley kissed her way down Hollis's body until she was on her knees on the floor. She reached up to unbutton Hollis's pants and removed them and her underwear, and before Hollis could feel the cool air, Ainsley's tongue lapped at her clit.

Hollis dug both hands into Ainsley's auburn hair, pulling slightly. This encouraged Ainsley and she moved her tongue in faster circles. Ainsley put an arm on each of Hollis's thighs and pushed them farther apart, giving herself better access. She plunged her tongue into Hollis's warm opening.

"Oh, Ainsley." Hollis barely managed to get the words out. She tightened her grip on her hair, not wanting to pull too hard, but needing to hang on to something. The warmth and wetness of Ainsley's skilled tongue coursed through her, and she could feel the pressure building inside her.

"Wait," she panted.

Ainsley looked up. "Everything okay?"

"I need to be closer to you." Hollis's chest heaved up and down as she tried to make words.

"Closer than this?" Ainsley slowly worked her tongue up the length of Hollis's slit.

"Yes. Come here." Hollis helped Ainsley up from the floor and pulled her sweatshirt off in the process. Ainsley stood in front and pulled off her yoga pants.

Ainsley stretched out a hand. "Let's go to the bedroom."

"No." Hollis still hadn't caught her breath.

Ainsley must have seen the desire in Hollis's eyes because she didn't fight her. Instead, she unclasped her bra, slid down her black silk panties, and climbed back on Hollis's lap. Hollis quickly shed her own shirt and bra until they were both naked on the couch. Hollis couldn't wait for the bedroom. She had just felt the tongue that she never thought she would again, and she couldn't wait a second longer.

Ainsley's wet center slid up and down Hollis's lap. Ainsley leaned in, rocking back and forth. "I'm not going anywhere," Ainsley said.

Hollis's stomach tightened. She ran her hands up the bare skin of Ainsley's back, taking all of her in.

Ainsley pushed Hollis's thighs further apart and traced a finger up and down her wet lips. Hollis was more than ready, she just needed to feel Ainsley closer. Hollis let out a sharp breath as Ainsley drove a finger inside her. She opened her legs even wider, exposing herself further for Ainsley. Ainsley took the hint and inserted another finger. Hollis kept one hand between Ainsley's shoulder blades, holding her in place. With her other hand, she found Ainsley's wet center and traced lazy circles.

Ainsley's breath caught and she seemed distracted by Hollis rubbing her fingers on her wet clit.

"You feel what you do to me?" Ainsley's voice turned husky. "You feel how wet I am for you?"

"Oh God." Hollis could barely contain herself as Ainsley drove her fingers in harder. Hollis took her hand and entered Ainsley, feeling her constrict around her finger as she pulsed inside of her.

"Yes. Right there." Ainsley's voice took on a new pitch as Hollis pushed her fingers into her, matching her rhythm. "Come for me baby," Ainsley said as she pressed her fingers into Hollis one final time.

Hollis didn't know she could orgasm on command until that moment. Ainsley had a hold on her that no one ever had. Wave after wave of pleasure washed over her as Ainsley kept her fingers firmly inside, careful not to overstimulate her. When the aftershocks subsided, Ainsley slowly exited her, and Hollis did the same. Ainsley settled in next to her on the couch as Hollis put an arm around her.

Hollis leaned her head back and looked at the ceiling. "What are we going to do when corporate wants you back in Raleigh?"

"What are you talking about?" Ainsley asked, still catching her breath.

"They are not going to let you stay out here. You are way too good. They are going to want you back at main headquarters."

"First of all, they paid a lot of money to move me out here. That means I'm going to be out here at least a few years. And second of all, how about some things we figure out as they come up?"

Hollis looked down and met the brown eyes gazing up at her. She was right. They couldn't plan their entire future together in one night. "Okay," she sighed.

"So you think you'll accept the job?" Ainsley asked.

"I think a new job could fit nicely into my revised five-year plan." Hollis kissed her. "As long as we're together, it can't be that complicated."

Epilogue

Hollis frantically examined the healed scar on her cheek in the bathroom mirror. The bright lights reflected off the white-tiled master bathroom of their new home and made the pink marks on her face stand out. For months, she experimented with different techniques to cover the thin scar, but nothing worked. Feeling this self-conscious hadn't been her reality since high school.

True to her word, Ainsley had sold her house, and they had bought a new one together that was close enough to HQ II. The bathroom was larger than her last apartment, and Hollis thought it was excessive, but Ainsley assured her that there would come a day when they were both getting ready at the same time and she would thank her for insisting on the extra space. Today was not that day.

Hollis checked her watch. She had exactly ten minutes to get out the door to be on time for the grand opening of the new Fitwear storefront. She stood in just her bra and underwear, unable to make a decision on what to wear. She looked at the four blouses strewn over the bathroom counter. She hated all of them. She couldn't find the pants she wanted. She couldn't find anything.

Like most real estate transactions, nothing about closing on this house had gone smoothly. They had a perfect plan. They would get the keys to the new house and then have two weeks to move out of Ainsley's house and Hollis's apartment. It would give them plenty of time to set the new house up the way they wanted and to go through all of their things to determine what they didn't need duplicates of.

But there had been issues with escrow and the seller kept asking for extensions. All things Hollis didn't understand, but Ainsley assured her were perfectly normal. When the dust settled, they had had exactly four hours to get completely out of their respective places and into the new house. In the two days since moving to their new house, Hollis hadn't found the time to unbox most of her belongings.

She picked up a purple blouse off the counter and examined it, hoping she would like it more. Something pricked her ankle, and she kicked her leg reflexively. She looked down to see Samson, their new black kitten, trying to eat her ankle. He latched his jaw onto her, and she bent down to pry him off. "Seriously?" she asked the cat.

"Hey, babe!" Ainsley called from the entryway. She was supposed to be meeting Ainsley at the grand opening. What was she doing home? Heels clicked up the wooden staircase.

"I just finished up with Andrew." She stood in the doorframe of the bathroom. "It's raining sideways, so I came to see if you wanted a ride." She motioned with her arms up and down. "But I see you aren't ready. Why aren't you ready?"

Hollis turned to face her. "I can't find my pants, that cat is literally trying to kill me from the ankles up, and I have the Great Wall of China tattooed on my cheek." She pointed to her face.

Ainsley just paused and shot her a confused look.

"You know, cause you can see it from space."

Ainsley picked up the black kitten. "Sammy here would never try to kill his mom," she spoke to him in a baby voice. "Look at this face? He is too cute."

"That cat hates me," Hollis said.

"What pants are you looking for?" Samson purred lovingly in Ainsley's arms.

"My black slacks. The lined ones."

"Oh." Ainsley set Samson down. "Those are hanging on my side of the closest."

"Why the hell are they hanging on your side of the closet?" Hollis snapped.

"Do you want to argue about why things are where they are, or do you want help?" Ainsley returned Hollis's tone.

Hollis slumped her shoulders. “Help please.”

Ainsley stepped past her and into the walk-in closet.

Hollis yelled over her shoulder. “We have to get this place organized this weekend. I can’t live like this. I can’t handle not knowing where things are.”

Ainsley returned and handed her the slacks on a hanger. “We already agreed that we are unpacking this weekend, and I know you are feeling really stressed about today, but I think this aggression may be misplaced.”

“I’m sorry,” Hollis said. She set the slacks down on the counter. “I’m just really nervous about the store opening. Why are you not stressed?”

Ainsley stepped closer to Hollis and pulled her. “Because I know the woman who planned the store opening, and I know that she planned every painstaking detail down to the second. In fact, I know that she did such a good job that she’s already been promoted to the nationwide rollout for twelve more stores.”

It was true. Hollis received the news last week. Even though the store hadn’t officially opened yet, the preliminary numbers showed it was outperforming expectations. The new role meant a co-manager, and she had insisted on Harrison. The two of them would travel the country ensuring that the remaining storefronts opened without so much as a hitch.

Ainsley squeezed her hips. “There is nothing left to do other than show up.” She glanced at her wrist. “And if we don’t get moving, we are going to be late, and that stresses you out even more.”

Hollis let out a sigh. “I’m nervous about all the cameras. Are you sure my face looks okay?”

Ainsley gently rubbed her thumb over the scar on Hollis’s cheek. “Your face looks great. It’s hardly noticeable.”

“But you notice it.”

“That doesn’t count. I know it’s there. Do I need to get Harrison to give you a second opinion?”

“I already called him. He’s with Greggory this morning.” She rolled her eyes. “I still can’t believe you gave him Greg’s number.”

"What can I say? He's charming." Ainsley went to the blouses that were strewn across the room. She grabbed a light blue one and handed it to Hollis. "This one."

Hollis eyed it, unsure. She hadn't liked it five minutes ago.

"Trust me. It brings out your eyes."

Hollis quickly buttoned the blouse and put on her slacks. She gave herself a once-over in the mirror and realized Ainsley was right, it did bring out her eyes. She started pacing, looking for her shoes. How was it she couldn't find anything in this house?

"Your shoes are by the door, babe." Ainsley was sitting at the end of the bed, waiting.

"Thanks." Hollis exited the bathroom. "Okay." She clapped her hands at her sides. "I'm ready."

Ainsley stood up and pulled her in again. "You look great."

Hollis blushed slightly. "Thank you."

Ainsley brushed a lock of hair behind her ear. "And I love your face."

Hollis smiled.

"I'll tell you what." Ainsley squeezed her. "We'll show up, make an appearance, get our face time with the higher ups—"

Hollis shot daggers at Ainsley.

Ainsley caught herself. "My bad. Poor choice of words. We'll get quality time with your new boss, and then we'll get out of there."

"I like the sound of that."

"And then we'll come back here, and I'll show you how proud of you I am and just how much I love your face." Ainsley kissed her cheek.

"Let's go." Hollis pulled her out the bedroom door. She wasn't going to be late.

"Oh," Ainsley said as she followed her down the stairs and to the front door. "I checked, and that ice cream place you like delivers here."

"Perfect." Hollis smiled as they left their house and shut the door.

About the Author

Kel McCord lives in a small town in Oregon with her wife, two kids, two dogs, and more gardens than she can possibly keep up with. When not writing, she enjoys reading, running, and finding new ways to make the perfect cup of coffee. *Uncomplicate It* is her first of hopefully many novels.

Books Available from Bold Strokes Books

An Extraordinary Passion by Kit Meredith. An autistic podcaster must decide whether to take a chance on her polyamorous guest and indulge their shared passion, despite her history. (978-1-63679-679-6)

That's Amore! by Georgia Beers. The romantic city of Rome should inspire Lily's passion for writing, if she can look away from Marina Troiani, her witty, smart, and unassumingly beautiful Italian tour guide. (978-1-63679-841-7)

The Unexpected Heiress by Cassidy Crane. When a cynical opportunist meets a shy but spirited heiress, the last thing she plans is for her heart to get involved. (978-1-63679-833-2)

Through Sky and Stars by Tessa Croft. Can Val and Nicole's love cross space and time to change the fate of humanity? (978-1-63679-862-2)

Uncomplicate It by Kel McCord. When an office attraction threatens her career, Hollis Reed's carefully laid plans demand revision. (978-1-63679-864-6)

Vanguard by Gun Brooke. Beth Kelly, Subterranean freedom fighter, is in the crosshairs when she fights for her people and risks her heart for loving the exacting Celestial dissident leader, LaSierra Delmonte. (978-1-63679-818-9)

Wild Night Rising by Barbara Ann Wright. Riding Harleys instead of horses, the Wild Hunt of myth is once again unleashed upon the world. Their ousted leader and a fey cop must join forces to rein in the ride of terror. (978-1-63679-749-6)

Heart's Appraisal by Jo Hemmingwood. Andy and Hazel can't deny their attraction, but they'll never agree on the place they call home. (978-1-63679-856-1)

Behold My Heart by Ronica Black. Alora Anders is a highly successful artist who's losing her vision. Devastated, she hires Bodie Banks, a young struggling sculptor as a live-in assistant. Can Alora open her mind and her heart to accept Bodie into her life? (978-1-63679-810-3)

Fearless Hearts by Radclyffe. One wounded woman, one determined to protect her—and a summertime of risk, danger, and desire. (978-1-63679-837-0)

Forever Family by L.M. Rose. Two friends come together after tragedy to raise a baby, finding love along the way. (978-1-63679-868-4)

Stranger in the Sand by Renee Roman. Grace Langley is haunted by guilt. Fagan Shaw wishes she could remember her past. Will finding each other bring the closure they're looking for in order to have a brighter future? (978-1-63679-802-8)

The Nursing Home Hoax by Shelley Thrasher and Ann Faulkner. In this fresh take for grown-ups on the classic Nancy Drew series, crime-solving duo Taylor and Marilee investigate suspicious activity at a small East Texas nursing home. (978-1-63679-806-6)

The Rise and Fall of Conner Cody by Chelsey Lynford. A successful yet lonely Hollywood starlet must decide if she can let go of old wounds and accept a chance at family, friendship, and the love of a lifetime. (978-1-63679-739-7)

A Conflict of Interest by Morgan Adams. Tensions rise when a one-night stand becomes a major conflict of interest between an up-and-coming senior associate and a dedicated cardiac surgeon. (978-1-63679-870-7)

A Magnificent Disturbance by Lee Lynch. These everyday dykes and their friends will stop at nothing to see the women's clinic thrive and, in the process, their ideals, their wounds, and a steadfast allegiance to one another make them heroes. (978-1-63679-031-2)

A Marvelous Murder by David S. Pederson. When a hated director is found dead in his locked study, movie star Victor Marvel, his boyfriend Griff, and friend Eve seek to uncover what really happened to Orland Orcott. (978-1-63679-798-4)

Big Corpse on Campus by Karis Walsh. When University Police Officer Cappy Flannery investigates what looks like a clear-cut suicide, she discovers that the case—and her feelings for librarian Jazz—are more complicated than she expected. (978-1-63679-852-3)

Charity Case by Jean Copeland. Bad girl Lindsay Chase came home to Connecticut for a fresh start, but an old, risky habit provides the chance to save the day for her new love, Ellie. (978-1-63679-593-5)

Moments to Treasure by Ali Vali. Levi Montbard and Yasmine Hassani have found a vast Templar treasure, but there is much more to the story—and what is left to be found. (978-1-63679-473-0)

The Stolen Girl by Cari Hunter. Detective Inspector Jo Shaw is determined to prove she's fit for work after an injury that almost killed her, but a new case brings her up against people who will do anything to preserve their own interests, putting Jo—and those closest to her—directly in the line of fire. (978-1-63679-822-6)

Discovering Gold by Sam Ledel. In 1920s Colorado, a single mother and a rowdy cowgirl must set aside their fears and initial reservations about one another if they want to find love in the mining town each of them calls home. (978-1-63679-786-1)

Dream a Little Dream by Melissa Brayden. Savanna can't believe it when Dr. Kyle Remington, the woman who left her feeling like a fool, shows up in Dreamer's Bay. Life is too complicated for second chances. Or is it? (978-1-63679-839-4)

Emma by the Sea by Sarah G. Levine. A delightful modern-day romance inspired by Emma, one of Jane Austen's most beloved novels. (978-1-63679-879-0)

Goodbye, Hello by Heather K O'Malley. With so much time apart and the challenges of a long-distance relationship, Kelly and Teresa's second chance at love may end just as awkwardly as the first. (978-1-63679-790-8)

One Measure of Love by Annie McDonald. Vancouver's hit competitive cooking show Recipe for Success has begun filming its second season and two talented young chefs are desperate for more than a winning dish. (978-1-63679-827-1)

The Smallest Day by J.M. Redmann. The first bullet missed—can Micky Knight stop the second bullet from finding its target? (978-1-63679-854-7)

To Please Her by Elena Abbott. A spilled coffee leads Sabrina into a world of erotic BDSM that may just land her the love of her life. (978-1-63679-849-3)

Two Weddings and a Funeral by Claudia Parr. Stella and Theo have spent the last thirteen years pretending they can be just friends, but surely "just friends" don't make out every chance they get. (978-1-63679-820-2)